New York Valentine

Carmen Reid

W F HOWES LTD

This large print edition published in 2011 by
W F Howes Ltd
Unit 4, Rearsby Business Park, Gaddesby Lane,
Rearsby, Leicester LE7 4YH

1 3 5 7 9 10 8 6 4 2

First published in the United Kingdom in 2011
by Corgi

A CIP catalogue record for this book is available
from the British Library

ISBN 978 1 40746 866 2

Typeset by Palimpsest Book Production Limited,
Falkirk, Stirlingshire
Printed and bound in Great Britain
by MPG Books Ltd, Bodmin, Cornwall

MIX
Paper from
responsible sources
FSC   FSC® C018575
www.fsc.org

CHAPTER 1

Lana all set for work:

Skinny black jeans (Diesel)
Sleeveless cowl-necked, belted, complicated top
(All Saints)
Skull and crossbones necklace (market stall)
White gym shoes (old PE kit)
Cloud of perfume (Gucci Floral)
Total est. cost: £215

'Oh Muuuuuuum!'

'**M**ove that great big, gorgeous bum out of bed now!'
The voice in Annie's ear was teasing but insistent.

'Right now!'

'Oh no,' she protested, 'no, no, no, no. You have got to be joking. It can't be time. I only went to bed five minutes ago. Seriously!'

But there was no mercy. The duvet was whipped

off and a playful, but still surprisingly stingy, smack landed on her behind.

'Owwww!'

'Up!' Ed instructed. 'Owen and I have to leave in five minutes. The twins are washed, changed, dressed and fed. The Princess of Darkness is in charge but you, my darling girl, need to get up.'

'Yes, I've got that,' Annie said huffily. Finally, she sat up, prised open her eyes and let the room come into focus.

'Someone should not have been out partying into the small hours when she has a full day of filming ahead. You're not 25 any more,' Ed pointed out.

'Thanks for reminding me.'

Annie's puffy eyes were properly opened now. She rubbed at eyelashes crunchy with last night's mascara and looked at her . . . *husband*.

Husband. Husband.

They had married in June, almost exactly three months ago now, but she still wasn't quite used to Ed, this lovely man, her boyfriend, step-dad to her older children, father to her twins . . . being her *husband*.

Her thumb moved instinctively to fiddle with the dainty diamond ring on her fourth finger.

Ed had understood her resistance to a traditional gold band. Annie had worn a wedding ring before, a ring which was now stored, in its leather case, along with a selection of other precious belongings – a memory box for the husband she'd lost. So Ed had married her in June with a sliver of platinum and a diamond as slight and sparkly as a fairy.

Through the crusty mascara Annie took an appraising look at him: he had broad shoulders and a muscular build, a kind face, a teacher's 'firm-but-fair' face, brought to life with the twinkle of mischief which rarely left his warm blue eyes and expressive mouth. Then there was unruly hair: sandy brown, curly and messed up whatever he did with it.

'You look foxy,' she told him.

'You think?' he asked modestly, but gave his slim hips a little shake for her benefit.

'Yeah, you've come a long way, babes. You have learned the ways of the well-dressed Annie-man.'

After a little snort, he pointed out: 'I picked out my clothes and put them on all by myself this morning.'

'Yeah, but it's taken *years* of living with me for you to make such good choices.'

Yes. From his sleek, indigo jeans, past the good belt, slim-fit dark blue shirt, nicely tailored grey tweed jacket up to the casually overgrown hair, he looked good. Really good.

'Goodbye kiss,' she said, opening her arms.

Although Ed was on a tight schedule, he knelt down in front of her, put his arms around her waist and pulled her in close. Pushing the peachy slip she'd worn to bed out of the way, he licked her breast.

'Good looking *and* frisky,' she said, crossing her ankles around his back.

'Lucky old you,' he replied.

They kissed long and lovingly before Ed had to break off because it really was time to go. Pulling on her dressing gown, Annie followed him out of the bedroom.

'I've got to say goodbye to my mini Alan Sugar.'

'More like your tiny Tony Soprano!'

They hurried down the narrow flights of stairs to the hallway where Annie's 14-year-old son, Owen, was already waiting, his heavy rucksack rumpling his blazer, his narrow trousers a little too high above scuffed black shoes.

'Come on!' Owen urged Ed, 'chop, chop, chop, let's look perky.'

He made an exaggerated movement towards his watch, slowly pulling back the cuff of his school shirt and flashing the bling golden timepiece on his wrist.

'Owen?!' Annie began, 'what piece of old tat have you been lashing your cash on now?'

'Genuine,' Owen said, tapping at the face of his watch.

'Yeah,' Ed shot the watch a glance, as he scrambled his bags, guitar and violin cases together. 'Genuine fake Swiss watch, made in China and flogged down the market by the Russian wide-boys.'

'You don't have to believe me,' Owen said, replacing the cuff and shooting his mum a smug smile.

He ducked his head slightly as she approached, but still allowed her to kiss him on the cheek and run a hand through his hair.

'That's my boy,' she said, realizing with a pang that he was just half an inch or so shorter than her. Any week now and he would overtake. He would be her big boy and she would have to look up to him!

He picked up his flashy sports bag and as he headed towards the door, gave her a wave which made the gold strap on his wrist twinkle.

For several months now, Owen had been making serious pocket money working on a market stall for his entire weekends. Just like his mum, after Owen had earned hard, there was nothing he liked to do more than spend hard.

Owen loved to work and he loved to buy and sell. Annie still found it funny, because Owen had once been very shy and introverted. The kind of little boy who'd found it easier to talk to his toy trains than to his friends. But now the trader Owen worked for at the weekends was paying him £90 a day, plus commission, because he was so good at his job.

Yes, there was a certain amount of ear-grating, market-stall lingo that Owen's family now had to endure. Annie could just about stand it because when Owen talked about his DVD stall, he just lit up with excitement. And wasn't that what you had to encourage your kids to do? Help them to find the things in life which lit them up?

Annie kissed Ed one more time, waved her two boys out of the door, then headed towards the kitchen where her nearly-18-year-old daughter Lana, who had definitely not yet found the things which lit up her life, was looking after the twins.

'Good morning, my love,' Annie said cheerily as she entered the room, her smile widening as she spotted the freshly made pot of coffee. Ed really was too good to be true.

Lana made a grouchy 'umph' in reply and carried on sipping from her mug, behind a curtain of long, dark hair. The babies, almost a year old now, began to scurry across the kitchen floor towards their mummy.

'Hello, hello, my darlings,' Annie cooed, squatting down and opening her arms wide to hug them both. They were far too big and heavy now to be picked up for a cuddle together.

'Mumma!'

First to reach her was Minette with her dark, soulful eyes and creamy cheeks. Micky wasn't far behind, nappy bottom waggling busily. They buried sticky faces straight into Annie's dressing gown but she didn't mind one tiny bit, just stroked their silky heads devotedly.

'Can you pour me a coffee, darlin' . . . and maybe, just because you're extra super nice, can you make me some toast?'

Lana let out a long sigh and dragged her slim, entirely black-clad body up from her chair.

'Thanks, Lana, you're a star,' Annie said, as

generously as she could, though really she'd have liked to seriously shake Lana or maybe even administer a little kick to her pointy, skinny-jeaned behind.

How many other teenage girls would *kill*, or at least donate vital organs, to be spending their gap year working in television? And did Lana thank her mother for arranging this amazing work placement? Did Lana look forward to her exciting day ahead at the studio? No. Lana was pretty much in a grump from morning till night and there didn't seem to be a thing that Annie could do about it. So because complaining about the grumpiness hadn't worked, Annie was currently trying to tune it out entirely and respond with relentless joy and positive vibes.

As she sat down to her coffee and toast, the babies, bored with cuddles, scuttled back to their play mat and the rolling balls, blocks and other drool-soaked objects of baby attraction.

Registering the time, Annie gulped her toast and swallowed the coffee with speed.

'Oh good grief! I've got to get dressed – have my usual morning melodrama,' she told Lana. 'Can you hold the fort for me down here just a tiny bit longer, babes? Dinah will be here in twenty minutes.'

'Oh Muuuuuuum!' Grumph, humph, harrumph.

'Thank you, sweetheart. You look great,' she added, not just to try and cheer Lana up, but also because it was true.

Lana was rocking the funky film crew look. She

was dressed practically enough for all the errands she'd be running and chores she'd be doing today. But the look came with dark eyeliner, a thick black fringe and just enough edge.

Annie had worried that maybe she was molly-coddling her daughter by arranging a job for her. But unlike her friends, who were planning trips abroad for work and travel, once Lana had left school with her impressive clutch of exam results, she'd been reluctant to make plans and didn't seem to have any ideas about her future. So finally, Annie had made the move and arranged the under-paid TV job because she hated to see Lana sitting about at home, becoming more and more gloomy.

The fact that Lana could only work up the bare minimum of enthusiasm for her new job drove Annie slightly wild. But what could she do? Over the years, she had discovered that she could not nag, trick, encourage or even bribe Lana into enthusiasm.

'OK, better get to my wardrobe. I'll try not to take too long . . .' Annie said, more to herself than to her daughter.

But this was the strange thing: everyone in her family now looked great, she thought. They all had their own individual-with-a-twist look and they worked it. Ed did groovy jeans, plus shirts and tweedy jackets. Owen was sporty labels with added bling. Lana did dark, skinny and moody. Even the babies had a look! Currently faded denim dungarees, Micky's with a blue top, Minnie's with pink.

But Annie, who'd been a personal shopper for years with one of London's best known fashion stores, who'd dressed women from every corner of London with every conceivable fashion dilemma, who now presented her very own *How Not To Shop* fashion TV show . . . *Annie* was the one member of the family who was having a bit of an image crisis.

As Annie opened her wardrobe doors and looked at the collection of clothes inside, it hit her once again. There was so much in here. So many outfits. But, aside from a trusted handful which she'd worn so often that even the TV crew were starting to poke fun, there wasn't anything she could wear because . . .

Annie looked down at herself. She was a *whole size* bigger than she used to be. An entire size. Possibly even, she had to admit to herself, two sizes; well, almost certainly one and a half. Even with *double* control pants (frankly a nightmare when you needed a wee), she could no longer fit into most of her wardrobe and there was no way, absolutely no way, she was buying new items in the dreaded new size – even though this was *exactly* what she would tell a client to do if they came to her for advice.

Buying new things in a bigger size would be giving up . . . it would be admitting defeat. She'd always been able to slim down and get back into her 12s and although she'd been dragging about the post-baby bulge for nearly a year now, she was not prepared to give up the battle yet.

Her hand went out to the stretchiest black dress she owned. OK, red leggings . . . the patent, peep-toed, very high red shoes . . . red lipstick . . . an amazing red and pearl necklace. These items would surely distract from the fact that she was wearing the black stretchy dress once again.

Another crimp on the shopping front was the promise she'd made to Ed about her mighty credit card debt.

Ever since she'd been old enough to own a credit card, Annie had been servicing, juggling, re-distributing and rearranging her great big designer-label-caused debt. But now she'd managed to bring the figure down to just within reach of £5,000 – the lowest she could ever remember it being. She'd promised Ed she would clear it, and only then would she be allowed to buy new items from some carefully worked out budget that Ed was apparently going to draw up for her.

Just £5,000 to go. It was still a lot of money to owe, but her card debts had once been close to ten times that amount. So now she was on track and almost certain that she could beat her promise to have it cleared by Christmas.

She'd thought that paying off a debt would just be pure denial and pain and, yes, seeing so much of her generous TV pay disappear in lump sums to Messrs Visa and MasterCard was difficult. But on the upside, being able to open those sinister white envelopes without the feeling of impending panic attack was much more rewarding than she'd expected.

As soon as she'd bound herself up in the two pairs of control pants and a minimizing bra, her mobile began to ring. After a quick search of the untidy bedroom, she located it.

'Annah!' came the booming, gushing, heavily accented voice of one of Annie's very best friends, Svetlana Wisneski.

Annie would probably have told anyone else in her life that she'd call them straight back as soon as she was dressed. But Svetlana, an extraordinarily glamorous former Miss Ukraine, who'd been married to not just one, but *several* of the wealthiest men in the world, was not a woman who waited for return phone calls.

So Annie sat down on the edge of her bed in the de-sexing beige pants and industrial bra and prepared to listen.

'In New York . . . is a *disaster!*' Svetlana exclaimed dramatically.

'Oh no! Has Elena's boyfriend left her?' Annie jumped to the conclusion, 'What's-his-name?'

'Sye? No. No. This all lovely little romance for them. Tscha . . .' Svetlana dismissed the thought, 'no this is bizzzzzzneeeeez. Elena not coping. Not coping one little piece. Her new American business

11

partner has left. Gone! Taken money, left debt with factory. *Disaster!*' she repeated. 'We have orders for dresses but we have no money and no factory to make them!'

'Oh no,' Annie sympathized.

Elena was Svetlana's lovely, determined and totally business-headed daughter. Although Svetlana had always sought fame and fortune by marrying the richest husbands available to womankind, Elena, a young twenty-something, was trying to turn herself into a business success story.

Svetlana and Elena's backstory was a little more complicated than most mothers' and daughters'.

In her early twenties, the beautiful Svetlana had had an affair with a married politician back home in the Ukraine. The affair had resulted in the unwanted baby Elena. When Svetlana decided to seek a husband, and her fortune, in the biggest, shiniest cities of Europe, Elena had been taken to the country-side to live with relatives. Svetlana had let many years slide by, hoping she wouldn't have to face up to her daughter again.

But two years ago when a furiously determined Ukrainian beauty had turned up on Svetlana's Mayfair doorstep, dressed in skimpy clothes and sporting a terrible hair-dye job, Svetlana had realized this was her past well and truly catching up with her.

Although at first they'd wanted to rip the blonde

tresses from each other's heads, it was still amazing to Annie how well things had settled down. Though, much to her mother's distress, Elena didn't seem remotely interested in rich husbands and mega-divorce settlements. In fact, she'd gone to business school, then earlier this year she'd persuaded her mother to found a dress label. Now Perfect Dress had small offices in London and New York and was about to launch a second, fledgling collection.

'What I do? What I do?' Svetlana was asking in a voice that sounded unusually frantic.

'Maybe you need to go over and see her,' Annie suggested.

'Ah no, is terrible timing. Just terrible. I'm too busy with Perfect Dress in London. So many orders – so many clients to talk to, visit, keep interested – and now possibility of no dresses! I can't go. Harry is too busy to look after everything when I am away and the boys . . . I can't leave my boys for so long. You know how Igor still worries me.'

Igor was Svetlana's last and most significant ex-husband. He was the father of her two boys, who were currently (though a former Russian volley-ball champion was working on this) the only heirs to Igor's vast Russian gas fortune.

Although Svetlana was now married to Harry Roscoff, a QC, a divorce expert and one of London's best legal minds, there had been Igor trouble before. Igor had once tried to sneak his sons out of the country and, although Harry had stopped the plan in its tracks, it had shaken Svetlana to the core.

She could hop to Paris or Milan at the drop of a hat for a business meeting or shopping weekend, but crossing the Atlantic and spending serious time away from her younger children just wasn't an option.

'Who do we know?' Annie asked, thinking out loud: 'who do we know who could go over and help? I take it Elena does *need* help? It's not that she wants to sort this out on her own?'

'Yes, of course! She need help!' Svetlana insisted, 'this biziniz partner take money. Un-paid the biggest sums and then exito! Elena in distressed. Big distressed. Not is knowing what's to do.'

Annie had known Svetlana long enough to recognize that when her English got all tangled up she was really quite upset.

'Who do we know who could help?' Annie asked again. She was looking down at her body in disgust. Control pants and minimizer bras only worked when you were standing up. As soon as you sat down, not one, but two uncomfortable rolls of flab bulged out, squeezed downwards by the bra and upwards by the pants. She'd have to get an all-in-one – but then where did the flab go? It had to burst out somewhere. Would she have monster shoulders and padded hips?

'We know *you*!' came the reply. 'You are needs go New York. *You*, Annah. You need to help Elena.' Taking a deep breath, Svetlana added, as calmly

14

and as grammatically as she could: 'I do not know one other person who could do this better.'

'Huh?'

For a moment, Annie was speechless.

Then her thoughts began to gather. Of course it was lovely, wonderful to be asked. But Svetlana never seemed to understand, or maybe she never wanted to understand, that Annie had a life too. Annie had a TV career and a family and tiny children, and could not just drop everything to be at Svetlana's beck and call.

'I can't go to New York . . .' for so many reasons, Annie told herself, but the one she began with was: 'I'm in the middle of filming.'

'For how long?' came the sharp question, 'how many weeks this go on for?'

'Another two months,' Annie said, also a little sharply.

Did everyone think that she just swanned about in front of the camera for a day or two then banked an enormous cheque? It wasn't like that at all. She slaved when she was filming. She slaved for long, long days and she travelled all over the country to incredibly non-glamorous destinations. Yes, she had long breaks, but they were precious – they were for catching up on all the family time she'd had to miss when she was filming.

'Annah, please, you cannot just take break and go out to help Elena? You know fashion. You great business lady. Remember the fashion show in Paris?'

How could Annie forget?

'We not have Perfect Dress without that show, Annah, and it was all because of you. Just for a few weeks . . . pleeeeeease?' Annie didn't think she'd ever heard Svetlana plead before.

'New York, Annah. Think how exciting . . .' Svetlana quickly moved into full-on persuasive charm mode. 'She have apartment in wonderful area, just off Fifth Avenue. You can go and stay.'

'No, Svetlana, I'm sorry,' Annie said quickly, batting the images of skyscrapers, yellow cabs, avenues and cocktails right out of her mind, 'I can't go. I would love to go. You know I would do anything to help the two of you. But right now it isn't an option. There's a whole crew, a whole filming schedule. Plus, my family. I have babies! Everyone's counting on me.'

Svetlana gave a strangled shriek of frustration before blurting out: 'But Annah, what are we going to do?'

CHAPTER 2

Melissa made-over:

Red V-necked knit tunic (Asda)
Pink frilled blouse (Mango)
Cropped jeans (Mango)
Purple funky Mary Janes (Camper)
Messenger bag (Kipling)
Total est. cost: £155

'Haven't a clue . . .'

Annie arrived at the studio by car. Not just any old car, the studio car, complete with driver wearing black leather gloves and a shiny peaked cap.

'Thank you, darlin'. Exciting day ahead for you, is it?' she asked him as she and Lana gathered their bags together and prepared to get out.

'Collecting James McAvoy from the airport next . . .' the driver revealed with a wink.

'Ooooh, is he coming here?'

'Nah, news studio in town.'

'Shame.'

As Annie headed inside, there was a flurry of activity as people saw her coming. Receptionists fluttered about with signing-in forms and visitor passes. A girl with a clipboard offered to walk her to her room and carry her bags.

'I'll be fine,' Annie assured her, smiling, 'I've been carrying my own bags for some time now, I'm sure I can manage a little bit longer.'

Lana, awkwardly trailing in the shadow of her mum, gave a quick wave before peeling off in the direction of the crew area while Annie headed to the VIP star suite.

The door was decorated with a handwritten sign which read *How Not To Shop*, stuck on with bright blue gaffer tape. As soon as she pushed it open, Annie registered the crowded room and the busy hum of activity.

'Hello my darlin's, look busy, I'm here!' she announced and all heads turned in her direction.

There was Amelia, the producer's PA, folders in hand, pencil tucked behind one ear, iPhone up against the other and something truly fashion-forward slipping from her shoulders.

In the corner was Ginger, the make-up girl, various other production bods and—

'Hi, you must be Melissa, lovely to meet you!' Annie greeted the woman sitting in front of the glaringly bright mirror as Ginger applied found-ation with a damp sponge.

'Yes . . . hello . . .' Melissa turned to Annie with a shy smile.

'How are you doing?' Annie asked, giving Melissa a friendly handshake. 'Don't worry, you're in good hands. Ginger is a genius. She can even make me look halfway presentable if I'm very, very nice to her, bribe her with free handbags and that kind of thing.'

'Ooooh!' Ginger smiled at Annie, 'have you got something exciting for me?'

'No, my darlin' not one exciting parcel has arrived at *How Not To Shop* towers for weeks. And . . . Amelia? We've not heard anything about the *one and only* bag, have we?'

Amelia shook her head sadly: 'I did call again, yesterday, but I don't want to pester . . .'

'No, no, we definitely do not want to pester,' Annie agreed.

Despite talk of the 'it bag' being dead and buried, anyone who worked in, around, or even within smelling distance of fashion knew that there was only one bag to carry this season.

It was chic and yet it was slouchy, it was structured, but casual, it came in many deep, subtle colours, including sea green with matt silver hardware. It was made by Mulberry. It was the bag Annie *had* to have. But the sea green was completely unavailable. Limited edition. Sold out before it had even made it to the shops!

Both Annie and Amelia had made several calls

to the head office to ask if there wasn't just one last bag somewhere which could be bought for Annie Valentine, you know, of *How Not To Shop*.

Annie still had a slightly odd feeling when she remembered how insistent the PR had been about the impossibility of sourcing a bag for her. Wasn't she cool enough? she'd wondered.

'It's not as if I want it for free . . .' she'd tried to make clear.

'No, we are absolutely sold out. Half of the waiting list has been left disappointed.'

'Couldn't you maybe make some more?' Annie had dared to suggest.

'That would just ruin the concept of limited edition!'

'Maybe you should think about making your next edition slightly less limited, then.'

Annie let out a sigh and told Amelia, 'It wouldn't happen to Alexa Chung, would it? They even named one of their bags after her. And who's the other really cool English girl in New York? You know the one who writes that column for *Vanity Fair*?'

'Emily Wilmington,' a little chorus replied.

'Yeah, it wouldn't happen to the lovely Emily Wilmington. Every time she leaves her beautiful Manhattan apartment, she's probably tripping over all the freebie goodies designers want her to wear,' Annie said, trying not to sound too resentful.

'Wasn't there a bag named after you?' Amelia recalled with a mischievous grin on her face.

Ah, the Annie V bag: that patent pink plastic disaster of the summer.

'Let's draw a veil, my love, let's draw a veil,' Annie said, not wanting to relive that memory.

'Now, Melissa, while Ginger makes a gorgeous job of your beautiful skin and oooooh green eyes, I am ever so jealous . . . tell me all about yourself. Why did you want to hand yourself over to the *How Not To Shop* team?'

'I love your show,' Melissa gushed, looking a teeny bit star-struck.

'Thank you!'

'And I've been ill and my husband had to give up his job to look after me . . .'

'Oh you poor thing,' Annie sympathized and reached over to squeeze Melissa's hand.

'So there's been no money or fun in our house for ages. But I'm much better now and he's just had news about a new job . . .'

'Fantastic!'

'. . . so I thought I'd celebrate by getting some new clothes and cheering myself up. But it's been so long, I've looked out there in the shops and . . .'

'You're lost,' Annie chipped in.

'Totally! Haven't a clue.'

'I know darlin' – it's all leggin's and *stonewashed* jeggin's and tunics, I mean – NEON!?! It's just about enough to make anyone over the age of nineteen scream!'

'There.' Ginger applied a final pat of powder to Melissa's nose.

'Can we just tousle her hair a little, make it a bit softer? Maybe use the tongs?' Annie asked, looking at Melissa's reflection.

'Just what I was thinking,' Ginger replied.

Once the tonging and tousling was done, Melissa looked herself over carefully in the mirror. She was trying to control the wide-eyed look of surprise from breaking out all over her face.

'Delicious,' Annie said. 'I hope you were watching her every step so you can copy all of this when you get back home.'

'Yes!' Melissa smiled.

'You better, she's make-up girl of the moment and one lesson with her would cost you over £300.'

'You're next,' Ginger instructed Annie. 'Sit down, gown up, phone off,' she said sternly, 'I'm not trying to apply the signature red Annie lips while you chitter-chatter on the mobile.'

'Yes, ma'am,' Annie gave a little salute, 'but let me just show Melissa the clothes we've brought in for her before you get started.'

Although Ginger gave a sigh, she nodded agreement.

'Come over here,' Annie instructed Melissa: 'this entire rack is just for you. We had your measurements, so we went out and scoured for the gorgeous new you.'

For a moment or two, Melissa just stood and looked at the rack as she was faced with a riot of fabric and colour.

'Go on, pull things out, hold them up, take a look – dive in!' Annie encouraged.

Melissa's hand went straight to a chiffon blouse sleeve in a vibrant red and pink print.

'Lovely,' Annie said, 'you can try that on first.'

'Oh no,' Melissa said immediately, 'I love the way it looks, but I wouldn't wear it.'

'Why not? If you love the way it looks, you should wear it, or at least try it!'

'No, no . . . too . . .'

'Stop! Shhhh! Whatever you're about to say, I've heard it before and I'm not listening. Too young, too bright, too feminine, too this, too that. Try it on! You might be surprised. This is the new you: healthy, cheerful, *well* Melissa. Recovery girl. Ready to go on out there again and be part of the world.'

Although this was delivered in Annie's most upbeat and encouraging voice, it seemed to make Melissa fold in on herself, and suddenly she looked upset.

'I know,' Annie said, putting an arm around her shoulder and squeezing hard, 'I know. It's a big step. A big change. Whenever people come to see me, I know it's a critical moment. They come before the big job interview, or after the divorce, or post-baby. They don't quite know who this new person inside is and they certainly don't know how to dress her.

'So they come to me for a few clues. Yeah, I might know about fashion and which figure looks best in what shape but deep down, I think *you* know what *you* really want and it's up to us to work it out together. So I know you want this blouse,' Annie said, and pulled it from the rack.

'We'll tone it down at first, have just the sleeves and the collar poking out from underneath this delicious soft red jumper.' She pulled a short-sleeved, V-necked knit tunic from the rack. 'You've got great legs, I've noticed,' she added, pulling tight cropped jeans from the rack, 'so now it's just shoes. Look down there at my selection . . . which ones make your heart beat faster?'

Encouraged, Melissa's hand moved along the row of shoes. All sorts of shapes and colours. All in her size! As her hand hovered over the violet Mary Janes, Annie said: 'Stop! I think those will be perfect!'

'I put on two stones being ill—'

'Shhhh!' Annie interrupted. 'I put on two stones having twins. We'll get there. We'll get it off. Slowly but surely. We'll get there.'

'No, but . . . what I was going to say was that I don't mind. Before, I'd have minded a lot. But now, I'm just so happy that I'm well again, that everything's working OK. That's why I want to dress nicely. Dress what I have. Just the way I am.'

'That's fantastic,' Annie agreed, feeling more than a hint of guilt. Wasn't that always what she was telling people to do? Dress the body they were in. Not the one they'd once had or hoped one day to have. Dress for the here and now.

As Amelia led Melissa away to try on her first outfit, Ginger ushered Annie into the make-up chair.

'Go on then,' Annie told her with a grin, 'see if you can make me ten years younger.'

'Easy,' Ginger said with a wink and zoomed in on Annie's eyebags with a corrector pen.

When the generous layer of matte, studio-lights-friendly warpaint had been applied, Annie smiled at herself in the mirror.

'Nice job,' she told Ginger.

There was a tap at the door and head cameraman, Bob, stuck his head round: 'Hey Annie, are we almost ready for act one, scene one?' he asked.

'Yep, we are.' Annie stood up and brushed herself down.

'How do I look?'

'Lovely,' Bob told her, 'but you're wearing that dress again. Ain't you got any time to go shopping, girl?'

'Oh shut up!' Annie told him.

Under the glaring studio lights, Annie introduced Melissa for the benefit of the camera, then ushered her onto the set.

'C'mon my lovely,' Annie said in full-on, upbeat presenter mode, holding out a hand for Melissa to grab. 'Melissa is here to show us how to do colours. We have red, we have pink, we have a splash of violet going on below. It's a sizzle. A riot.

25

I'm here to tell you: never worry about the rules your mum might have given you: if you love it, wear it!

'Life is absolutely too short to worry about "does blue go with green?" If it looks good to you, go for it. I've had enough of people in black and navy and beige. Stand out from the crowd. Look lovely! And wear the colours you just can't get enough of,' Annie instructed.

'Melissa hasn't been well, she's spent months in drab hospital wards so you can't blame her for wanting to break open the paintbox and wear delicious reds and pinks all in one go.

'And doesn't she look *gorgeous*?'

Even Melissa nodded her head at this.

'I love my job,' Annie said straight to camera with a big grin, 'I really do love my job. If you are in a wardrobe rut, don't know what to wear, can't make sense of what's out there in the shops, have a big milestone event ahead or are just generally *freaking out* about what you should be putting on, get in touch. Email me: we can feature your problem on the show, or even better, I'll get on the phone and we'll have you right here, just like Melissa.'

The door to the studio opened, distracting Annie from her speech.

'And cut . . . just for now,' the director said, her attention caught as well. Everyone turned to see who had committed the crime of opening one of the large double doors and allowing a shaft of light into the darkened studio.

Someone was walking through the darkness on sharp, metal-tipped heels.

One of the lighting crew swung a spotlight in the direction of the footsteps. Tamsin Hinkley, the show's producer, was striding towards them.

Usually Annie was pleased to see Tamsin, and not just because she was always beautifully dressed. Tamsin was Annie's biggest fan, who had believed in their programme right from the start and had ensured the last series was a major ratings success which was immediately re-commissioned.

But today, Tamsin was not smiling. In fact, she looked thunderous.

'Hello everyone,' she said in a voice that sounded tense and angry.

'Hi.'

'Hello.'

'Hey Tamsin.'

A range of voices answered back.

'What's up?' Annie asked. 'You don't look happy.'

'No. I'm not happy at all,' Tamsin replied. Then she scraped her long hair away from her face and just held it there, hand clasped at the back of her head: 'I don't know how to tell you this,' she began.

Several people in the room started to fidget nervously.

'Channel Four has de-commissioned this series,' Tamsin announced, letting her hair fall and trying to stand up tall and look professionally around the room, 'I'm afraid they've pulled the plug on us.'

There was a slight wobble in her voice as she added: 'And there's absolutely nothing I can do. I know this because I've been on the phone to my lawyer for the last hour.'

There were gasps of astonishment. Someone burst into tears. The director began to protest. Melissa looked crestfallen.

Only cameraman Bob, who'd been with Annie right from her first TV job on an iffy digital channel, seemed unfazed. 'Oh yeah,' he said, as he calmly began to dismantle his equipment. 'Happens all the time.'

Annie stared at him in shock. 'But it can't be happening *now*.' She heard her voice, all high and thin: 'please just pinch me and tell me it can't be happening.'

'It is, Annie,' Tamsin confirmed. 'I'm so sorry,'

CHAPTER 3

Mimi-Jay looking deeeeeelightful:

Black button-up short sleeved jacket (salon's own)
Silky black harem trousers (Topshop)
High yellow patent heels (New Look)
Bright pink push-up bra and thong (Dorothy Perkins)
Oversized pearl and gold necklace (Topshop)
Yellow and pink striped nails (Blaxx salon)
Total est. cost: £145

'No moanin' and groanin' now.'

'So it sounds as if Ed has been cool about it,' Connor said, although his voice was muffled because he was lying face down on Mimi-Jay's beautician's couch, head inside a fluffy white towel, enjoying some full-on Blaxx salon attention.

'Yeah, Ed is as cool as I am stressed,' Annie replied from her own couch, where she lay smothered in a face mask, 'he was unbelievably calm.

As if TV shows just come and go, as if I breeze in and announce my entire series has been cancelled every day of the week.'

'Well, it has happened to you once before,' Connor pointed out, 'and for a while there it did look as if you wouldn't be in the second series . . . so you can't say he'd had no warning – owww!' Connor exclaimed as Mimi-Jay yanked the wax-covered cloth from his shoulder blade, pulling a strip of back hair with it.

'C'mon man,' Mimi-Jay protested, 'you're a big strong, muscular guy, no moanin' and groanin' now. It's bad for business. You know I'm gonna be quick.'

'Eeeek!' Connor squeaked into his towel when the next strip was ripped off. He didn't dare disobey Mimi-Jay. Nobody would. She was a six-foot-tall black girl with biceps as broad as a boxer's. If she said 'no moanin' and groanin',' then there would be no moaning and groaning.

'Annie, I don't know if you should be eating crisps lying down,' Dinah pointed out from her couch on the other side of Connor's. 'You could choke and, adorable though the twins are, I don't know if I want to be their step-mum as well as their nanny.'

Through a half-crunched mouthful, Annie replied: 'They're not crisps, they're nachos, and anyway, I thought you could do the Heimlich manoeuvre.'

'Theoretically,' Annie's sister replied, but waving

her drying fingertips in the air, she added, 'It would seriously spoil my manicure, though.'

This made Annie laugh, despite the nachos, because it was so un-Dinah. Her younger sister was a grown-up art student who wore Birkenstocks, Oxfam treasures and homemade things and whose idea of 'grooming' was washing her below-the-shoulder hair and twice a year taking tweezers to her shaggy eyebrows.

'Why am I getting a manicure anyway?' Dinah wondered. 'I'll just be wiping bottoms tomorrow.'

'But with baby-pink nails,' Annie pointed out, 'so much nicer.'

'Didn't you eat a bag of nachos on the way over here?' demanded Dinah.

'I'm addicted,' Annie had to admit. 'Ever since the show got canned, I can't stop eating them. I think it's because they crunch. I think it's angry eating.

'It's not just me – now Lana has no gap-year job she's going to be mooching round the house in a total sulk wishing she could join her best friend Greta, tracking yetis in the jungle or whatever it is she's up to.'

'Yetis? Don't they live on mountains?' Connor asked.

'Dunno,' Annie said, chomping another mouthful.

'This nacho habit is not good, my darling. Maybe you should try popcorn?' Dinah suggested: 'air-popped, no oil.'

'Oh yes, oh saintly wholemealy one. Maybe I could just try chewing on a bit of string?'

Annie sank her hand into the bag once again.

Along with the bling-est nails ever seen outside the Bronx, the 'beauty treats with friends' room was a Blaxx speciality. It consisted of three couches in one treatment room and often three therapists working at the same time, gossiping up a storm.

'So what is your plan of action now?' Connor asked Annie. 'Tamsin must be trying to get another channel to buy the show. Right?'

Connor was a well-known actor who was years ahead of Annie in the TV career game. He had spent the past fifteen years trying to get on TV, being on TV, finding fame on TV, then, inevitably, being thrown off TV. He was currently trying to get his foot back in the door in a meaningful and long-term way. So he knew much more about the industry than Annie.

RADA-trained *acTOR* Connor was so tall, olive-skinned, dark-haired, snowplough-jawed and generally knicker-droppingly handsome that it was hard to believe why any TV executive would keep him from the small screen. In fact, Annie had to sit up and take a little look at his face and rippling torso just to cheer herself up. In the way that she might look at a painting or fashion photograph, just for the sheer aesthetic pleasure.

Of course, as Annie knew, every truly maddeningly handsome man came with a catch: too vain, too stupid, too flirtatious – there was always a fatal flaw. With Connor, there had been two. Number one: she was introduced to Connor by the man she was desperately in love with, and number two: Connor was only interested in equally gorgeous men.

Ah well. Never mind. Over the years, he'd become one of her truly best friends.

'Yeah,' Annie said, lowering another nacho into her mouth, despite the danger of a monosodium-glutamate overdose. 'Of course Tamsin's out there selling hard. And there's a campaign on Facebook: save our *How Not To Shop*. Owen's getting my website sorted and apparently I need to Twitter.'

'Oh yes, you must have a tweeting twategy,' Connor said from the depths of his towel.

Riiiiiipppppp went another wax strip.

'But Tamsin's the lynchpin,' Annie added: 'she's the one who needs to sell it to someone else. That's my best hope.'

'So you're not offering yourself around as a presenter yet?'

'No . . . do you think I should?'

'Definitely. Meet agent. Discuss.' Connor instructed.

'Please tell me that everything's going great with you again,' Annie said. 'You were the star of a much bigger TV show than I was, you got dumped but now you're back in the saddle again. Aren't you?'

'It's never been quite as comfortable or quite as secure a saddle, let me tell you,' Connor admitted.

Mimi-Jay's wax strips were travelling lower,

Annie noticed when she glanced over. Surely Connor wasn't getting his buttocks waxed? Not right here in front of her and her sister?

'The *Elephant Man* series has nearly finished shooting,' Connor went on. 'All hopes of it translating into a West End play are fading fast, because the guy who was going to write the script is ill. So in just a few weeks I'll be as footloose, fancy free and frightened about the future as you. Unfortunately.'

'You're kidding. What are you going to do?' Dinah asked.

'First of all, I'm going to track down Gawain, the best personal trainer I have ever experienced, so I can chisel my abs and beef up my arms. Then I'm going to look for parts which demand physical perfection. I want to be an action hero, or at the very least, a dangerously threatening English bad guy – all the major movies have one. I think I'd be *fabulous*.'

With that, he turned his beautiful square jaw, sculpted cheekbones and dark eyes towards Annie and gave her 'sultry and smouldering'.

'Ooooh, yes, you would be good,' she agreed, '*we* know this. It's just getting everyone else in the world to see it.'

'I know,' Connor gave a sigh and not just because Mimi-Jay was now smearing molten paraffin onto his left buttock.

Annie closed her eyes. She didn't need to see more. Really, she didn't.

'What am I going to do?' she asked Connor, sounding a little more worried. 'I loved my show. It can't just end like this.'

'You've got to stay visible, be visible. Call Tamsin and your agent every second day if you can bear it. Keep totally plugged into all the TV industry news. If there's a whisper of anyone making anything that might be good for you, you get your agent to chase it. Or do the chasing yourself. Have meetings! Get out there. But there's something I have to tell you and you're not going to like it . . .'

'Oh?' Annie sat up, propped on her elbow.

Just at that moment, Mimi-Jay whisked away the towel preserving the very last of Connor's modesty and instructed: 'On your knees and I hope you had a very thorough wash before you came here.'

Annie and Dinah watched wide-eyed as a totally naked Connor raised his knees so that his bum stuck right up into the air.

Totally professionally, Mimi-Jay began to apply molten wax to his . . . *inner* (eek!) buttocks.

'What's up wichoo two?' Mimi-Jay asked. 'Did he not tell you he was getting a back, crack and sack?'

'Whoa,' Annie said, putting her hands over her eyes. Yes, she liked to appreciate Connor and his physical beauty, but this was an overdose.

'Hey, apparently straight guys are getting this done now,' Connor said between gritted teeth. 'Girls too want their men smooth all over. But what would I know?'

35

Mimi-Jay pulled off the cloth, and Connor gave an 'Owwwwww!' of pain.

'I think this is progress,' Dinah pointed out. 'It goes some way to making up for the female torture known as the Brazilian. I did that once and never again.'

'Still Brazilian-ing, Annie?' Connor asked, the nervy fear of what was to come next obvious in his voice.

'Every now and then I like to hack the undergrowth from the runway so in the event of an unscheduled landing, I'm prepared.'

'Sex life that good, huh?' Connor asked. 'And you two used to be so h-ot!'

Obviously, things were getting hotter for Connor too. The wax was being layered on fast.

'Connor, shut up,' Annie replied grumpily. 'You've never been a parent. We have babies. No one with babies has a sex life. I'm bloody grateful that we're still talking.'

Annie lay back down on her couch. 'What were you about to tell me that I wasn't going to like?' she asked, hoping to distract Connor from whatever excruciating pain was coming right up with the sack wax.

'This business is all about looks,' Connor began, 'and it's very tough. Dog eat dog. There are thousands of young, beautiful, talented females queuing around the block to fill your shoes, Annie Valentine. It's staring you right in the face, baby. For TV, you look big. Way too big, honeybun.

When I find Gawain, you are going to come and train with him too. And for God's sake girl, put those nachos down. Step *away* from the nachos. Uh oh . . .'

'Bite down hard,' Mimi-Jay warned.

Rrrrrriiiiiippppp.

'Aaaaaaargh!'

CHAPTER 4

At home Annie:

Very forgiving black dress with extra stretch
(Betty Jackson)
Purple leggings (Lana's wardrobe)
Red lipstick (Chanel)
Black sheepskin slippers (uggggh) (Ugg)
Total est. cost: £170

'Are you on drugs?!'

Annie stared at the computer screen in front of her. She had phoned Tamsin (again). She had phoned her agent (again). She had updated her Facebook page, Twittered her Tweets, replied to all the latest comments made by her very sweet and loving fans and now she had nothing else to do.

Absolutely nothing.

She looked at the corner of the screen. It was only 10.17a.m. She'd been at her desk for forty-seven minutes exactly. Listening hard, she could just make out Dinah's cheerful voice as she chatted to the babies downstairs.

Employing her sister as her full-time nanny had been one of the best business decisions Annie had ever made. And even though she was at home now, she wasn't going to cut Dinah's hours, because there was going to be more work. She was determined there was going to be more work. For everybody's sake.

Her phone bleeped with a text and she snatched it up, anxious for a development of any kind at all.

'Surviving?' the text from Ed began, 'you are wondrfl. Sthg will happn. Dnt PANIC. Pls. Xxx'

It wasn't the agent/producer news she'd been hoping for but at least it made her smile.

When the babies were tiny, Ed had taken months of unpaid leave to look after them. But finally, in the summer term, he'd gone back to his job as head of music at the mightily posh and private St Vincent's – the school Annie had *slaved* to send her children to. It still made Annie smile to think that she'd first met Ed on a parent–teacher night.

When Ed and Owen had rushed out of the house at 8.15 this morning, Annie had felt so jealous of their need to be somewhere by a certain time. As she'd stood in the hall, ready to see them off, she hadn't quite been able to believe that once again she was adrift, at home, without a job.

Ed had kissed her goodbye and told her as cheerfully as possible: 'Keep busy, keep smiling. This is only day four. And this is *you* we're talking about. You always get through things. You are always OK. I know you!'

But staring at the computer screen now, it was hard to believe in herself. As usual, she had no back-up. Tamsin was the one and only executive she knew in the TV business. She hadn't a clue who else to speak to about finding a job. Well no, that wasn't quite true. She'd worked on another programme before. Although almost everyone who'd been involved with that had been a complete idiot.

Apart from Bob, the cameraman. He'd been so incredibly good, she'd immediately put him forward for the *HNTS* job.

She called Bob's number up on her phone.

'Hello Annie,' he answered almost immediately.

'Hey, how's it going? Have you recovered from the shock yet?'

'Yeah, yeah . . . you've got to be prepared in this business. I've been in it long enough to know that. I'm working on a nice little documentary up in Wales. Old friend of mine put me on to it.'

'You've got another job? Already?' She tried not to sound too resentful.

'Yeah . . . lot easier for me, though. I'm just the guy behind the scenes with the camera skills. You're the talent, you're the big name. It's much harder to find a new vehicle for you. Is there any word about *How Not To Shop*? Do you think someone else will go for it?'

'There's an online petition to bring it back.'

'I know, I've signed.'

'That's sweet. But, so far no word. Tamsin says she has a whole load of meetings lined up so here's hoping something will come of them.'

'Here's hoping . . . Catch you soon, girl, but I've just seen the director, so I'm going to have to look busy.'

Once the call was over, Annie was left staring at her screen again.

'Mulberry,' she typed in: 'sea green leather.'

There were several links to the purse which matched the bag she was desperate to get her hands on, and one article by a fashion editor lamenting the scarcity of the bag in green. But no further leads.

She phoned the number of the biggest Mulberry store in London.

Several minutes later and she had established that there were no green bags left anywhere in Britain.

'I know . . . isn't it such a shame?' the sales assistant sympathized, totally understanding Annie's distress. 'Do you have a friend in New York? Because apparently our Manhattan branches have still got a few greens. The colour's not been such a big wow over there as it has been here.'

As Annie put the phone down, she wondered if Elena, struggling with her failing business, would be in any sort of state to go on a little handbag errand for her. How was the dollar/pound exchange rate these days? Would it be cheaper or more expensive to buy the bag in the US?

She looked online, purely in the interests of theoretical research. Of course. And as she looked, she began to sniff.

There was a weird smell.

Annie got up from her desk and went out into the hallway. 'Dinah?' she called down the stairs, 'is something burning?'

There was no reply, no sound at all from downstairs. Dinah must have taken the twins out when Annie was on the phone.

But now it seemed to Annie that the smell was coming from upstairs. Lana and Owen's rooms were up in the attic . . . and the smell was something like burning hair.

'Lana!' Annie called up the staircase, 'are you OK?'

There was no reply.

With a jolt of worry, Annie began to hurry up the attic staircase, taking the steps two at a time. *She's just straightening her hair . . . she's just done something weird to her hair. It will be fine.* Annie told herself as she hotfooted it to the top of the house.

'Lana!' she called out again.

She tapped on Lana's door and when no reply came, she pushed it open.

'Lana, what's burn—?' Annie asked, but she could see immediately what was causing the smell.

Lana was lying on her bed, headphones on, eyes

closed, mouthing to the music. In her hands was a fat cigarette.

Was she out of her mind? Was she on drugs?! Was this some kind of cry for help?!

Annie stomped over and yanked the headphones lead out of the iPod. Lana opened her eyes and looked at her mum in surprise.

'What do you think you're doing?' Annie demanded, 'you are lying on your bed SMOKING! What's going on? Have you gone stark, staring, raving mad?'

Before Lana could even get a word out, Annie, hands on hips, went on: 'Is that what I think it is? Are you on drugs? Here? In your own bedroom?'

Lana rolled her eyes.

Then she leaned over and dropped the cigarette into the half-drunk mug of coffee at the side of her bed.

It fizzled and sank, making an even more horrible smell.

'Well?!'

'Calm down. It's herbal. And horrible. I'm not going to bother lighting up another one. OK? Happy now? Greta sent it to me, from Morocco.'

Lana pushed a package across the bed towards her mum. Annie unfolded the pages covered in Greta's tiny handwriting, and a bundle of photos and packet of herbal cigarettes tumbled out.

'She wrote a letter and sent you pictures? That's very twentieth century.'

43

'No internet where she's working, not even enough electricity to charge up her laptop. It's pretty far out.'

Annie looked at the photos and saw small boys and girls smiling, dressed in tatty, bleached-out clothes. In the background was a wood and mud hut. No, laptops didn't really fit in with this scene.

'I thought she was in the jungle . . . with yetis?'

Lana rolled her eyes again.

'She's in the Moroccan countryside, teaching English to schoolchildren. Suzie's the one in the Amazon. Planting trees. No one is doing anything with yetis.'

Greta had left in the second week of the summer holidays and, to be honest, Lana hadn't really cheered up since then.

'Do you wish you'd done something like this?' Annie asked gently.

Lana nodded slowly, and gave a great sigh: 'Well, you know why I didn't, because I still have to sort out what I'm going to do next. I have to read prospectuses and fill out application forms and go for interviews and try to decide what the hell it is I am going to do with my life.'

She sank back against her pillows as if just the thought of it was exhausting her.

'Lana . . .' Annie began gently, 'I'm really sorry the TV job has come to an end. Not just for me but also for you.'

Lana scowled.

'No, I have been thinking about you too, honestly.'

Lana had already spent most of the past three days hiding in her bedroom in a gloomier mood than ever, causing Annie a great deal of worry.

'We're both out of work right now,' Annie told her. She risked taking hold of her daughter's hand and patting it gently, 'I'm sorry darlin', you've not been through anything like this before. But I have. The worst thing you can do is lie on your bed and get depressed. You've got to get out there, keep busy. Why don't you go and see some of your friends who are still in town?'

'Ha! Everyone is either abroad working or so busy with their jobs here that they can't even see me on a Saturday, let alone an afternoon right in the middle of the week.'

'Well, there are still evenings, babes. Don't make it out to be totally bleak.'

'I haven't got any money to go out in the evenings anyway,' Lana huffed.

'I'll give you some money . . . maybe Owen will give you some money. He's the only one in the house who seems to have endless amounts of cash,' she joked. 'Maybe Owen would let you help on his—'

'Muuuuum,' Lana growled. Obviously doing any kind of work with her brother on his market stall was absolutely out of the question.

'OK, forget that,' Annie said.

Lana pushed the headphones socket back into the iPod and turned the music up again. This conversation was over.

She closed her eyes as further indication that her mother should leave the room.

But Annie stood there staring at her daughter in concern. What was Lana going to do now? It would be hard enough getting another TV series off the ground with a place in it for Annie. She was almost certainly not going to be able to bring her daughter along as part of the package.

If Lana had been at all enthusiastic about her film crew work, Annie might have been able to ask Bob to help her find a lowly paid position somewhere . . . but it had been obvious to Annie from the start that Lana was just going through the motions.

Annie couldn't use her retail contacts to fix Lana up with a shop assistant job either, because Lana had already refused point blank. And Ed couldn't find her any sort of classroom assistant work because she'd already declared: 'over my dead body'.

In fact, despite hours of conversation with her, no one was any clearer about what Lana was interested in doing.

Watching her daughter lying bored on the bed listening to music, surrounded by pictures from her best friend's new and exciting life, Annie worried. What if Lana became really unhappy? What if she got depressed? Suicidal, even?

Something had to be done. Drastic action was needed and Annie was the one who was going to have to take it.

Besides, she was in danger of slipping into a deeply unhappy place herself if all she could do now was hang about the house waiting for the phone to ring with good news.

'Lana?' Annie said loudly, hoping to be heard above the music, '*Lana*!'

The music went off and Lana looked grumpily up at her again. 'What?' she demanded.

'What do you think about going to New York?'

'Huh?'

'Would you like to go to New York?'

Lana's face looked blank, but she was at least sitting up now.

'Elena, you remember her?'

'Yeah, of course . . .'

'Well, Elena's having loads of problems with the dress company she's trying to run in New York and she's asked me to go over and help her. At first, I said no—'

'What?!'

Lana leaned forward, eyes wide. She even pushed her great heavy fringe out of her face.

It was the most animated Annie had seen her daughter in about two years.

'Well . . . I said no because of the filming schedule.'

Not to mention the babies, and my family and my husband . . .

'But?' Lana was just about panting.

'Well, now . . . now that I've no filming schedule, maybe I should offer to go over for a few weeks to help out . . . and since you're not doing anything else right now—'

Lana leapt off the bed and grasped her mother's arm. 'So?' she asked desperately 'So? You're going to go and you're going to take me with you? Is that what you're saying, mum?'

'Well, I'm just thinking about it. To be honest, my love, this has only just come into my head . . . I've not even . . .'

But it was too late. Like some deranged dervish, Lana, headphones still in her ears, was dancing and leaping about the room chanting, 'I'm going to New York! I'm going to New York!'

CHAPTER 5

New management Paula:

Tight grey jacket with wide lapels (Vivienne Westwood staff discount)
Bright blue body con dress (Hervé Léger staff discount)
Black suede gladiator heels (Jimmy Choo staff sale preview)
Total est. cost: £570

'We have a lovely little pink bolero . . .'

Annie pressed her flushed cheek against the cool glass of the underground carriage window. To say that Ed hadn't exactly warmed to her idea of a business trip to New York was an understatement.

Ed had a lot on his plate, Annie reminded herself, determined to try and see things from his point of view, at least a little. He'd only just returned to his very busy job as head of music at the precious and precocious St Vincent's after taking almost a whole year off to look after their babies.

The babies still didn't sleep every night through, so both parents were operating on a degree of grumpy frazzledness at all times. Still, she wasn't sure if that *entirely* excused him from calling her a 'hare-brained lunatic'.

'But Annie, you're supposed to be *here*,' he'd said last night. 'You are supposed to be right here, on standby in case your agent or producer calls with news about a new deal. For all we know, that could happen any day.'

In sheer stress, he managed to drop the salad bowl, breaking it into four jagged pieces and splattering the table, the wall and floor with green leaves, oil and vinegar.

The great big, guilt-inducing 'what about the children?' question came next.

'I was only planning to go for three weeks, four at the most,' she insisted. But at that, he'd landed a big juicy baby in her arms, making her feel like a guilty traitor for even saying the words.

'Lots of mummies have to travel for work. It's not the worst thing I could do.' She'd run her traitor's hand over Minnie's soft as a kitten curls.

'Maybe there won't *be* another TV job for me, Ed. Have you thought about that? Maybe I'll have to hope that I can go into business with Svetlana and Elena,' she told him as he picked salad from the wall.

'Of course I've thought about that!' he replied.

'I usually think about that in a cold sweat in the middle of the night when I'm also thinking about our vast mortgage, the twins' future school fees, Lana's next phase of education, your credit card bills and all the other expenses in my life.'

'You're the one who just took a *year* off,' she'd snapped back, regretting immediately how nasty it sounded. 'Don't think I'm not intending to earn just as soon as I possibly can.'

'Will they pay you for this New York trip?'

'Flights yes, and there's somewhere to stay.'

'No, Annie,' Ed had insisted, shaking his head. 'No I really think this is crazy. In another week or so, Tamsin will have sold *How Not To Shop* to another channel and you'll forget all about this. You loved that job! You're forgetting how much you loved that job, Annie.'

'But what about Lana?' It was her last attempt. 'She thought it was an amazing idea. She couldn't wait to get on the plane. I have four children, not just the twins. I have to think about Lana too.'

But Ed had shaken his head emphatically. For the time being, the discussion was over.

The tube train braked hard for Knightsbridge station, bumping Annie's cheekbone against the glass. She made her way off and hurried through the station until she was standing in the beating heart of London's swankiest shopping district.

Annie was supposed to be here to preview The Store's Autumn/Winter collection for a featurette on her TV programme. She just hadn't had the heart

51

to phone up and cancel. The Store staff were her most loyal fans and she couldn't bear to tell them in a bald phone call that the show had been cancelled. The least she could do was go in person . . . and maybe also just take a little look at some of the new things. Not that she was buying, obviously. But she could never, ever resist a peek.

As she clipped along the pavement in her platform-heeled, morale-boosting shoes, she looked up at the glittering windows of The Store now straight ahead of her.

The Store was a department store dedicated to fashion. Every important label, every major designer, every item needed, wanted, longed for and lusted after could be found at The Store. Well, if it was that hot, it would probably have sold out, but not to worry, once inside the shiny doors, you'd be certain to find something else to take its place in your heart.

To most Londoners, The Store was a chilly and intimidating place, full of four-figure price tags and ultra snooty staff. But for Annie, breaking into a smile as she pushed against the familiar glass revolving doors, The Store still felt a little bit like home.

She'd spent years of her life working here, progressing from sales assistant to personal shopper. Many of her good friends were still at The Store – the staff who'd lived through many of her past adventures with her – then there was the loyal client base who still had Annie on speed-dial for wardrobe advice in a crisis, and then there were the labels. What was Vivienne doing this season? And Stella? And Matthew? And Miuccia? Fashion, labels and the brand new season's collections had been a part of Annie's life for so long that she was always bursting to know.

For Annie, new clothes, new styles and the latest looks were a comfort, a fresh start . . . a source of hope and optimism.

'I know just exactly what you should do, Annie girl, you should come back and work for us. Even temporarily. You know we'd welcome you back with open arms. We're rushed off our feet,' Paula said as soon as Annie explained what had happened to her TV series. In The Store's Personal Shopping suite, a little crowd of staff had gathered round and now murmured in agreement.

'That's a lovely offer, but you have so totally filled my shoes,' Annie said, giving Paula the once-over and a significant wink.

Paula didn't just look amazing – it's hard for a six-foot-something black girl with a lithe figure to look bad – she also, for the first time, looked glamorously grown up.

The jacket over the bod-con dress was sober and serious. There was simple gold jewellery around her wrist and neck, and her long nails had been given an unusually elegant manicure. Not a zebra stripe or diamanté stud to be seen.

'Have you been promoted again?' Annie asked.

'Oh yeah,' Paula winked back, 'head buyer for this floor. Didn't I tell you?'

'Nooooo! Trips to Paris? And Milan?'

'Not yet, but they are coming right up.'

'Congratulations.' Annie dared to hug Paula again, even though embracing this gazelle made her feel like a small squashy frog.

'Come back to us,' Dale, from Menswear, repeated and the other assistants nodded eagerly.

'I can't yet,' Annie told them, 'it's too—'

She broke off because she definitely didn't want to hurt their feelings. But coming back would be too much of a step backwards. She'd been the presenter on her own TV show – she just couldn't return to personal shopping at The Store, no matter how welcoming, familiar and easy it would be.

'I still think a new TV thing will happen,' she told them instead. 'I had over a million viewers. There's an audience out there who like me and hopefully my producer can sell the show or a slightly different version to someone else. Fingers crossed.'

'What about your friend Svetlana?' Paula asked, 'wasn't she setting up a dress label with her daughter? Weren't you involved with that? In fact, we've got some of their dresses on order.'

'Fantastic! I love their dresses. I think the label is going to do brilliantly well . . . I even thought about going over to New York to help over there . . . but . . .'

'Excuse me?'

A voice interrupted the animated conversation.

All heads swivelled towards a woman standing at the entrance to the suite.

'I was just wondering about personal shopping . . . well, I've never been personally shopped . . . do I need an appointment? Do you charge?' she asked hesitantly.

'Come on in,' Paula said with an expansive sweep of her arm, 'our dedicated personal shopper isn't in this afternoon . . .'

Ah . . . how well Annie remembered her treasured weekdays off, designed to make up for the hectic blur of Saturdays at work and often Sundays too.

'Oh . . .' the woman at the door hesitated. She was holding a jumble of dark clothing and hangers in her hand.

'No seriously, come on in,' Paula urged, 'you're going to be in very safe hands today.' She gave Annie a wink as she said this: 'I'm the head buyer for the floor, but I'm having a quiet day. This is our former personal shopper who now does makeovers on TV and I have a feeling she's not going to be able to help getting involved. What are you looking for?'

'A dress . . .' the woman uttered the word with a degree of dread; despondence, even.

'That's good, we have lots of dresses,' Paula encouraged. 'Special event?'

'Ye-ees.' Again this sounded hesitant.

'Step into our boudoir,' Annie urged the woman, 'this is a nice problem to have and we're going to enjoy solving it for you.'

Just half an hour later, the woman – a fifty-something psychiatrist called Joanne Kettner – had sipped her way through one glass of complimentary champagne and abandoned the two severe black dresses she'd brought into the suite with her.

'Black is so strict,' Annie said, 'plus, I think it drains you. You don't want to have to wear tons of make-up if you don't usually. So, we'll try out a dress in a better colour that does all the brightening and tightening for you.'

For the first ten minutes or so of Joanne's session, Annie had tried hard to take a back seat. She'd tried to busy herself browsing the enormous rack of new season's clothes which Paula had set out for her to look at in her TV capacity.

But although Paula was good with Joanne, Annie just hadn't been able to stop herself from getting involved. Because she loved to shop for other people, maybe even more than she loved to shop for herself.

'My husband's going to be given an award at the kind of swanky ceremony I usually run a mile from. Most of the time I let him go to that kind of thing with work colleagues,' Joanne confided. 'But this one means a lot to him, he's asked me to come and I want to dress up, make the effort, go the extra mile. But . . . I'm a psychiatrist, I don't do fluffy or floral or flouncy or . . .'

'Fussy?' Paula suggested.

'No,' Joanne pulled a face at the very thought.

'So we want to go glamorously feminine, just a touch, an elegant ruffle or two, something just a little softer,' Annie chipped in, holding out two long silk cowl-necked dresses: one ivory with bold watercolour style pink and black flowers, the other violet with long, silky purple sleeves.

'Oh they are too pretty,' Joanne said, 'almost too pretty to try on.'

'Don't be mad, dresses *need* someone to try them on,' Annie insisted. 'That's when they come alive.'

Minutes later, Joanne stood before them in the ivory dress.

They all agreed it was beautiful, but Joanne didn't like the bare arms: 'I'm nearly fifty-three,' she protested, 'I think my arms need less attention.'

'We have a lovely little pink bolero . . .' Paula suggested.

'I've seen the price tag on this number,' Joanne said with a smile. 'There's no way I'm buying a bolero to go with it. We'll give the other one a go.'

When she stepped out in the violet and purple dress, Annie and Paula definitely had the 'that's it' look on their faces, but Joanne still looked troubled.

'It's beautiful,' Paula assured her, 'I love the way the neckline sits, and the drape at the front is so flattering.'

'It's lovely,' Joanne agreed, but she was still peering at herself critically.

'What are you thinking?' Annie had to ask. 'What are you telling yourself?'

Joanne turned from the mirror to look at her dressing guide properly: 'Which show is it you're on?' she asked.

'I had my own programme, called *How Not To Shop* – we did makeovers and shopping tips for real people and lots of fun slots. It was great,' Annie said sadly, 'I really loved it, but unfortunately, the plug has just been pulled. We were filming series two then boom . . . end of story.'

'I'm very sorry. Do you think you'll get another show?'

'I'll have to wait and see, but times are tough and there are so many other presenters who've done much more than me waiting in the wings.'

'Did you get any unexpected results?' Joanne wondered. 'Did you buy people new jeans, restyle their hair and suddenly find they were dumping their husbands and riding off into the sunset?'

'All the time,' Annie said with a grin. 'Almost everyone who applied to the show was on the verge of a big new change. I'm a psychiatrist too, you know, but with dresses, not drugs.'

Joanne laughed at this: 'Did you have a good producer who can get you more work?'

'Tamsin Hinkley, yes, she's fantastic, if anyone can get my show re-commissioned, it's her. But we're way off track here. We're supposed to be looking at you in this amazing dress. Are you

worrying that the dress is wearing you?' Annie
wondered.

Joanne smiled at this.

'That's exactly right. The dress is wearing me.
I'm so unused to a dress like this, I don't know
how to get back in charge.'

'No shoulder pads, no white-collared shirt,
you're all to pieces,' Annie teased.

'First of all, we need the shoes and the bag,'
Paula said and headed off to the shop floor to
find them.

'Then we need a little restyling . . . wait right
there,' Annie instructed her. 'Do not go anywhere.
I'm posting someone on the suite door to make
sure you don't flee.'

Within minutes, both Paula and Annie were
back. Joanne was buckled into four-inch strappy
silver evening shoes and handed a patent clutch.
Meanwhile Annie clipped on earrings, applied
lipstick and hairsprayed Joanne's short locks out
of her face.

'We want to counteract any hint of a move south.
Earrings are moving up, hair is moving up, lipstick
gives that central focal point – am I getting a bit
technical?' she joked.

When Joanne looked into the mirror this time,
she was just as poised and elegant as they hoped
she would be.

'Very good, girls,' Joanne smiled. 'Very well done.
The dress, yes, the bag, yes. I'm not even looking to
see how much it is because I'll be too horrified and

change my mind. Earrings yes, so long as they're costume jewellery, not real. I'm even going to buy the lipstick but the shoes . . .' she lifted one foot out from under the hem of her dress: 'no way the shoes. Even if they were the last shoes in Britain. No way!'

'Oh come on,' Annie urged her, 'you've got the whole of your life to be a sensibly dressed psychiatrist, wife and mother. One night in a pair of fantasy shoes isn't going to kill you.'

'I'll need lessons in how to walk.'

'Just swing your hips, baby,' Paula instructed and began in her four-inch heels to demonstrate the kind of shimmy that suddenly made her look giggly, Bambi-ish and 21 all over again.

'So what will you do if you don't get another job in TV?' Joanne asked Annie. 'Will you come back here and do this? You're very good, but I'm sure you know that.'

'What about New York, Annie? You were just about to tell me what you might go and do in New York,' Paula reminded her.

'When I rudely interrupted?' Joanne asked.

'Well . . . New York,' Annie couldn't help giving a little sigh, 'I have these friends who've set up their own dress label. They wanted me to go over and help out in New York . . . just for a bit. Nothing permanent. I was desperate to go, because I really can't stand sitting about waiting for something to happen . . .'

'But? I have the feeling there's a but coming,' Joanne prompted.

'But my husband thinks it's a mad idea. I was going to take my oldest daughter with me, she's just left school, but that would leave him in charge of the other three – and the babies are only a year old.'

'But New York?!' Paula insisted. 'Working for a label.'

'I know! I would have *loved* it. Even for a few weeks. But he won't agree. And I think I might have to accept that. I mean, he has a point. There are lots of reasons why . . .'

'Didn't you just tell me I've got my whole life to be a wife and mother? And a psychiatrist in sensible shoes?' Joanne asked gently.

She had clear, grey eyes and a soft smile. Her head was titled slightly and Annie felt as if the eyes were staring into her deepest thoughts, reading her mind and smiling knowingly at what she'd found there.

'It's our biggest challenge,' Joanne added, 'working out how to do the best we can for the people we love while remaining true to ourselves.'

True to ourselves.

The words rang in Annie's mind for a moment.

'You're good,' she told Joanne, 'but you probably don't need me to tell you that.'

'You have to be true to yourself or it eats you up inside, eventually. Trust me here. I've heard it so many times from so many different people.'

For several moments there was a thoughtful silence, then Annie snatched up her bag and rummaged about for her phone.

'Booking the flights to New York?' Paula wondered.

'No. Calling Ed. There's still five more minutes of lunch break, I might be able to catch him and then . . . I'll have the chance to talk to him again.'

'To tell him you're going to New York?' Paula persisted, excitement in her voice.

'Well . . . I won't put it quite as baldly as that . . . but . . . YES!'

CHAPTER 6

Plane Lana:

Black vest top (Topshop)
Black skinny jeans (Primark)
Pink pointy pumps (New Look)
Pink and black fringed scarf (Vintage Miss
Selfridge via Oxfam)
Overwhelming scent sensation (duty-free)
Total est. cost: £50

'Oh look! Look at that!'

'So you're going to be fine. You're going to be absolutely, totally fine? Do you promise? You won't let one single thing go wrong?' Annie asked, aware that her heart was racing at panic-speed.

'Yes,' Ed said simply, solidly, utterly reassuringly. He placed his hands on her shoulders as if to weigh her down and bring calm to her frantic mind.

'So you're going to go and see Mum this

weekend, to give Dinah a break. And you'll take the babies, but Owen will obviously be at the stall. But you'll be back in time to give him dinner and—'

'Shhhh,' Ed soothed.

'Mum said something about Stefano going away for a fortnight,' Annie remembered suddenly. 'I don't know if that's soon, or if maybe she's just got confused. You need to speak to him and find out. Because if he's going away, Mum can't be on her own, she'll have to come and stay with us, so we'll need to know when that is. And I hope I'll be back by then otherwise you'll have too much to—'

'Annie! Stop it! I'll speak to Stefano on Saturday. I'll get the dates of his holiday and the recipe for his chorizo casserole. OK? You were the one who wanted to go on this trip,' Ed reminded her, his hands sliding to the tops of her arms, which he squeezed affectionately.

'Yes, yes . . .' she said distractedly because now that the boarding card was actually in her hand, now that her entire family was assembled around her at passport control ready to say goodbye, now she just wasn't quite sure if she really could manage to go.

Ed put his hand under her chin and turned her face towards his.

Oh no. Oh no, it really was going to be time to say goodbye.

'Look, you've convinced me that this is a good idea. That it is really important for you,' he reminded her, 'so now you have to go. Stop worrying about us. We're going to be fine. And you're going to be great!' he encouraged her.

'Is it too late to change my mind then?' Annie whispered, her eyes fixed on his.

'Your luggage is checked in! That would cause all kinds of complications. Plus,' he leaned over to whisper against her ear, 'Lana would kill you.'

This was probably true.

Annie hugged him very, very tightly, then pushed her lips against his in a deep kiss. Suddenly a gap of four weeks and the entire Atlantic Ocean seemed very real and very frightening.

'Do we *have* to watch this?' Owen asked from his place behind the twins' buggy.

Lana nudged her brother with her elbow. 'We have to say goodbye too,' she reminded him.

'Yeah, well, don't think I'm going to kiss you.'

'You'll be sorry if our plane stalls, dives into the sea and we're never seen again.'

'Lana!!' Annie pulled away from Ed and made a horrified face, 'don't even joke about it.'

'Please don't cry over the babies,' Ed warned her, 'you'll just make them upset.'

Annie knelt down in front of the buggy and both Micky and Minnie began to giggle and babble, delighted with her attention.

'I'm going to see you later, buddies,' Annie told them as cheerfully as she could, with a big smile across her face, although now that she was really doing this she felt as if her heart might crack.

Minnie, who was an acutely sensitive soul, seemed to pick up that all was not well and an anxious look began to build in her face.

Annie decided to unbuckle her and wrap her up in a big hug.

'Bye-bye Min, see you very soon. Very, very soon,' Annie said, rubbing her hand over her baby's back.

Her baby girl nuzzled her face against Annie's shoulder.

'Daddy's here, and Owen and Aunty Dinah. Mummy and Lana will be back soon.'

'Mumma,' Min said, squeezing her podgy arms tightly around Annie's neck.

If Min cried or protested, Annie wasn't sure if she would have the strength to walk through the departure gate.

'Boo!' Owen had crept up behind Annie and now popped up under Min's face, causing her to break into a giggle. 'Come to big bruv,' he said, holding out his arms and grinning.

Min let go of Annie and accepted a lift from Owen without the slightest worry.

'You're a star, Owen,' Annie said, and bent over to kiss him.

'Watchit!' Owen warned, 'no lips! One on the cheek is all you're getting.'

'A hug? At least a hug . . .'

He gave her a brief, one-armed squeeze because of Min. 'And remember my DVDs. The full list plus the money is in that envelope I put into your bag this morning. All right?

'Take care,' she told him, swallowing a lump in her throat the size of a potato.

'We'll be sweet as a nut, Mum. You go off with Lana and have a ball. And next time you're going to New York, you're definitely taking me, OK?'

She kissed him again and ruffled his hair, just to annoy him: 'I love you, *all right*?'

Then it was time to squeeze the life out of Micky and give Ed one last, long hug. Until the build-up of tears behind her eyes was at danger level.

'You'll be fine. You'll be more than fine,' she whispered, 'you're the best Dad ever and you run the house like clockwork.'

Feeling his arms hold her tight and his curly hair brush her face, for a moment she thought of when she'd first been invited into Ed's basement of chaos. So much had changed. Imagine if she'd known then that he would become her totally domesticated husband and they would have *twins*!

'OK, see you in four weeks!' Lana called out. She was incredibly cheerful and excited. Ever since the flights had been booked, the cloud of boredom and gloom hovering above her for so long had completely evaporated.

She whirled round her family, landing quick kisses on cheeks then took hold of Annie's arm. 'C'mon Mum, it's time to go. New York is waiting for us!'

As soon as her family was out of sight, Annie cried hard.

She cried all the way through the security process and on into the departure lounge. There, Lana marched her to a bar and made her buy a glass of buck's fizz, even though it was eight in the morning. Only when the entire drink was downed, did Annie finally stop sobbing.

She blew her nose and began to look around through streaky eyes. There was a full ninety minutes till boarding.

'We could try on a lot of perfume in ninety minutes,' she pointed out, with a final sniff.

'We could,' Lana agreed with a grin.

'You're supposed to stick to three or four . . . apparently the nose gets confused.'

'Right.'

Annie hadn't managed to doze for even one moment on the flight, and neither had Lana. It was cramped, chilly and claustrophobic on the plane. How had transatlantic travel managed to become like a marathon bus ride? Where was the glamour? People had once arrived in New York by steam liner with bellboys in pressed uniforms ready to trolley their initialled leather trunks behind them.

Annie pulled the lump of fibre held together by static which passed for a blanket around her shoulders.

Once the champagne buzz had worn off, the first hour of the flight had been hard. Watching the coastline of Ireland slip away beneath them and the great steely grey expanse of water begin, Annie had brooded on the fact that the entire Atlantic Ocean was going to be between her and Ed, Owen and her babies.

An ocean! What had she been thinking? She couldn't help feeling that there was no way she was going to last four weeks. This would be impossible. But it hadn't seemed fair to mention such doubts to Lana, who was glowing, tingling, just about out of her mind with excitement about landing at JFK in a few hours' time.

Whenever Annie's face looked worried, Lana had made her order another glass of fizz. So now, six hours later, Annie was gulping water and trying to recover from the effects of high altitude early morning drinking.

Plus, the concerned look on the face of their American air hostess was becoming a little bit off-putting. There had been no denying the reprimand in the last: '*Another* glass of sparkling wine for you, ma'am? Ok-aaaaay.'

Lana had shut down the in-flight entertainment and was now looking out of her window with unmistakable delight. When Annie peered over Lana's shoulder to get a glimpse of the view, she too felt a jolt of excitement. Below was a bright blue sea and a long blond strip of coastline.

'Wow! Could that be New England?' Annie asked.

'Maybe. Doesn't it look beautiful? There are islands . . . maybe it's the Hamptons. Maybe we're almost there.'

Annie took a glug from her bottle of water and tried to run calming hands over her hair. But it was no use: static from the blanket, from the fuzzy velour seats, from the very atmosphere of the plane was making her hair crazy. She poured a little mineral water into her hands, then smoothed wet fingers over her short blonde bob.

'Better?' she asked Lana.

But Lana didn't even turn; her eyes were glued to the window. She pointed with her finger and her mouth dropped open in awe.

'That's it,' she whispered, 'the skyline. Ohmigod! We're here. Look, Mum. LOOK!'

Lana moved her shoulder back so that Annie could see out of the little glass oval. There was a tiny, postcard-perfect view of a jagged square centimetre of Manhattan skyline. Now Annie had to gasp too.

'Oh look! Look at that!'

'The buildings are so *big*. The island is so *small*. Oh this is amazing.'

The plane wheeled around in the sky and suddenly they were looking at blue ocean, tiny toy ships and—

'There! It's the Statue of Liberty! So small!'

'But it must be so big! Compared to that ship . . .'

'We are nuts.'

'This is soooooo brilliant.'

'I can't believe we've done it!'

'I can't believe we're really going to New York!'

70

'We're going to New York, we're going to New York!'

'I still can't believe it.'

'This is the best trip I've *ever*, ever been on,' Lana announced, grin right across her face.

'Babes, we've not even landed yet. We might still crash . . . or land up in some flea-pit with cockroaches . . . or get mugged – murdered, even.'

'Mum, this is the best ever trip. The best ever idea. Thank you!'

To Annie's amazement, her sulky, grumpy, slouchy, grouchy teenager was suddenly throwing her arms around her.

'Thanks, Mum.'

'It's OK. I would never have been brave enough to come on my own, babes. Thank you for forcing me onto the plane,' Annie admitted.

As they hugged, Annie dared to stroke her girl's hair, just as she'd done when she was little. A prickle of tearfulness welled up in her eyes and nose.

'We're going to have a ball, babes. A totally wonderful ball.'

All the horror of queuing for two entire hours in the cramped, windowless space of JFK's arrival hall evaporated when Annie and Lana got into their bright yellow New York cab and began the journey into Manhattan.

When the Brooklyn Bridge and then the skyscraper skyline came into view, they began to shriek at each other in a fever pitch of excitement.

'There's the Empire State!'

'No *that's* the Empire State!'

'Look at that!'

'Look over there!'

'This bridge is amazing!'

'Everything's amazing. Look at the size of the buildings.'

'Look how many cabs. How much traffic.'

'We have to shut up. The driver is laughing at us. He thinks we've come in from a farm or something.'

The driver did begin to laugh at this. 'Where yo from?' he asked, pushing back a sweaty baseball cap.

'London,' Annie admitted.

'No skyscrapers in London?!'

'Not like this. Not all jammed together like this,' Lana told him.

It was hot. They hadn't been prepared for the wave of heat shimmering off the tarmac as they'd climbed down the aeroplane steps. And now, inside the taxi, the black plastic seats were sticky with heat and humidity. Annie had brought choice items from her autumn wardrobe; she wasn't prepared for the knockout heat of high summer.

'Is it always like this in September?' Annie asked the driver.

'No ma'am, for September this is *hahht*,' he replied.

'Hahht,' Annie repeated, enjoying the accent. She couldn't stop looking out of the cab window at the looming Manhattan skyline, hazy in the early afternoon heat.

This was heaven.

She'd only been to New York once before for a magical long weekend with Ed and she'd forgotten how brilliant it was: the excitement, the hustle, the crazy feeling of everything at once being brand new because she'd never been before and yet so strangely familiar because she'd seen it all so often on the screen.

'Wow . . . wow . . . double wow . . .' Lana repeated in a reverential whisper.

'Here and loving, loving, loving it! Thank you. Could not be here without you.' Annie texted Ed.

Once they were over the bridge, the cab joined the traffic swirling through the Lower East Side towards the address in lower midtown which Svetlana had given them.

'So where are we going?' Lana asked, eyes still fixed to the window: they were passing a play park and it was so different from London because the kids were all in baggy vest tops bouncing and chasing a basketball. By the side of the road, a man with a bucket was washing down an enormous shiny brown car with a white roof which looked like it had driven straight out of an Elvis movie.

'We're heading for East 16th Street between Fifth and Sixth,' Annie replied. 'Doesn't mean much to me . . . but that's what it says. Building 1157, apartment 121. You know Svetlana, it vill be simply vonderrrrrful.'

'Yeah but don't forget, this is Elena's end of the business.'

'Hmmm.'

Lana had a point. While Svetlana was a woman used to luxury, a woman who could not in fact see the point of life without luxury, her daughter Elena was very different.

Elena was thrifty, ambitious and tough. She had been brought up by relatives in the Ukraine on the £50 a month or so which Svetlana, busy scaling the London super-rich scene, had billed as 'manicure' and used to fund the upbringing of the daughter she hadn't wanted then, but was so very fond of now.

Despite their very different styles, the business had been working well. Until their New York partner had messed things up and bailed out with lots of their money, obviously.

The cab was on a wide, four-laned avenue now, the traffic jumpy, snarled and impatient and the driver blaring his horn and yelling at everything ahead.

Annie couldn't help gaping at the shops. Huge glass window fronts, making chain stores like Gap look as glossy and important as major department stores.

'You do like Elena, don't you?' Annie asked her daughter all of a sudden. 'I mean, she's a bit different from how she was when she stayed with us. Do you remember?'

Both of them laughed at the memory of Elena on their doorstep in high heels and micro-mini with bad blonde hair dye and dodgy male friends. The very picture of Eastern European chic.

'She's better dressed for starters,' Lana pointed out.

'Oh yes, very smart, very businesslike. And she's so good at her job, so efficient. I can't really believe she let a partner mess her up like this.'

'I bet she's glad you're turning up to help her out.'

'I can't wait,' Annie admitted, 'I've been bored out of my nut sitting at home waiting for the phone to ring.'

'This is yo street,' the cab driver announced, then, turning a sharp right at a huge window display of the most gorgeous handbags Annie thought she'd ever seen, he drove into a narrower one-way street with a mixture of tall apartment blocks and smaller old brownstone houses on both sides.

'Nice neighbo'hood,' the driver commented.

Lana and Annie scanned the street for the right number: 1123 . . . 1141 . . .

'Isn't that what's-her-name?' Annie said, pointing to a girl who was standing at the door of one of the brownstone houses, searching in her bag . . . maybe for a set of keys.

'Who?' Lana asked.

'That girl, the English one, she writes for *Vanity Fair* . . . Emily . . . ? Emily Wilmington. I'm sure that's her. In DVF, carrying a very nice bag,' Annie added approvingly. 'We're staying on the same street as Emily Wilmington! Amelia and Ginger will never, ever believe me.'

'Get a photo!' Lana suggested.

But too late: the girl had opened her front door and slipped inside.

'There it is!' Lana exclaimed and pointed to a high, ten- or twelve-storey building, of red brick. Rows and rows of bells were lined up beside the double glass front doors.

Once they were out of the taxi and standing on the pavement, Annie and Lana couldn't help exchanging glances . . . both feeling a heady rush of excitement and astonishment.

'We made it!' Annie told Lana. 'We're here. We're standing in East 16th Street, midtown, between Fifth and Sixth!'

'We came up Sixth,' Lana said, 'so that—' she pointed a short distance ahead to the junction on the other end of the street – 'that must be Fifth Avenue. Right there.'

Annie smiled: 'This is sooo cool. C'mon, find bell, let's get in, let's see Elena, let's dump luggage and let's get out again!'

Lana found the right number and pressed the buzzer. Several moments later, a fuzzy 'hello' came out of the intercom and the front door clicked open.

Inside, the lobby was dark and cool, lined with locked letterboxes and four elevators with shiny golden doors.

'Tenth floor,' Annie instructed Lana, looking at her scribbled instructions.

The lift brought them out into a nondescript corridor lined with brown doors and hideous wall lights. Checking numbers, they walked left, then turned down another long corridor. At number 121 they stopped and Annie knocked at the door.

Several moments later and Elena was standing in front of them. But she looked nothing like the Elena they remembered.

'Are you OK?' Annie asked straight away.

Elena's long blonde hair was hanging lank and limp round a pale, exhausted face. There wasn't a trace of make-up to hide the circles under her eyes and she was wrapped up in a short silky dressing gown. Even though it was lunchtime in NYC, Elena obviously hadn't made it out of her pyjamas yet.

'No, not OK,' the deep, accented voice replied gloomily, 'and I asked my mother to tell you not to come.'

CHAPTER 7

Elena miserable:

Floral silk dressing gown (Victoria's Secret)
Worn white T-shirt (borrowed from Sye)
Chipped pedicure in Fire Engine Red (Thai
Blossom nail boutique)
iPhone (Apple)
Total est. cost: $600

'End of business. End of story.'

'**B**ut we're here to help you!' Annie exclaimed, putting her bright smile of greeting back in place and trying not to feel too winded by Elena's less than enthusiastic welcome.

'Huh,' came the unwilling response.

'But your mother thought I could be lots of help, darlin',' Annie insisted, 'and Svetlana thought it would be useful for Lana to come and help us all out too. Free workers – that's got to be a good thing.'

Elena couldn't have registered Lana at first, because now she brightened slightly, peered over Annie's shoulder and said, 'Lana, I not know you here. Please come in.'

For a moment, Annie wasn't sure if this meant she had to stay outside.

But Elena repeated: 'Come in,' and she did seem to mean both of them.

She opened the door wide and stood back to let them into the tiny corridor. This opened out onto a bright room with a white-tiled floor which contained a kitchenette, a fold-down sofa, a TV, a tiny café table scattered with papers, and all in a space about two metres square. Now that all three of them, plus Annie and Lana's bags were in the room, it felt claustrophobically small.

'There is only one very small bedroom,' Elena explained, 'You will have to stay here.'

Lana gave a little gasp of surprise while Annie dismissed the idea as bonkers, quickly trying to work out if she could afford to move them into a hotel. But four whole weeks? That would just be totally beyond the budget. Impossible. Almost as impossible as trying to live in a tiny kitchen, on a fold-down sofa . . . with Lana!

Annie was conscious that she needed a long, cool, thirst-quenching drink. A long bladder-relieving pee might also have been a nice idea, not to mention a comfortable seat and a degree of pampering. But, nevertheless, she turned to Elena and tried to concentrate on the poor girl's woes.

'You look very upset. Has it been a terrible time?' she asked soothingly.

Elena sank her long-limbed, lanky frame down onto the corner of the squashy sofa which Annie had been eyeing up for herself and threw her head dramatically into her hands.

Lana and Annie pulled up the two spindly café table chairs and prepared to listen.

It was a fraught story.

The partner had disappeared, taking with her a sizeable chunk of company money and leaving unpaid debts, including at the factory which had made the last run of dresses. Elena had no intention of pursuing the ex-partner through the courts because: 'this America – lawyers and doctors are the most expensive people. Once you get involved you can never stop paying.'

There were many orders to fulfil: a whole range of high end shops had placed requests for the next collection of Autumn/Winter dresses. The shops were expecting those dresses within weeks but there was no money to buy material, or to have the dresses made up. The factory in Hong Kong was not going to make a single dress for Elena until she had paid her bill for the last order.

'I don't know how to get out of this,' Elena confessed. 'I think I will have to tell everyone who has ordered dresses that we can't deliver. But then we will be finished. End of business. End of story.'

She glanced up as she said this and Annie could see that she was close to tears.

'I don't know what to do,' Elena added in a shaky voice.

There were so many questions Annie would have liked to ask, so many possible suggestions, solutions, areas to explore. But just then Elena's phone bleeped. As she picked it up and checked the screen an unexpected smile flashed across her face.

'Sye is at the door. He's coming up,' she beamed, looking up at them.

Ah. Sye. Of course.

Annie remembered now.

Sye was a very handsome, utterly charming photographer, based in New York, who'd met Elena at the first Perfect Dress fashion show in Paris, back in the spring. Sye, with his dreamy eyes and hippie cool hair, was very possibly the reason 22-year-old Elena had been so keen to quit London and her mother's comfortable Mayfair mansion in order to open up the New York Perfect Dress 'office'.

Yes, having a New York 'office' sounded very impressive, but the New York Perfect Dress office was in fact, Annie suspected, the little spindly-legged coffee table she was now sitting at.

'How is Sye?' Annie asked.

It was amazing how Elena's face had brightened.

'He's good,' she replied, 'he's very good. He always makes me feel better about everything.'

'OK, so, when you're ready, we will talk about the business. You'll tell me all about the problems and we'll think hard about what we can do to solve them. I promise you, I've had all kinds of financial ups and down in the past and I want to do everything I can for you.'

With a shy smile, Elena replied: 'I know. You are a very good person. Think of the fashion show. It would never have happened without you and I would never meet Sye and sell the first dresses. I'm sorry I not very kind when you arrive. Sorry,' she smiled apologetically first at Annie, and then Lana.

'Fogeddaboudit,' Annie said, trying out her new 'transatlantic' twang. Lana nodded in agreement.

There was a tap on the door and Elena jumped up to answer, running her fingers through her hair as she did so. She disappeared behind the small partition wall which screened the living room from the door.

Annie and Lana smiled at each other as they heard the exchange of 'Hey baby's and the long, smoochy kiss that followed. Then Sye came into the room, Elena draped around his waist and shoulder.

'Hey there,' he said with a big grin.

'Hi,' Annie and Lana replied.

'Nice to see you again,' Annie told him, 'you look well.'

'You too . . . Just off the plane? You must be exhausted.'

'No! Too excited. Too much to see. Too much to do,' she told him.

'I know – this city is the best,' he said with a grin.

Sye was as scruffily handsome as Annie remembered, dirty blond curls, heavy stubble, tanned face, strong tanned arms emerging from his rolled up shirtsleeves. Broad shoulders crisscrossed by at least two camera straps.

Annie wouldn't have thought at first glance that Sye was the man for Elena – and certainly Svetlana could not stand the thought of her daughter hooked up with such an ordinary mortal, when she wanted Elena married off to a multimillionaire 'at least' – but it was obvious Elena and Sye were devoted to each other.

Maybe Sye's easy charm and relaxed friendliness were the perfect foil for Elena's intense ambition and nerviness.

The pair sat down on the sofa and after several moments of watching them trying and failing to keep their hands off each other, Annie realized that she and Lana needed to be out of the way.

'Are you as hungry as me?' she asked Lana.

'Definitely.' Lana looked away with something of a blush as the hand around Elena's waist slid down to her buttock and squeezed.

Elena moved one leg over Sye's and the two sat entangled together, jiggling, finding it almost impossible to concentrate on anything else but each other.

'I think we'll go out, Elena,' Annie announced. 'Get some food, walk around the neighbourhood . . . step out onto Fifth Avenue for the first time.'

'Good idea. Eat first. We talk later,' Elena agreed, then floated a kiss onto Sye's earlobe.

'We'll call you when we're thinking of coming back. OK? Or maybe meet you somewhere out?'

'Hmmm mmm . . . ya . . .' Elena was looking deep into Sye's eyes. She brushed his hair out of his face and he nipped her hand with a hungry kiss as it passed his mouth.

'You're not changed. We should go to your room and get you changed,' he told Elena in a voice which was intense and urgent. It was as if Lana and Annie had already evaporated.

No time to fix her hair, no time to change her shoes, Annie just snatched up her handbag and headed for the door. She pulled Lana along with her. It was definitely time to get out of here, before they were watching a live show.

CHAPTER 8

Most handsome passer-by:

Freshly pressed pink shirt (Gant)
Freshly pressed white jeans (Levi's)
Brown boat shoes (Timberland)
Gold-rimmed sunglasses (Ray-Ban)
Brown mailbag (Dooney & Bourke)
Fresh, clean scent (Calvin Klein)
Total est. cost: $950

Flirty smile

'Did you know it was going to be as hot as this?' Lana said, instantly regretting the fact that she was still wearing her travelling jeans.

'Air conditioning,' Annie said, 'you get all cool and comfortable and then you can't adjust to the real temperature outside again. Relax, we'll walk slowly, on the shady side of the street. Fifth Avenue first?'

'Oh yeah!'

The irrepressible, wild with excitement smile had returned to Lana's face. The one she'd been wearing as soon as the taxi had carried them over Brooklyn Bridge and into this amazing city.

Down the street they went, past a bookstore, a swanky interiors shop and a smart café. The pavement widened as they approached the Avenue and then – pow! They were standing *gobsmacked* in the vast canyon of one of the most famous avenues in the world.

Both Annie and Lana had to look right, left, up, right, left and up again to take in the vast scale of this road.

It was wide, wide, wide with multiple lanes of honking, jangling traffic. And it was so high! Five-, ten-storey, even twenty-storey buildings on each side and in the distance skyscrapers, but with the Avenue cutting a vast concrete valley between them.

'It's fantastic!' Lana gasped and did a little dance, 'I can't believe it! Look, there's the Empire State, finally! Right ahead of us. It looks like we could just walk in a straight line and be there.'

Annie was too overwhelmed to speak. She was trying to take it all in: the vast Avenue, the gleaming shop windows all around, the hustle of the crowds rushing past them, the stifling heat, and the overwhelming adrenalin buzz of the place.

Just looking at this street was like chain-drinking espressos. It was incredible!

'I'm never leaving,' Lana announced. 'I'm going

to stay here for ever. This is my spiritual home, Mum.'

'Me too,' Annie agreed, 'let's walk!'

So they strode side by side through the lunchtime bustle, Annie – eyes on stalks – checking out the shop windows, each more enticing than the next, and then, of course, the New Yorkers themselves.

There was a definite New York summer look: pencil thin figure, bright sleeveless dress, big hair, big sunglasses, high heels or manicure with flip-flops plus blingtastic bag.

In the last minute she'd seen a Prada, three Coaches, a Marc Jacobs and a rash of Louis Vuittons: possibly real, possibly fake. These girls loved their arm-candy.

'Don't they look amazing?!' Annie said, meaning the women.

'I have never, ever seen so many good-looking guys in such a short space of time,' came Lana's astonished reply.

Annie gave her a nudge, but now that she looked, she could see it was true.

New York men all seemed to be tall and lean with immaculate hair, sunglasses perched on their heads, tight jeans, clean pressed polo shirts. And they had muscles! Teeny waists! High buns!

'They can't all be gay . . . can they?' Lana wondered.

Several blocks on, the irresistible window of the 21st Street Deli drew them in. Inside was a salad bar on truly epic New York scale.

'I don't know what to get,' Lana wailed in front of the triple rows of salad on offer. 'I'm not even going to have room in my box for a bit of everything!'

When they were sitting in front of a huge glass window eating salad and sipping iced tea in the air-conditioned splendour, Annie's mobile rang.

'Hello.'

She recognized Ed's voice straight away.

'Hi there!' she replied.

'You've adopted the lingo then.'

'I've adopted the city. I'm a New Yorka now. You guys are going to have to pack up and move over to join us. Kidding!' she added quickly. 'Is everything OK?'

'Yes. We're just phoning to say good-night,' Ed said.

'Good-night?!' She looked out of the window: the Avenue was still bathed in blazing sunshine.

'It's 9.30p.m. Babies in bed, Owen in shower, me thinking about turning in early,' he said and gave a yawn.

'Long day at school?'

'It's always a long day at school.'

'And you're all OK?' she asked again.

We're fine, Mick and Min have had a lovely day. Don't worry about us. We're all coping. Are you having a great time?'

'As a tourist, fabulous. As a dress-business consultant . . . we'll have to wait and see. Elena is all over the place. But I'm hoping we'll be able to help. Lana's fantastic. She's in love with New York – aren't you, darlin'? Ed, there haven't been any calls, have there? Tamsin? Anything like that? No,' Annie answered her own question, 'they would phone my mobile.'

'No. Nothing. Have you told her you're in New York for four weeks?'

'Well, not exactly. I said I might be out of town for a . . . bit . . .'

'Annie!'

'It'll be fine. Honest. OK, we shouldn't talk for too long, should we? Transatlantic phone bills.'

'No,' Ed agreed.

'Well, bye for now, babes, I love you.'

'Love you too.'

Then the line went dead and for a moment, Annie felt the pang. London was so far away. If anything happened . . .

But Lana's excitement brought her right back to the lure of New York.

'Where are we going to go next?' Lana wanted to know. 'Shall we keep on walking? Shall we take a cab somewhere?' She pulled her well-thumbed guidebook from her bag and began to flick through the pages she'd marked up.

'What about Wall Street? Or Central Park? Or the Flatiron Building . . . it's really close by. Or the Empire State? Or the Statue of Liberty?'

'Lana! It's OK,' Annie assured her, 'we're going

to be here for *four weeks*. We don't need to see the whole of New York in a day.'

It was 1a.m. British time when Annie and Lana finally flagged enough to venture back to Elena's apartment.

It was 8p.m. in New York but the pace of the city hadn't slackened in the slightest. In fact it almost seemed busier. The shops were open till 10p.m. *most nights*! Annie felt torn between glee because the shopping would never end, and sympathy for the sales staff. Their shift rotas must be nightmarish.

'D'you think Elena will be in a better mood now?' Lana asked as they stood in front of the row of bells once again and prepared to buzz.

'Yeah . . . I'm sure,' Annie replied, 'when I phoned her to say we were on our way back, she sounded much better.'

But when Elena answered the door to her apartment, she looked just as distraught as she had done earlier in the day.

'What's the matter now, my love?' Annie asked, fearing a fresh calamity on the Perfect Dress front.

'It's Sye,' Elena gasped, clearly on the verge of tears.

'Is he OK?'

Elena nodded.

'Has he broken up with you?'

Elena shook her head.

'Then what is it?'

Elena stepped back from the door, letting them and the several bags of shopping they seemed to have acquired into the little apartment.

'He's going away,' Elena wailed, collapsing onto the sofa.

She was freshly showered, Annie noticed, wet hair wafting a delicious scent, but her shoulders were slumped and she looked totally miserable.

'Where's he going?' Lana asked.

'On a shoot, in Venezuela, for *six days*.'

Annie couldn't help the smile that crossed her face. Elena must have it bad if a six-day absence was the cause of this much grief.

'But, Elena, that's what Sye does,' Annie reminded her. 'He's a fashion photographer! You should be proud of him. And he's obviously totally mad about you, anyone can see that just by the way he looks at you.'

'But this man. This beautiful man,' Elena exclaimed miserably, 'he will be surrounded by beautiful models all day long.'

Annie couldn't believe this lovely girl could be so insecure. 'He'll be fine, Elena. You're the one he wants to be with,' she said, 'try and remember that. Now, we need to talk about business.'

'Oh yah,' Elena gave a shrug, 'more bad news. Someone who give us £10,000 to start up Perfect Dress wants money back. So now we have close to zero.'

CHAPTER 9

Annie does New York:

Purple sleeveless draped dress (Banana Republic)
Nude peep-toe platforms (Marc Jacobs)
Oversized sunglasses (Nina Ricci)
Blue patent leather tote bag (DKNY)
Total est. cost: $920 (Ooops)

'Everyone has setbacks.'

Bright sunshine peeped through the small blind-free window of the tiny kitchen-meets-sitting room, waking Annie at the ungodly hour of five the next morning. But as it was 11a.m. in Britain, she felt as if she'd had a luxurious lie-in.

Despite having to cope with a new sleeping partner in a cramped bed, Annie had slept soundly. She glanced over at Lana and saw that her daughter was still fast asleep, despite the noise of the bin-men now rattling and clanking metal dustbins down in the street below.

She broke into an excited grin. Even the noise of dustbins being emptied was thrilling because they were New York dustbins . . . *trash cans*, she remembered.

Annie stole out of bed quietly and after a visit to the pocket-sized bathroom, stuffed with more toiletries and products than Annie had seen in many chemist shops, she clicked on the coffee machine, sat down at the tiny café table and decided that Elena couldn't mind too much if she took a look through the large pink files all neatly labelled: Perfect Dress.

Despite a talk with Elena about the business yesterday evening, Annie felt she needed to see all the documents, the invoices, the facts and figures. Only then would she really have a clear idea of how to launch a rescue plan.

Besides, she'd been invited in as a partner. Surely, there couldn't be a problem with looking through the books?

She suspected Elena would be asleep for at least another two hours. After crying on first Annie and then Lana's shoulder, Elena had dressed up and headed out for her last evening with Sye before he left for Venezuela. Annie knew that Elena had come home because her bag and leather jacket were slung over the other café chair.

Sipping at her coffee, Annie looked through pages and pages of orders, invoices and printouts of email exchanges. Then she came to the photo-copied papers with the latest dress designs. A talented Italian designer, based in London, was the person who translated Elena and Svetlana's 'creative vision' into the kind of paper patterns which factories could use.

Annie looked through the pages carefully with her seasoned shopper's eye. The drawings were beautiful. Truly lovely designs that managed to combine fashionable with classic, stylish with wearable. So very clever. Annie remembered what had made her invest some of her own money in the Perfect Dress label.

Svetlana and Elena's inspired idea was to make comfortable dresses which could be dressed up or down for every occasion. These were swishy, fluid shirtdresses and wraps in bright colours and luxurious but machine-washable fabrics. Dresses that could do the school run in boots and a denim jacket, but then a dinner party in heels and a necklace.

They hovered between the £200 and £300 mark: just above the high street, but below designer label prices.

From her understanding of the files in front of her, Elena had tens of thousands of pounds' worth of orders to fulfil but debts with her factories and now absolutely no money left in the bank. What she needed was to raise some advance cash, money which would let her make the dresses to meet these orders. When the order money came in, she'd be able to pay off her factory debts, then her creditors, and she'd still have money in the bank to get next season's dresses lined up.

Despite the financial hiccups, Annie was convinced the dress label was still a great idea. Look how many shops had placed orders! Bloomingdale's had ordered close to ninety dresses for the period between September and February. Annie remembered now that Sye's mother had something to do with Bloomingdale's and this was how Perfect Dress had gained its first foothold in the US.

So, in a nutshell: they just had to raise some serious funds and find a dress factory that would run their order . . . that was all.

Annie glanced again at the Bloomingdale's order to see when the first dresses were expected. In *three weeks'* time!! So what on earth was Elena doing lying in bed at 5.45 in the morning? She needed to be up, drinking coffee and starting a full day of phone hustling on both sides of the Atlantic.

Lana sat up on the couch. 'Hi, Mum. You keeping busy?'

'As a bee. I'm going to work all day today, love. What do you want to do with yourself?'

Lana flicked a glance at the large clock on the wall.

'I think I'll have a shower, then head straight up Sixth Avenue to be first in line at the Empire State Building. It opens at 8a.m.'

'No! You're not allowed to go up it without me!'

'Mum, I am,' Lana insisted. 'I'll go up this morning and then you can come up with me when you've got the time. I'm going up more than once. Greta says it's the best thing in New York.'

'It is,' Annie agreed. 'Ed and I went up at sunset and the city below was all golden . . .'

'Very romantic,' Lana said, nipping embarrassingly dreamy memories in the bud. 'Did you sleep OK?'

'Yeah fine, you?'

'Not bad. I was so tired but as for you . . . you snore! Did you know that?'

'I do not snore. There is no way I snore. Ed has never complained about me snoring.'

She must have said this a little too loudly, for the bedroom door opened and, floral dressing gown flung about her once more, Elena slouched moodily into the kitchen.

'Vat time is it?' she said, eyes screwed up against the sunshine.

'Just after six,' Annie said brightly, as if this was a totally reasonable time to wake up the person who's been forced to have you to stay for four weeks.

'Six!' Elena hissed.

'Would you like a cup of coffee?'

Elena shrugged her shoulders, which Annie interpreted as a yes. She turned to the coffee machine and tried not to sigh too audibly; just as the one moody girl in her life seemed to have finally cheered up, she'd landed herself with another.

Elena perched on the end of the sofa bed

because there wasn't enough space for her to get across the room to the table.

'I've been looking through the company books,' Annie said, pointing to the files, 'I hope you don't mind. The orders are fantastic. You've got to be pleased about that.'

'Ya, but vat point if no dresses?' Elena gave another listless shrug.

'Hey, this isn't like you,' Annie said, wanting to inspire a bit more confidence and optimism, 'and this definitely isn't like Svetlana. If your mother was facing a problem like this, she would do something. She would be on the phone every minute of the day trying to solve this. That's what you and I need to do. Get on the phone, get talking to people and think of a way to raise some money.

'If we could just find a new factory . . .' Annie added.

Elena laughed at this.

'If you could get enough money together to make the first run of dresses . . .'

Elena laughed at this too.

'But once the money for those first orders comes in, you'll be back in business,' Annie persisted.

Elena shrugged and took her coffee cup back to her bedroom.

She didn't come out again until she heard the front door close. Maybe she thought Annie and Lana had both gone out together, when it was Lana setting off for the Empire State Building. Annie was still waiting at the table, fresh coffee cup in hand, to give Elena another team talk.

'OK. Sit down beside me and listen,' Annie began. 'We need the list of all the people who put money into Perfect Dress in the first place. Then you, me and Svetlana will call them all up and ask for just a small further investment. We'll say we have an incredible amount of orders – which is true – and a minor cash-flow problem – which is also true. We'll tell them they're going to get this money back in just two months' time, with interest.'

Elena, still in her dressing gown, looked at Annie with a pale and uncertain face, then took the seat offered to her.

'Elena, you've got a book full of orders and people are expecting dresses in three weeks' time,' Annie said sternly. 'I'm really sorry about the woman who messed things up for you . . . but we have to do something before it's too late.'

'Juno Harper. Not even her real name,' Elena muttered in disgust.

'I'm sorry this has happened to you. But it doesn't have to be the end of the world unless you want to make it the end of the world. You can get out of this. Your mother wants to help you, and so do I.'

Elena sighed, ran a hand through her long hair and looked dangerously as if she was about to cry.

'Everyone has setbacks,' Annie continued, 'believe

me, I've had plenty, and especially in business, I promise you. Handling success is easy-peasy, it's how you handle the setbacks that marks you out. Hey, I bet even Ralph Lauren and Donna Karan had some really bad times. I bet they've sat at the kitchen table in pyjamas wondering how on earth they were going to make it work from here.'

Elena gave a little slip of a smile at this.

'Why don't you have a shower?' Annie suggested: 'wash your hair, do your make-up and put on one of your Perfect Dresses. Remind yourself how good they are. Get a little bit of fire back in your belly. Surely your inner Ukrainian doesn't want to go down without a fight?'

Elena smiled more broadly at this. 'You right,' she agreed finally, 'not without a fight.'

'How much money do we need to make the dresses for these orders?' Annie asked.

After several moments' thought, Elena replied: 'At current factory and material prices, we need about £30,000.'

'Easy,' Annie said immediately, but really she wasn't so sure. 'Go shower and dress, I'll phone Svetlana.'

By the time Annie had spoken to Svetlana back in London and they'd divided up the list of previous investors between them, Elena had washed, dried her hair, applied the recommended make-up and put on a pale lilac dress.

As she stepped out of her bedroom again, she looked almost cheerful.

'You look gorgeous,' Annie told her, which was true. 'Now, here's your list. The first person to get an investment has lunch bought for them . . . Talking of lunch, is there anything we could have for breakfast, babes? I'm really not at my best on an empty stomach.'

'Café two doors along sells muffins to die for.'

'Shall I go?'

'Yes, I make start on calls.'

The Village Bakery was indeed a muffin-eater's paradise. Unable to narrow down the choice, Annie brought back two bagfuls: white chocolate chip, cinnamon and apple, maple and pecan, blueberry and finally banana. Along with two steaming lattes.

She'd thought the muffins would be divided out between herself, Elena and, later, even Lana.

She hadn't counted on Elena nibbling at barely half of a blueberry muffin and leaving her latte untouched. So, in between the tricky phone calls in which she tried to make funding Perfect Dress sound as positive, breezy and tempting as possible, Annie somehow managed to chew her way through three New York sized muffins.

As one New York sized muffin is the size of a baby's head that was a lot of muffin.

By the end of the first hour, sixteen calls were made: ten by Elena, six by Annie – she found that she could keep people talking for longer – but not one single penny was reeled in.

The second hour was tougher. To keep her spirits

100

bright and her enthusiasm up, Annie put Elena's latte in the microwave and used it to wash her way through muffins four . . . five and then . . . oh good grief, six.

'But we already have the orders,' she explained patiently to the grumpy man at the end of the line, 'I'd hate for you to be sorry when this is a thriving business and you could have made the big money by getting in early . . .'

'The only thing I'm sorry about is lending Svetlana £10,000 in the first place,' he retorted. 'So far, I've only had £3,000 back and there's no word about when the rest is coming. So don't even think about asking me to risk more!'

The line went dead.

When Elena put down her phone, the two looked at each other. 'I'm depressed,' Elena said.

'Well . . . this is only the first morning.' Annie tried to sound more upbeat than she really felt.

'But we do everyone on the list. There are no more names to try,' Elena pointed out.

'Shall we phone Svetlana? Maybe she's had some luck with her names.' Then Annie had to ask: 'Couldn't *she* give us some money to cover this tricky patch?'

'She gave as much as she could when the business start,' Elena replied, 'now she has no more liquid cash for "tax reasons" or something . . . when you are as rich as Svetlana, money is always complicated. Anyway, I make this problem, I want to solve this problem.'

'Right . . .' Annie tried to understand, but really, if she wanted to, Svetlana could probably just sell off some tiny, unloved earring to cover this short-fall.

The call to Svetlana's phone registered busy. But Annie's phone began to buzz in her hand with a text.

'Still on top of ESB. Brilliant! Cm join me!! L xx'

ESB . . . it took a second to register that this was Lana texting from the top of the Empire State Building. Maybe she should go. Sunshine was streaming in through the kitchen window; it was another amazing day in this unbelievable city. Maybe Annie should get out there. If she and Elena had called every name on their lists, they'd have to think of another idea, and what better place to go for inspiration than the Empire State Building?

'We need a break,' she told Elena, 'I'm going to go and join Lana. Then let's meet up somewhere bright and inspiring and see what else we can think of.'

As she headed to the tiny bathroom, to reapply lipstick and make all the other little adjustments required before she was ready to face the immaculately groomed streets of New York, Annie wondered out loud:

'Is there any factory anywhere that might give us the credit, based on our order books? Then we would just need to find money for the material.

Just a two-month credit window? Even one month, if we could get everyone to pay on delivery . . .'

Once again, Elena shrugged. 'No,' she said in a deep and mournful tone: 'I think is hopeless.'

CHAPTER 10

The Greenwich Village shop assistant:

Blue silk pussy bow blouse (Ann Taylor)
Blue and white pleated skirt (Miu Miu)
Orange patent belt (Century 21)
Orange patent sandals (Gucci via Designer Shoe Warehouse)
Total est. cost: $470

'Isn't that bag just soooo . . .'

'I love this!! I love it! I'm never going home. I'm never even coming down!'

These were Lana's words of greeting as she caught sight of her mum stepping out on to the viewing platform up on the 86th floor of the Empire State Building.

Annie was feeling a little robbed. In the twenty-five minutes since she'd entered the building and been whisked up the escalators to the ticket-buying floor, she'd spent more money than she could ever have imagined . . . and all on a view.

There had been the extortionately expensive ticket, then straight through to the queue for the photo . . . click . . . $25 . . . all ready to be super-imposed on the Empire State Building backdrop. The $10 for the pop-up souvenir map she already knew she'd only look at for five seconds. She'd even thrown a dollar into the machine which gave you back a penny . . . embossed with the Empire State Building, yes, but still a good way of turning a dollar into a penny.

Plus, she had a feeling there was going to be a huge, dazzling array of things she would absolutely just have to buy for her family as soon as she hit the ESB gift shop.

'Tourist,' Lana accused her, pointing at the $10 map in her hand.

'Yeah right and you're such a New Yorker, standing on top of the Empire State Building gawping. Look at you, eyes out on stalks. Are you having a lovely time?'

'The best,' Lana replied and turned her face back to the chain-link fence which protected tourists from the dangers of being up here; including being so overwhelmed by the sight of Manhattan Island stretching out before them in every direction that they just faint and topple over in sheer wonder.

It looked amazing. Annie hadn't expected it to look anything else. Just to the north was the luscious greenery of Central Park, surrounded by the breathtaking apartments it probably took *generations* of mega-wealth to acquire. Downtown a whole cluster of skyscrapers shimmered in the city haze.

'Look over there.' Lana pointed to a fat spire which seemed to be entirely covered in gold: 'Gold roof tiles, just how over-the-top is that? And over there – look, there's actually a three-storey house, with a garden, on top of a skyscraper. Look at that! I'm sooooo loving this. I've decided I'm going to marry the next really fit looking guy I see and become an American and just stay here for ever. Simple.'

Annie smiled. What else could she do? She smiled even though there was a silent voice inside shouting, *Of course you're not moving to the other side of the Atlantic from me. Don't even joke about this!*

'Do you know what it is about this view that is so exciting?' Lana went on, finding it hard to tear her gaze from the glittering buildings downtown. 'It isn't the highest building in the city, but it's high enough and so central that you feel right here, right in the heart of things. This is a view of the whole beating pulse of the place.'

'The beating pulse,' Annie repeated, 'I like that. You're right. This place just throbs in a way that London doesn't. Maybe it's the extremes – the height of the buildings, the length of the avenues, it all takes your breath away. London's a town that gradually sprawled out into a city. Much more planning went into making New York amazing.'

'D'you know how big London was when Samuel Johnson said: "Tired of London, tired of life"?'

'No,' Annie looked at her, intrigued.

'Just two square miles, or something like that . . . back in the 1700s.'

'Clever clogs . . . so what do you think you're going to do next then, darlin'? What's the clever Lana brain going to focus on now?'

Annie asked the question gently, hoping it was a good moment. So many conversations about Lana's future plans had gone badly that she was becoming very careful of raising the subject.

'I'm thinking about it very hard,' Lana answered, not taking her eyes from the view, 'I'm going to look into some things and I'll tell you, just as soon as I know more.'

It was the calmest, most focused reply Lana had given her in weeks.

Annie was just about to tell her daughter how absolutely fine this was when something thrilling, something green and shiny caught her eye. For a moment, she thought the woman walking past was carrying The Bag. The one Annie had longed for ever since she had first set eyes on it in a small and dimly lit show preview video. But no. It wasn't The Bag, just a cheap imitation. It reminded her about The Bag, though. How could she have forgotten that the last few remaining sea-green Mulberrys were still, just possibly, somewhere in this very city?

All at once Annie's passion to find The One was reignited.

'We have to go!' she told Lana.

'Really?'

'Yeah. We're definitely coming back. Maybe every day. Well, I would if I could get a season ticket or something.'

'So where are we going?'

'To Greenwich Village . . .' Annie looked through her current handbag to see if the little scrap of paper with the very important bag shop address was still there.

'Why?'

'You'll see . . .'

'Is this for work?'

'Sort of. Well . . . not exactly, but it's important.'

'This is a shopping quest, isn't it?'

Annie nodded. Lana didn't laugh, or even let her eyebrows twitch a little. She knew a shopping quest when she saw one and understood just how important it might be.

'So, to Greenwich Village – at top speed. In a cab, maybe?'

'Yes . . . cab. Definitely.'

When the cab pulled up outside the familiar looking shopfront, Annie felt a burst of anxiety. Was there really still a chance that The Bag would be here?

She glanced at the shop window, almost hoping to see it hanging in splendour, centre stage. But then again, she also didn't want it to be there, attracting too much attention and causing someone to snatch it from her now.

She waved the fare at the driver and hurried out

of the cab, Lana at her heels. As she opened the door to the shop, they were greeted with a delighted: 'Hello, and how are you today?' from the nearest glossy assistant.

'Hi,' Annie smiled, but after fleeting eye contact, she began to scan the shop slightly feverishly. Was it here? There was navy, and periwinkle blue, a rich, autumnal burgundy, then browns and blacks, of course. But where was the sea green?

'Oh!'

There! Over there, from the corner of the store came the flash of green. A perfect blue-green. Not too wintery, not too summery, just exactly perfect for this fashion moment. It would go with red, blue, black, purple – all her favourite colours.

She couldn't stop herself from hurrying over.

'Oh look!' she urged Lana, 'here it is. Isn't it absolutely perfect?'

Lana smiled but couldn't agree wholeheartedly. 'You know I don't really get the bag thing,' she had to admit.

Annie had already taken the bag down from its stand and was 'trying it on', holding it this way and that, slipping it over her shoulder and critically assessing its proportions and whether or not they went with hers.

The bag was beautiful, perfect in every way. There was no way now that she'd taxied all the way here that she was going to let it go.

She looked at her reflection in the long mirror. Nothing at all was wrong with the bag. But everything was wrong with her. She had the boobs she'd always wanted, yes, but it was all the other lumps and bumps. For the very first time, she saw something a little too like her mum's lovely, comfortable, cuddly body staring back at her and she felt far too young for that.

Round cuddly bodies looked good on grannies. They did not look good with beautiful bags, statement shoes and expensive dresses. Plus, she was going to run out of designer sizes soon. Only a handful of proper labels could be found in a SIXTEEN.

Just thinking of the word made prickles of sweat leap out from her skin, despite the chilly air-con.

'Hi, how are you? Isn't that bag just soooo fabulous?'

Annie was now in the full glare of the shop assistant who'd stepped out from behind the counter, to reveal a brilliantly thought out blue and white outfit with inspired splashes of orange.

'I'm *loving* it,' Annie agreed, 'never taking it off.'

Her mobile began to bleat, so she fished it out of the handbag over her other shoulder and looked at the screen. Ed was calling.

For a split second Annie was torn. On the one hand it was Ed and it was always lovely to hear from him: on the other hand, she was in a handbag shop, about to consider a major purchase. Just exactly the kind of purchase Ed would have a fit about.

But then, what if something had happened and he was desperately trying to get hold of her? She pressed answer immediately.

'Hello! It's me, is everything OK?' she asked.

'Yes, of course. We're all fine . . . do you want to say good-night to the babies?'

Good-night? It seemed just too weird to be standing in Greenwich Village, in a handbag shop, in the middle of a blazingly sunny day about to say good-night to her babies who were going to bed thousands of miles away in London.

While Lana rolled her eyes, Annie listened to the babbling of each baby in turn and felt a very physical longing to have these little people right here in her arms.

'That was lovely,' she told Ed, when he was back on the line. 'It's not upset them?'

'No. They seem pleased. It's not upset you?'

'It's totally upset me,' she confessed, 'but I wouldn't have it any other way. Is everything really fine?'

'Yes!' Ed assured her. 'Where are you right now? Paint me a picture.'

Annie glanced about the shop. This wasn't exactly a picture that Ed would like. If Lana did not get the bag thing, there was definitely no way at all that Ed got the bag thing.

'*But it's just a bag,*' he would declare every time Annie brought home one of her hand-crafted masterpieces. '*Men don't even need them – we have pockets. Don't you see this is all just a conspiracy to keep women poorer! Every £200 or £300 you squander on those things is lost for ever.'*

Every £200 or £300! The poor man had no idea. And anyway, the money wasn't lost for ever, Annie still had a busy presence on eBay, 'recycling' all the beauties she'd grown tired of. Just very occasionally, she still bought a treasure or two on eBay. But you had to be very, very careful who you bought from. There were so many fakes and scams out there.

'We've been up the Empire State today,' Annie replied, deciding to avoid the question completely. 'It was amazing. Almost as good as when I went up there with you,' she added quickly, so as not to leave him out.

'And now . . . let me guess? There's some retail therapy going on?' Ed asked.

'Just a tiny little bit. Honestly, considering how fantastic the shops are over here, Lana and I are being *unbelievably* restrained.'

'So far.'

The assistant had the sea-green beauty in her hands and was holding it above a stack of tissue paper, gesturing to Annie.

Annie nodded enthusiastically.

'You work very hard for your money, Annie, don't let it slip away between your fingers too easily.'

'Ed,' she warned.

'Just not handbags,' he pleaded, 'please do not spend any more money on expensive handbags. At the last count, weren't there—'

'Ed!' she warned again.

'Talking of your hard-earned money, Tamsin phoned . . .'

'Did she? What did she say? You didn't tell her I was over here, did you?'

'Have you honestly not told her?'

'Have you?'

'Well, what *did* you tell her?' Ed asked, a little exasperated.

'I said I was going to be away for a bit . . . a little trip . . . I didn't want her to think I was bailing out or anything. You haven't told her, have you? Not about the dress business or anything?'

'I don't think so,' Ed admitted. 'I did say you were in New York, though. But she wasn't phoning with news, she wanted to let you know that the money had come in for the work you've done up till now on the series.'

'How much?' Annie wondered.

'£15,000,' Ed replied.

'Wow . . . I wasn't expecting that much.'

'There's tax, agent commission and all those other things to come out of it,' Ed reminded her: 'it won't be as much as that when everyone's had their share.'

'I know, I know . . . so let's call it £10,000.'

The tissue paper was going round the bag; the assistant smoothing and folding with as much care as if she was lovingly wrapping a beautiful gift.

'Ed, do we need that money right now?' Annie asked next.

'Well . . . yeah, we always need the money to keep everything going. Keep the show on the road.'

'But do we need it right now? This month? Or could it wait just for a month or two?'

'Depends.'

'Depends on what?'

'Depends on what you're going to do with it.'

'I'm going to lend it to Elena.'

Silence.

So Annie jumped in with all the reasons why she should make Elena's business the loan. The order books, the temporary cash-flow situation, the virtual promise of getting the money back quickly – with interest.

Finally Ed said cautiously: 'Well . . . it's your money. If you want to stake it, you can do that. But please, Annie, be aware that you are staking it. You might not get it back.'

'Svetlana spends that amount of money in a day. She could get it back to me with a click of her fingernails,' Annie reasoned, ignoring the whole 'no liquid cash' and 'tax' situation.

'Maybe you want to take out a contract with Elena, have something in writing?' Ed suggested.

Annie handed her credit card over to the assistant.

For a little second, she felt an unusual hesitation. If Elena's business was such a good bet, shouldn't she try and put some more money into it? Instead of blowing her cash on another bag?

Just a little corner of the green leather poked out from between the sheets of paper.

No. An executive, an investor in an amazing new fashion label, should definitely carry a wonderful new power bag just like this one.

'Where is it made?' Lana asked, as they perched at a sidewalk café table, sipping at a celebratory coffee.

'What? The bag?'

'Yeah, it's not actually English, is it? It's not really made in England.'

'No. I think a lot of their things are made in Turkey and finished in England.'

Annie's phone bleeped and she saw she had two messages. One from Owen, the other from Connor.

Mum, can you add the new Twilight film to my list. It's just come out on DVD over there. Thanks. Luv ya. O

Annie replied:

OK missing you. Police or fire dept. T-shirt? Mum xx

Then she opened the message from Connor:

Think I've found Gawain. He's in NYC like you.

She quickly typed back:

> Forget it, me not hunting at gay gyms for
> yr Gawain.

'Is anything still made in England? Or in the US?' Lana wondered.

'I don't know . . . it would be interesting to find out. We could do a special programme about . . .' Annie tailed off, remembering with a jolt that there might not be any more programmes at all. 'I need to phone Tamsin – see what's happening,' she said, mainly to herself.

'Weren't loads of clothes all made in the US once?' Lana asked. 'Wasn't it a huge producer of cotton and cotton clothes, cotton T-shirts, denim? But now, pretty much everything is made in Asia, isn't it?'

'Yeah. Did you know that cotton jersey, the stretchy stuff, was invented in Jersey? You know, the island off England. And apparently Coco Chanel's lover wore jersey polo shirts – probably to play polo in – and she loved the stuff so much she ordered bales and bales of it from England to make dresses . . . and during the first world war, she used cheap grey military fabric she bought in from Spain to make these amazing creations for Parisian ladies.'

Annie and Lana's eyes met. There was a spark of inspiration there. They both caught it at the same time.

'Cotton jersey,' Lana repeated, growing enthusiasm in her voice.

'Made in the US!' Annie added, her eyes lighting up.

'Elena needs to get in some really basic material,' Lana said, thinking out loud.

'Yeah,' Annie agreed immediately. 'And forget about the cheap Chinese factories. That could be her unique selling point – she could have dresses made in the US of A. Come on, let's get back to the flat, fire up the laptops and start looking.'

CHAPTER 11

Lana hits Manhattan:

Green and white summer dress (Anthropologie)
Yellow high heels (borrowed from Elena)
Green messenger bag (Fossil)
Total est. cost: $180

'A Flirtini? Go on, Mum . . .'

As soon as Annie told Elena about the £10,000 she was prepared to invest in Perfect Dress, spirits rose in the tiny apartment.

Then the idea of an American factory, of dresses 'Made in the USA', appealed to Elena too and for the rest of the afternoon and early evening the trio were extremely busy trying to find out what they could do to make this happen.

They Googled, they searched, they phoned. Annie found herself having a long and involved conversation with Pete from the American Cotton Council. Emails flew out, telephone enquiries were made. The optimistic energy began to infect them all. Now that there was some money, even just this little bit of money, everything suddenly felt possible and doable, if they just put their minds to it. The hours flew past.

'We need to take a break and go out,' Elena declared from her bedroom, where she was working from her bed with her laptop and mobile.

'Uh-huh, I am totally burned out,' Lana, on the sofa with Annie's laptop, agreed.

'Yeah, there's just one more guy I want to get hold of,' said Annie. 'I have his mobile number so I'm going to try him right now.'

She plugged in the number, but the answering service clicked in. 'Voicemail,' she told Lana, 'it's probably a sign. A sign that I need to unwrap my unbelievably lovely new bag, dress it up and take it out to play.'

She could just get dressed up and go straight out, Annie realized with a hit of astonishment. There was no babysitter to arrange, no putting babies to bed, no leaving an entire list of emergency numbers taped to the fridge – she really could just slip into another outfit, apply make-up and leave the building. Not even knowing where she was going to go!

The dizzying sense of freedom this gave her was like a rush to the head.

'Where can we go? Where's good to go?' she called out to Elena, not that there was really any need to raise her voice as Elena's bedroom was only two feet away from the kitchenette.

119

'I know very hip bar. Very cool, lots of Sye's friends go there. Is on Seventh Avenue, close to Condé Nast building, many magazine peoples go there.'

Annie caught the astonished look on Lana's face. 'Cool!' Lana breathed.

'Fantastic,' Annie enthused, though honestly, she was experiencing an inner dither. Had she really packed an outfit finger-on-the-pulse enough to withstand entry to a bar frequented by glossy magazine types? Yes, the new bag could probably endure the gaze of *Vogue* editor Anna Wintour herself, but Annie couldn't get inside the bag. She would have to think of something to wear with the bag.

Lana was looking properly excited at the evening ahead.

'I'm going to put on my new dress,' she began: 'you know, from that amazing shop we were in on the first day. I'll go and shower first. Is that OK, Elena?'

While Lana showered, Annie rummaged through the clothes in her suitcase. There was no space to unpack in the tiny apartment, so she and Lana were trying to live out of their bags as neatly as possible. There was also no washing machine, so at some point in the near future they would have to make use of the communal laundry room, which apparently was down in the building's basement.

Dress . . . dress . . . Annie needed something

lightweight but with long sleeves, something that went with the bag and her highest heels.

'What are you going to wear?' she asked Elena, who sounded as if she was rummaging about in her bedroom.

'Something new, maybe . . . I go out this afternoon to Century 21. So cheap there, I always find something.'

Elena appeared at her doorway still wearing the lilac dress she'd put on earlier in the day.

'You should wear a Perfect Dress every time you go anywhere,' Annie told her, 'you're so lovely, you're a walking advertisement. Then whenever anyone asks you where you got your wonderful dress, you whip out a business card and get them to place an order. You are still going to sell online as well, aren't you?'

'Website is a mess,' Elena confided. 'Mother supposed to be looking after it. But she say she is very busy.' This came out a little dismissively. 'She does not care about the business so much as me,' Elena added.

'Maybe you need to get someone else to do the website then.'

'Maybe,' Elena shrugged. 'There is so much to do . . . too much to do. I don't know where to—'

'Shhhh!' Annie soothed her, because she didn't want Elena's shoulders to slump down once again and that pained expression to return to her face, 'you'll get there. We will all get there. We made huge progress today. Huge!'

★ ★ ★

121

When the trio stepped out of the apartment building and into the brightly lit whirl of evening on Fifth Avenue, Annie could not wipe the smile from her face. She was in New York City, dressed to the nines and hailing a cab to the bar of the moment.

Her bag was delicious, her shoes were fabulous and, even better, despite the muffin fest, her dress did up. She felt very happy, although she had to admit to herself it was the two girls on either side of her who were pulling all the admiring glances.

Elena, glammed up, looked just as sensational as Annie had expected, all tight fabric, big blonde hair and legs.

The more unsettling surprise was Lana. In her strapless flowery dress and borrowed shoes, with her long dark hair falling in a sleek curtain down below her shoulders and a light touch of make-up, she looked so sophisticated. She was nearly 18, Annie couldn't help reminding herself. She was so very nearly a grown-up. Annie was hugely proud of her beautiful girl, but it was a little difficult to adjust to all these guys turning their heads in Lana's direction. Lana was definitely noticing, but she just raised her chin, tossed her hair a little and kept striding on in the tricky pointy shoes.

Elena effortlessly hailed a cab and it manoeuvred them in and out of side streets and over several huge, six-laned junctions until they were speeding up Seventh Avenue. Back-lit water fountains, fluttering American flags, breathtaking shopfront displays flashed past until they drew to a halt at the bar.

Elena slipped her arm through Lana's, and on their long legs the girls pulled slightly ahead of Annie as they walked inside.

The bar was dark and very swanky – all grey leather banquettes with dark wood and mirrored touches. Low, jazzy music played, the kind that Ed would be able to name in three notes. The loud, crashing, siren-blaring Avenue outside was totally forgotten because, in here, it was as glamorous as an old black and white movie, except the girls were in much shorter dresses and the guys had elaborate hairstyles, not hats.

After a little look around, Elena spotted her friends and began to walk towards a table where four beautiful young twenty-somethings, three guys and a girl, were deep in discussion.

'Hey,' Elena said, totally cool.

'Hey, Elena,' the nearest, a very blond-haired guy with a round, handsome face replied.

'I bring some friends too, from London,' she added.

There was a general 'hi' of greeting and some shuffling as the four moved down the banquette to let everyone else in. Elena and Lana fitted onto the ends, but Annie was left without an obvious place to sit.

'I'll see if I can find a chair to put on the end here . . . does anyone want a drink?' she offered.

Seconds later, she found herself trying to memorize an order for six cocktails.

Even Lana had said: 'A Flirtini? Go on, Mum . . . I've always wanted to try one.'

'You're under-age,' Annie had whispered back.

'No one's asking,' Lana pointed out, head cocked defiantly, blinking blue eyes up at Annie the way she'd done ever since she was tiny.

'Just one,' Annie said, relenting in the face of those melting eyes, as usual.

'And no maraschino, it's very important,' the girl with a short and severe brown fringe added, 'I'm like totally allergic to food colouring. I'll go into shock and you'll have to EpiPen me.'

'Oh dear God no,' one of the guys laughed, 'not again!'

Annie managed to make her huge cocktail order at the bar, adding on a glass of wine for herself. The barman got down to the elaborate production performance, shaking ice cubes about here, flipping cucumbers into the air there, sliding glasses up and down the bar. Maybe it would have been fun to watch if she hadn't been standing all on her own at the bar, feeling like the heaviest, oldest person in the entire world: an invader in the world of twiglet-like, young, gilded, beautiful people.

The row of glittering drinks was set before her on two silver trays.

'And no maraschino,' the barman repeated, putting the last cocktail into place.

As her glass of wine was added to the tray, he informed her: 'That'll be $238.55.'

Although this was almost double the amount she'd expected to pay, Annie managed to rein in her gasp. A quick check of her purse and she found the relevant cash: a $100 bill, then another, then two twentys.

She put the money on the counter.

The barman looked at it, then looked up at her. 'Is there a problem?' he asked.

What?

'No . . .' Annie wondered if she'd misheard. Maybe it was $338. Maybe these were the most expensive cocktails in the universe and she'd somehow been crazy enough to order six of them. Maybe it was $538 and she wouldn't have enough to pay. She'd be flung into a New York jail and never see her other children again because by mistake she'd wandered into the most expensive bar in Manhattan and ordered a round of drinks.

'What have I done wrong?' she asked, panicky now. 'I'm not from New York, I don't know the rules.'

At this, the barman leaned on his elbow towards her. He was yet another perfect New York physical specimen. What was it about this town? Did they round up the ugly people at the bridges and refuse to let them in?

'Aha, OK new-to-New-York lady. Here we give great service because we expect a great tip.'

'Oh.'

'And not some pussy 10 per cent tip either. If I did a good job, it's 20 per cent minimum. Only pay less if you want me to spit in your next drink.'

Urgh.

'Right, OK, I see . . .' She began to rummage in her bag again, doing the maths. She owed him another $46! He was pocketing $46 per round of drinks. No wonder he looked so gorgeous and well-dressed.

She put another $50 on the counter and asked if he would at least help her take the drinks to the table.

'No problem,' he said, rolling up the money and stuffing it into his back pocket.

As the drinks were handed out, Annie searched for a spare chair to add to the end of the table and finally found a plush velvet stool. Unfortunately, when she sat down, she was about eight inches lower than the banquette.

Plus everyone else was in a hubbub of conversation and although they were quite happily sipping at the drinks she'd bought, they didn't exactly seem concerned about letting her into the conversation.

Lana, who would have cared, who would have made sure her mum was involved in the chat, had been moved along to the very far end of the table.

Annie sipped at her wine and watched: three girls, three guys, all young, all full of the excited energy of a night out; the adventure and possibility that lay ahead.

The blond-haired guy was laughing with Lana, who turned all of a sudden in Annie's direction, pointed to her and announced: 'My mum's on TV, you know,' kindly trying to bring her into the group.

This caused a little ripple of interest. Everyone now turned to her with curiosity.

'In TV? Over here? Which network?' one of the guys asked.

'No, in Britain. I was doing a show with Channel Four,' Annie replied. 'Sort of a fashion, magazine-style thing. I was the presenter.'

'You're on TV?' the blond guy couldn't really have looked more surprised.

'Yeah,' Lana dug him playfully in the ribs. 'Over a million viewers every week.

'How many seasons have you done?'

'Is it filming right now?'

The questions came in thick and fast until the moment when Annie had to admit that the show was 'taking a break' and there was no new commission at this exact moment.

Then the faces turned away again, the interest faded to nothing and Annie was left gazing at her wine glass.

Nice.

When Elena went off to the bathroom, Annie dared to slip from her little stool up onto the banquette.

Really, she wanted to hear what the blond guy was talking to Lana about, but once she was up on the leather bench, severe fringe girl suddenly wanted to talk to her.

'Jeeeeeeez, they just love real-looking people on British TV, right?'

This was her opening line.

'Real-looking' didn't exactly sound like a compliment.

'Yeah, I think they do,' Annie replied. 'But it was a girls' show. It was for girls, by girls and we made people feel good by not being too perfect. We were keeping it real.'

'Yeah . . . smile,' the girl instructed Annie.

Annie did, wondering if the girl was going to whip out her phone and take a picture.

But no, instead, Miss Fringe said: 'Real British teeth and everything. No Botox. That is just so unusual. Over here, you could not be on television. No way.'

Annie was feeling more than a little insulted now.

'What about you?' Annie decided to change tack, 'what do you do?'

'I'm at *Elle Decoration*. I'm an editorial assistant.'

'That's great and what about your friends?'

'Well, Taylor, he's the blond guy who seems sooooo interested in your daughter, he's doing an internship at *Vogue*. He's at college, majoring in journalism. Then Mick is at *Elle* with me. He's one of the contributing editors, he writes about architecture and Donald is a news photographer. He's with the *New York Post*.'

'And you all kind of know Elena because of Sye?' Annie asked.

'Yeah. He's crazy about her, I don't think she has any idea.'

'No. I don't think she does.'

Silence.

Annie looked over at Lana again. Handsome blond – Taylor, she remembered – was leaning right over her; he looked as if he was about to kiss her.

Annie felt herself bristle.

But instead, Taylor turned and whispered in Lana's ear.

'So I guess,' Miss Fringe went on, 'even though you're on television, you must eat carbs and everything. That would never happen over here. I know this girl who's trying to get into presenting. She's way, way thin and they still keep telling her she's too fat to make it.'

Now Annie was bristling all over.

She turned to her wine glass, but she'd emptied it ages ago. No one had offered to buy her another and she wasn't going up to the bar to be charged twenty quid for a second glass.

'We have to go,' she said, standing up abruptly, 'Lana, do you remember? We said we'd have to be at the . . . the thing before midnight . . . so we have to go now.'

Lana looked up at her in dismay.

'Vat thing?' Elena asked, back just in time to hear this.

'It's a private thing,' Annie said and now she felt torn. She didn't want to drag Lana away, but she couldn't take this any more. Carbs. Carbs! Of course she was allowed to eat carbs even though she was on TV. These people were absolutely mad. Obsessed. She couldn't bear to sit beside them for another second.

'Please, Lana,' Annie added in a voice which was a little too pleading.

Lana turned to Taylor: 'Lovely to meet you. I really mean that. I'm in New York for a few weeks. I hope we'll bump into each other again.'

'Bump into each other?' Taylor asked, looking confused.

Obviously this was not an expression which crossed the Atlantic well.

'See each other . . .' Lana began but then blushed and came to a halt. Because even she knew what 'seeing each other' meant in US-speak.

'Good-night.' She smiled at the others then began to pick her way out of the banquette.

'See you later,' Elena offered.

As soon as they were outside the bar, Lana turned to her mother full throttle.

'Why are we leaving? I was having the best time. I do not want to go home now. It's early. You could have gone home on your own you know, you didn't have to bring me into it. I'd have been fine with Elena.'

'I didn't want to leave you with Elena and those

130

people. They all seemed really, really shallow,' Annie said. She was feeling flustered.

'Shallow? Because they work on magazines and take photos? You used to work in a fashion store and now you work in TV. I don't think that makes you one teeny bit more deep and meaningful than they are,' Lana stormed in reply.

'You're just angry because that guy didn't ask for your number.'

'So? Why shouldn't I want him to ask for my number? Maybe if I'd been able to stay there and talk to him, he would have asked. Instead, I'm being dragged home by my mum like some six-year-old.'

'Ouch.'

'What did that girl say to you, anyway?'

'What girl?'

'You know, the one sitting beside you. One moment you were chatting away, the next you were standing up, wanting to leave. What did she say?'

'Nothing.'

For several seconds they walked along the side-walk together. A brisk wind had picked up and it felt surprisingly cold walking along in thin summer dresses without any coats.

'Was it about your weight?' Lana asked in a much calmer, gentler voice.

At first Annie said nothing.

Then she finally admitted: 'Maybe.'

'New Yorkers are very weight conscious.'

'I'm very weight conscious,' Annie protested, 'but that doesn't seem to help me. I just get bigger and bigger.'

'Poor old Mum,' Lana said and slipped her arm round Annie's waist.

'Can we have less of the "poor" and less of the "old"?' Annie said, putting her hand over Lana's and patting it. 'I'm not even forty and I've got this gorgeous grown-up daughter who completely overshadows me. It takes getting used to, babes, it takes some getting used to. I can tell you.'

'You're lovely and you're famous,' Lana added kindly. 'Can you walk in those shoes?'

When Annie nodded yes, Lana insisted they walk some of the way home.

'I'm not going to get thin just by walking,' Annie protested.

'It's a start though,' Lana insisted.

'I didn't think Taylor looked very nice,' Annie confided, 'he was too handsome and very full of himself.'

'Mum! Don't say that. I really, *really* wanted him to ask for my number.'

'Did you?'

'Yes!'

'And you still came with me?'

'Yes!'

'That is very, very kind of you,' Annie said.

'I know. Too kind. But maybe he'll ask Elena for *my* number. What do you think?'

CHAPTER 12

Librarian Lana:

Green capri trousers (Miss Selfridge)
Pink shirt with ruffles (New Look)
Green messenger bag (Fossil)
Yellow heels (borrowed from Elena)
Highly kissable pink lip gloss (Mac)
Total est. cost: $220

'Shut up!'

hen the first rays of sunshine stole in through the little kitchenette window the following morning, they found Lana deeply asleep on the sofa bed, her head shrouded with dreams of noisy New York streets and handsome New York men.

Annie was already at the café table, quietly tappity-tapping on the laptop. She was reading through her business email about fabric and factories, checking her personal email and looking at the photos Ed had just sent through this morning.

Her lovely babies were sitting on Owen's lap eating something which looked worryingly like chocolate brownie! Ed must have been in charge of that. Dinah would never, ever let the twins have chocolate brownies.

'What are they eating and should I be worried?' she typed to Ed, knowing that he wouldn't be able to reply for hours because he was already at school. She'd phone Dinah later in the day and make sure the babies were really absolutely fine. Dinah would tell her just exactly how well Ed was coping without her around.

Meanwhile, Annie had three factories not far from New York to call. She also had a list of discount fabric warehouses in the area. If they could somehow find some very cheap fabric, maybe they could use the remaining few thousand pounds just to get the very first dresses off the production line.

She and Elena were going to have a very busy day, so after switching on the coffee machine, Annie also decided to turn on the TV news at low volume to gently wake the household. It was 6.45a.m. Time to kick New York ass, no matter what time it had been when Elena had stumbled over their sofa bed in the dark last night.

With something of a groan, Lana opened her eyes, but then immediately put her hand up to shield them against the sunlight.

'Just be grateful I only let you drink one Flirtini,' Annie said.

'What time is it?' Lana asked.

'Nearly 7a.m.,' Annie replied.

'Too early!' came the shout from next door.

'It's never too early for New York,' Annie called back, 'we've got a busy day. I've got a whole list of factories and fabric suppliers, you need to drink coffee and help me call them all.'

A long, loud groan came from Elena's bedroom.

'Yeah and if you drank enough cocktails at that place to make you groan, you're going to need to sell a serious amount of dresses.'

Elena entered the kitchen in her by now very familiar micro floral dressing gown.

'Hey, Lana, I have message for you,' she began, after a lengthy yawn. 'Taylor give me his number for you. He make interview at New York Central Library today, he say if you come at 12.30, you can get special visitor library tour with him. Exciting, no?'

Lana sat up in a shot. 'Really? *Really*! He wants me to come?'

The grin on Lana's face was a joy to behold. Even though Annie thought Taylor was dangerously handsome and far too full of himself.

'Uh-oh,' Annie couldn't help teasing, 'very handsome young blond alert. Shark in the water, swim for your life.'

'Muuuuum! Shut up!'

'No, honestly, I think that's lovely. A date in a library. A library tour – that sounds incredibly sweet, it sounds like the kind of date a mother dreams of her daughter going on.'

'We talked about the library . . . but he never said anything about me coming along . . . what time, Elena? 12.30?'

Lana was already getting out of bed. She looked touchingly panicked.

'Ya,' Elena confirmed.

'You can always call him to check,' Annie suggested. 'Take the number he gave Elena and call him after breakfast – even though I didn't think he looked nearly nice enough for you.'

'Muuuum! You didn't even talk to him,' Lana protested, 'how can you tell what someone's like just by looking at them?'

'Life experience, darlin',' Annie said, but then immediately felt 100 years old. 'I've met enough men to be able to size them up in seconds. Just based on their haircuts and taste in shirts, I can tell you so much about them . . . but you – you've got to get out there and meet many more before you can make judgements as quickly as me. So you have to call him.'

Lana looked at her in astonishment.

'What?' Annie asked. 'It's not as if I've asked you to marry him . . . just call him. No big deal.'

'Ya. NBD,' Elena added.

'I have a date, at the New York Central Library with a writer who's working at *Vogue*. This is way cool. This is beyond cool,' Lana gasped, then she began to rummage through her things in search of her mobile.

'Let me guess? There are some important people

who need to be kept up to date with this exciting development?' Annie asked.

'Definitely! Susie is not going to believe me. I'll have to take pictures to prove it. Do you think you're allowed to take pictures there?'

'No idea,' Annie replied.

'What's your hot date outfit?' Elena asked.

When Lana looked blank in response, Elena kindly offered: 'You can come look in my room, see if something you like.'

'Not too . . .' Annie began, but then bit her lip, it was just too strange when you heard warnings your own mother had once made issuing from your lips. Not too *short*, not too *tight*, not too *sexy* . . . was, of course, what she wanted to say. But Lana was almost 18, she had the total hots for this boy and probably wanted to wear the shortest, tightest, sexiest thing she could get her hands on.

'Not too . . .?' Lana asked her mum with a mischievous smile.

'Not too fashion,' Annie replied, 'boys don't understand fashion.'

'Even if they work for *Vogue*?'

'Oh yes . . . he works for *Vogue*. Well, that's different then.'

'Come and help me choose something,' Lana offered and then made Annie's heart melt by adding: 'you're always good at helping me decide what to wear.'

'Aw!' Annie said and in an instant all the stand-up rows she'd had with Lana in changing rooms

right across London were forgotten. Well . . .
temporarily.

As Lana and Annie stood on the threshold of
Elena's tiny bedroom for the first time, they realized that they didn't have a hope of actually
entering. The sliding doors of her fitted closet were
open and a mountain of clothes was spilling out.
Plus every inch of floor space was taken up with
bulging carrier bags, piled on top of each other
in untidy heaps. In one corner of the room they
reached all the way up to the ceiling.

'Whoa, I don't want to see your excess luggage
bill when you head back to London,' Annie said
jokily, thinking, *Unless this is all sample dresses in
sample sizes . . . then hello, we have a problem.*

Some of Elena's helpless shrugs and despond-
ent moods were making a little more sense to
Annie now. How could someone living in a room
like this ever feel she was going to get anything
done?

Maybe Elena was feeling a lot worse than Annie
had imagined. Everyone had a weakness, everyone
had a thing they did when they were stressed out
and all was not going well. Annie had somehow
become a stress eater. Elena was possibly a stress
shopper.

Lana gazed at the room in silence. Her own
room back home was, on occasion, messy, just like
any self-respecting teenage girl's. But *this* . . . to
Lana this was a crime. She knew Elena must have

loads of fabulous things to wear in this room, but how on earth could she even find them?

'You know what? There's a pair of cute capris in my bag and a lovely shirt to go with them. I think I'd really like to wear those,' Lana announced, not wanting to stand and look at this chaos any longer, let alone be invited into it.

'Why don't you get dressed too, love?' Annie suggested to Elena. 'Tomorrow, we have a factory to visit, upstate. Today, I have three fabric warehouses in Brooklyn on my list. You have to come with me because I'm definitely going to need your help to find enough fabric to make 300 dresses for £3,000.'

'Impossible,' came the response.

'Nothing. Absolutely nothing is impossible and you have to believe me here because I've got so many ways of proving that.' Annie shot her a little wink, then closed the bedroom door, so Elena could get dressed in her clothes whirlwind in peace.

Annie suddenly felt a rush of maternal feeling for Elena. She was only 23, she was trying to run a big and brave new business and she had a pretty unusual family backdrop. Svetlana was her real mother, but had only been in her life for a couple of years. Elena could probably do with all the support she could get.

Annie went back into the little sitting room and tidied away the sofa bed, waiting for Lana to emerge from the bathroom.

'A triumph!' Annie declared when she set eyes on her daughter, who was in a pink ruffled shirt and mint green capris, her face all dewy lip gloss and blusher.

Sexy? Yes, as the shirt was unbuttoned low, but she was still sweet and perfect for a library date . . . even one with a *Vogue* writer.

Annie smiled as she realized that, back in London, Lana had only ever worn black.

CHAPTER 13

Elena over-dressed in Brooklyn:

Pink, yellow and green dress (Missoni via
Svetlana)
Brown belt (Gap)
High green suede sandals (Gucci via Designer
Shoe Warehouse)
Purple tote (Marc Jacobs sale)
Total est. cost: $450

'Eighteen per cent.'

The subway from Manhattan to Brooklyn was underground all the way downtown and underneath the East River but it came up out of the tunnel at Carroll Street station. From here, it moved through the streetscape of this New York neighbourhood giving Annie and Elena a view of everything that was going on.

All around Carroll Gardens, the beautiful old brownstone buildings were cleaned up, repaired and restored to their former glory. There was fresh paint, gleaming front doors, window-boxes, bright

141

green gardens, and along the sidewalks nannies pushed babies about in designer prams. The play parks were full of small children, water fountains and yummy mummies.

But within a stop or two, the landscape began to change. Still the same brownstone, picturesque, nineteenth-century four- and five-storey houses. But here they looked shabby and run-down. Windows were broken, hung with towels or boarded up. Graffiti sprawled across abandoned play parks. On the street corners, gangs of teen boys hung about looking tough.

'I thought Brooklyn was all fashionable and up and coming?' Annie asked Elena.

'Maybe only has one nice part?' Elena suggested.

The two women looked out of place in the subway car now. For a start they were white, when every other person was black. Plus, they were just too showily dressed for a trip to this part of town. For the first time, nice shoes, nice bag, nice dress made Annie feel vulnerable instead of powerful.

It hadn't escaped her attention how segregated parts of New York were compared with London. According to Elena, even Central Park was carved out into black, white and Hispanic areas. There were no fences, it was all voluntary, but people just kept to their respective areas and seemed to feel more comfortable that way.

As the train pulled up, Annie stood up and took a long look out of the window. It was a grey and grimy urban scene. Low brick warehouses were decorated with loops of barbed wire on their roofs and graffiti murals all over their walls.

'And I thought working in the fashion industry in New York would be sooo glamorous,' she told Elena as they stepped out onto the platform and took surreptitious glances at their map, so as not to look like total victims.

'Bet there are places much tougher than this in the Ukraine?' she asked as they walked out of the subway station and towards Discount Fabric Warehouse number one.

'Ya, of course, and I stay away from them,' Elena answered. But she was carrying herself tall and confidently all of a sudden, like a girl who knew just how to act when she was in a rough street.

Not that this part of Brooklyn looked terrifying. It was broad daylight, grannies were out with their small grandchildren, shopping in the tiny Korean stores. It just looked shabby and poor.

'So where did you grow up? Did you have nice people looking after you?' Annie asked. She'd never dared to ask Elena this before, but now that they were walking along together with their mission ahead of them, Elena seemed slightly more at ease and more approachable.

'I grew up in the countryside,' she replied. 'A very kind woman, Baba Boska, look after me. The family of her sister live in the house beside us and those children feel just like my brothers and sister. I've not been back to them for three years and I miss them. I don't think they really believe my life now. Ever since I go to university in Kiev is very, very different life from theirs.'

'Difficult . . . very difficult for you to adjust to,' Annie sympathized.

'Ya,' Elena said and gave her shrug, 'the money. The money is unbelievable. How much money people have. How much money people need. When I was growing up, my mother sent enough money for a manicure to Baba Boska every month. This keep me and Baba fed, clothed, in our house, pay for everything we need. But we need much, much less. No car. No bus journeys, not even a bicycle.'

'Did Svetlana pay for you to go to university?'

'No, I get scholarship.'

'I remember now . . . engineering?'

'Yes.'

'But then you did business studies in London?'

'Yes.'

'Does Svetlana still send Baba Boska money?'

'No.'

Annie glanced over at Elena and noticed that she drew her lips angrily together.

'But I do,' Elena added, 'she's getting old. I worry about who will look after her and maybe she will have to pay for doctors soon. She can never move . . . this would be like uprooting a tree.'

'You have a lot of things to worry about, darlin' – the Perfect Dress business, Baba Boska's health, impressing the new mother in your life . . . I can

144

understand why the stress relief has got a little out of hand.'

When Elena looked at her with a puzzled expression, Annie added gently: 'The shopping. The shopping habit has got out of your control, maybe?'

Elena's pace slowed. 'In Svetlana's London everything seem to cost more than I can ever imagine,' Elena began, 'but she give me money. More money than I can ever imagine. Here, I find everything is so cheap compared to London. Designer clothes, 70 per cent off, designer shoes 80 per cent off. The drugstore, buy one get one free. And I still have money from Svetlana, she pay me salary for this business, even though we not make any money yet. But now . . . on my credit card . . . all these cheap things, all this money off, and I owe . . .' Elena stopped walking altogether now, as if the thought of the figure had stopped her in her tracks.

'It's OK, you don't have to tell me,' Annie assured her.

'Maybe I need to tell someone. Every time I think of it, I want to be sick.' She took a deep breath. 'Twenty-four thousand,' she blurted out.

Annie covered her surprise. 'Pounds or dollars?'

'Dollars.'

'What's the interest rate?'

'Eighteen per cent.'

It didn't take long to make the calculation. Annie had learned a lot about credit card debt in the many lessons Ed had given her.

'About $4,500 a year. That's what it's costing you just to have that debt. Before you've even paid a penny back,' Annie told Elena.

'I know. Of course I know. I go to business school! But I still can't help myself . . .'

'Please try not to worry too much. It can be sorted. We'll talk about it. We'll talk about it all, but right now . . .' Annie came to a halt and pointed across to the other side of the road: 'here's the warehouse, so we better start thinking about Perfect Dresses.'

'Here?' Elena looked at the low, ugly building with the metal shutter doors in undisguised horror. A faded sign above the entrance read: 'Frederico's Fabulous Fabrics'.

'Nothing fabulous here, I promise,' Elena said.

'Shhhh! Don't be such a spoilsport,' Annie nudged her. 'Seek and you will find.'

CHAPTER 14

Taylor's smart casual:

White cotton shirt (Ralph Lauren)
Blue linen suit (Brooks Brothers)
Dark blue silk socks (same)
Brown lace-up brogues (Tods)
Total est. cost: $1,600 (Mom paid)

'You have to have the New England clam
chowder.'

Lana stood in front of the marble-columned splendour of the New York Central Library and acknowledged the terrifying thud-thud-thud going on in her chest. She took a deep breath and let it out slowly, the way her mum had taught her.

She was going to be fine. Really. She was going to walk calmly, coolly, up this amazing flight of stairs and into this building. There she was going to find Taylor, because it was already 12.36 and 30 seconds and in his text he'd told her to be on time.

Lana took another deep breath, let it out slowly and began to step through the office workers snatching a quick lunch break on the stairs.

No sooner had she set foot inside the vast, creamy marbled entrance hall when a voice called out: 'Hey Lana! Hi!'

She turned, smiled immediately, but felt just about weak at the knees at the sight of Taylor. He was so blond and so beautiful. His hair slicked back, his deep summer tan set off against the white shirt and blue suit he was wearing for work.

He approached and kissed her right on the lips before she could even think about it.

Just smack! Right like that. Lip to lip. She didn't even have a moment to close her eyes. Was just suddenly tasting mouth, saliva, toothpaste, coffee. Looking at the golden cheek right up close. Then, just as suddenly, he'd broken off.

'Glad you could make it,' he said and flashed her a smile. Compared to her he seemed completely un ruffled, as if this was how he said hello to every girl he met. Maybe it was, Lana thought with a sudden sinking feeling.

'Come and meet Linus. He's fantastic, you're gonna love him. He's gonna tour us around. Just me and you because he loves the piece I'm doing on the library and . . . pretty girls,' he added in a whisper. 'So, charm him.'

Then he took Lana's hand in his and led her along to the reception desk where an elderly, uniformed guard was beaming at them expectantly.

Her hand. He had her hand in his. Naturally, casually. As if this was just the way it always was, had always been.

Lana had worried intensely, all morning, about possible hand-holding and a possible first kiss. How would it happen? Who would make the first move? Would he make a move? Would she? Would she want him to make a move? And now . . . they had already kissed! Just like that! And he was leading her round this amazing building, by the hand!

This was nineteenth-century Manhattan: marble, elaborate plasterwork, leather-bound chairs, wood panelling. Funny how she'd always thought of New York as being shiny, brand new, ultra-modern. She'd never considered for a moment that it had history.

Taylor's hand felt just right in hers. Not too hot, not at all sweaty. Just cool and perfect. Although Linus was talking to them and no doubt telling them something fascinating, Lana kept thinking about the kiss and then an electrifying buzz would pass through her and it was almost entirely impossible to concentrate on a single word.

She had never, ever had such a good time in a library.

Far, far away from marble columns and gilded reading rooms, Annie and Elena were stepping into the cavernous, dimly lit warehouse of Frederico's Fabulous Fabrics.

The entire badly lit, bare concrete walled space was crammed with enormous metal shelves filled with rolls and rolls of fabric. More fabric than Annie could ever remember seeing before.

'We'll find stuff here,' she encouraged Elena, 'we'll work our way through the whole place if we have to. Just remember nothing can cost more than $6 a yard.'

Not exactly a big budget, Annie would be the first to admit, but somewhere Frederico would have something for them . . . please!

A full forty minutes of searching later and Annie was deeply disheartened. How had she imagined that this would be easy? This place was where Crimplene came to die.

She'd looked at hundreds, maybe thousands, of rolls of fabric but nothing was good enough. Nothing seemed even vaguely suitable. And when she had occasionally come across something that might just do, it had a price tag three or four times more than they could afford to spend.

There were still two more warehouses to visit, so she didn't want to be gloomy and have Elena shrugging and moaning at her already. But, secretly, Annie wasn't entirely optimistic . . . this was the biggest warehouse, this was the one with the best reputation. If there was absolutely nothing to be found here, she didn't rate their chances.

Elena appeared to be stress shopping. She was at the till with a square piece of waterproof fabric saying she needed something to cover the café table back at the apartment. Then she bought two yards or so of velour, muttering something about Baba Boska and cushions.

Annie watched the way Elena knotted the top of the carrier bag then put it inside another carrier bag, and she recognized that much more complicated feelings were at work here. This was not just normal shopping.

But she said nothing and together they made the ten-minute walk along grimy, characterless streets to the next warehouse.

This place was dingier, less well stocked and after twenty minutes of looking around, Annie knew that there was nothing for them here. Although Elena once again bought a small piece of waterproof fabric for the café table.

'Two pieces is better,' she explained to Annie. 'When one gets dirty, we can use the other one.' Then she started up with her complicated bag-knotting system again.

As they trekked along the charmless, industrial-looking road towards the third warehouse, Annie warned Elena: 'Don't think that we *have* to find something here. If there's nothing we like, we'll go back to Manhattan, look up more warehouses and keep on trying. Maybe we'll have to revise the fabric budget and scrape money together from somewhere else so we can afford to pay more.'

'I'm going to have to tell the buyers that the dresses are not coming,' Elena began. 'People are expecting these dresses in less than three weeks'

151

time. If I don't warn them, they will have low inventory. Nothing on the shelves. Maybe I need to tell them so they can order other things.'

'No!' Annie protested. 'Not just yet. Give it just another day or two. Elena, we have a potential factory lined up, we just need some fabric and then we are so close to solving the problem. Please!' she went on, 'don't tell anyone about dresses not arriving on time yet. Just avoid those calls and ignore the emails. Just for a day or two. We're going to know very soon if we can turn this around.'

Elena was looking closely at the map in her hand: 'We should be there by now.'

Instead they were walking along a pavement with a high wall on one side and a row of scruffy houses on the other.

There was a break in the wall for a metal gate. Annie peered through the bars of the gate.

'Maybe this is it?' she suggested.

The gate wasn't locked, so she pulled back the bolt and let it swing open. In front of them was a tarred car park, empty, and beyond the car park, a fabric warehouse, shuttered up and obviously closed.

Not just for the day, but closed down.

'I guess there wasn't much call for DIY dress- and curtain-making out here,' Annie said. She scanned the car park looking for any signs of life.

To the side of the building was a big metal skip which seemed to have rolls of fabric poking from the top of it.

'Boy, his stuff must have been really bad.' She pointed at the skip so Elena looked over too. 'He couldn't even give it away. He's actually throwing it out.'

Annie gave Elena a little glance.

'Shall we go over and just have a look?' she asked.

'In the bin?!' Elena said incredulously.

'We've come so far . . . my feet are killing me, it would be crazy not to just have a look. You never know.'

'But it's so high!' Elena protested. 'How will we look?'

'You just give me a leg up, then I'll hold onto the edge and take a peek inside.'

'Take a peek? What is this peek?'

'I'll just look,' Annie explained.

'Maybe we get in trouble,' Elena worried.

'But there's no one around.'

This was true, but not in a good way. Both the car park and the warehouse were deserted. But they had the creepy, desolated look of unloved areas in scary neighbourhoods. Annie knew this was exactly the kind of place where two women from Manhattan Island might well lose their bags, their money and anything else a mugger wanted to take without asking.

But she was still walking briskly towards the skip, mainly because Annie believed in luck. Well, no, she didn't really, but she believed in the thing her mother had told her over and over again: 'Lucky people make their own luck.'

If she looked in enough places, Annie would find the right fabric at the right price, and looking in enough places included looking in a skip beside a warehouse in some shitty, tumbledown corner in the bad part of Brooklyn.

'OK,' Annie said, reaching up to put her hands on the edge of the skip and sending flakes of rust showering down, 'just boost me up a bit.'

Elena understood and locked her hands together into a sort of stirrup. Annie stepped in and scrambled up so that her elbows were on the edge of the skip and she could look inside.

Countless rolls of material had been thrown in there, along with food wrappers, bulging black bin bags, empty cans of beer, old tools, including a rusty spade and a broken bucket.

She reached over, grabbed at the nearest rolls of material and pulled them towards her. Luckily, there had been no rain for over a week, so they weren't wet or soggy.

The rolls were all of a dark, drab fabric: navy blue and charcoal grey.

Upper arms burning with the effort of dangling, she instructed Elena: 'Just lift me up a bit more – hold my legs.'

Then Annie managed to use her thumb and first two fingers to feel the quality of the fabric, something she'd been doing all afternoon.

It wasn't half bad.

The fabric was thick, but stretchy. It felt like proper, old-fashioned cotton jersey. The kind that cost $25 a yard and more. She took hold of one roll and with a huge effort managed to edge it over the side of the skip.

'More coming,' she told Elena.

Four rolls – two navy and two grey – were eased over the top of the skip and onto the ground beside Elena.

Elena was desperate to take a look at the fabric, but she was too busy holding up Annie's legs.

'I'm going to have to go in,' Annie decided: 'there's more stuff over in the corner.'

'No, Annie, not into the beeeen,' Elena warned, sounding horrified.

'Yes, into the beeeeeeeen,' Annie said, imitating Elena's accent as she scrambled forward and managed to swing one leg and the patent high heel at the end of it over the edge of the skip. This is tricky, she thought, as she wobbled dangerously above the concrete floor. But with another push, she was slithering down into the skip, dress snagging on the rough metal sides.

Very gingerly, she picked her way over the bin bags and rolls of nasty nylon and netting until she was close to the remaining rolls of material in the corner.

I'm in a skip, she told herself, where I'm 'sourcing' 'unique', 'limited edition' dress fabric for a truly 'one-off' collection. Oh the glamour!

'Annie!'

Elena's voice sounded extremely anxious.
'Yes?'

'There's a dog! There's a very big, big dog! And he coming this way!'

'You have to have the New England clam chowder. Do you like clams?'

Before Lana could reply to Taylor's question, he was off again: 'Or maybe the lobster salad. Seriously, it's better here than anywhere else on the Eastern seaboard. The fish and seafood at this place is the best. The best!'

The waiter hovering at Taylor's elbow beamed with pleasure: 'That's very kind of you, sir.'

'Hey, I'm only telling the truth,' Taylor grinned at him.

Lana was so in awe of everything that she could hardly speak.

Here she was in a proper fancy, grown-up restaurant with starchy white tablecloths, wine buckets, waiters in full dress . . . and with the most sophisticated guy she'd ever met.

He was only 20, she'd established that. He was still at university – 'college' as they called it over here – but he was spending his summer vacation in Manhattan working at *Vogue* (his mom had a little connection, apparently).

Only 20, but he already knew where the best seafood restaurant was and how to get a good table on a busy lunchtime. And *he* was taking *her* out to lunch!

'You order for me,' Lana said, glancing up shyly from the menu.

Taylor did, then told the waiter, 'Well, we don't want to be carded, so we better drink mineral water. Do you have the Apollinaris?'

'Yes sir, an excellent choice. The champagne of mineral waters.'

'Exactly!'

Lana restrained her mouth from gawping open. The champagne of mineral waters! Jeeeeeeeeez.

'Didn't you just love the library tour?' Taylor asked, turning to her with his utmost attention.

'Oh yes,' she replied, 'it was wonderful. Thank you for letting me come along.'

'So what are you doing tonight?' Taylor's bright eyes were so intense, Lana could hardly look into them for more than a moment or two.

'Tonight?' she repeated, trying not to squeak.

'I want to spend as much time with you as I can,' Taylor said, reaching over to touch her arm.

Then Lana felt a physical symptom she'd never experienced before. The blood rushed and stuttered in her chest with excitement and it really did feel as if her heart had fluttered.

'Your lobster salad, Miss,' the waiter announced. He lifted the huge silver lid from the dish and set it down in front of Lana. Then her crystal glass was filled with the extravagant fizzing water.

Glancing at the next table, Lana saw two women in designer suits and power jewellery gossiping over salads. One had a bright yellow ostrich skin Hermès bag perched in her lap.

Could this *be* any more glamorous?

Annie heard a clang as the tip of Elena's pointy shoe hit the side of the skip. Then came an undignified scrambling sound, and finally Elena appeared, then tumbled straight down into the bin bags and roll ends.

Annie looked out across the car park and saw a huge black and brown beast running at full stretch towards them.

The chain collar around his neck clinked ominously as he bounded up. When he reached the foot of the skip, he began to bark ferociously.

'I'm sure he's all talk and no trousers,' Annie said loudly, trying to be heard over the furious barking.

Good grief! Look at the beast! Foamy saliva was flecking the dog's jaws as he barked and barked like a mad thing.

'I never used to like dogs, but we have one now and they're really not that bad. They just like food . . . all they're ever after is food,' Annie said, trying to sound as calm as she possibly could while she wondered how on earth they were going to get away from the Hound of the Baskervilles down there.

Elena was cowering low. She was obviously not a doggie person.

'Hello boy, hello there. Good boy,' Annie said

over the edge of the skip, in the brightly cheerful, slightly insane tone she'd heard doggie people use.

The dog stopped barking, sat down and looked at her expectantly.

'See, he's not so bad.'

'No, no . . .' Elena said in a whimper, still crouching down in the rubbish.

Unless Annie could think of a way of getting rid of the dog, it looked like they would be stuck in the skip for some time. She wondered if there was a security guard somewhere . . . but then he probably wouldn't exactly be impressed to find two Manhattan fashion types going through his trash.

She looked at the scrunched up takeaway packaging dotted across the skip. Maybe she could find some scraps of food in one of those that would pacify the dog?

As she reached over to pick up one of the bags and look inside, it seemed to stir, rustling slightly. She hesitated for a moment, but then, determined, she reached over and snatched it up.

She didn't mean to shriek, but she couldn't help it: when you see the big brown furry back of an ugly urban super-rat, instinct takes over.

'Aaaaaaargh!!!'

'What?!' Elena jumped up, horrified.

'There's a . . . *mouse* . . . a small mouse,' Annie exclaimed, trying to play it down, but now her flesh was crawling and more than anything she

159

wanted to get out of this place. She was wearing peep-toes! Any moment now she might feel rat fur brushing against her bare feet.

Uuuurgh!

'I'm going to give the dog the hamburger left-overs in here' – she held up the rustling bag – 'and see if I can get him to like me.'

Given the choice between dogs and rats, Annie would try her luck with the dog any time. Gingerly, she reached inside the bag, feeling for the cold, greasy scraps of burger and fries and hoping she wasn't going to come across another horror: a dead rat bit or live rat baby.

'Here boy, good dog,' she said, tossing the bit of mouldy chicken nugget or whatever it was to the ground.

The dog wolfed it down, then looked up at her expectantly. Were they making friends? Or was the dog just hoping she would taste as good as that?

The big brute began to bark again, loudly, as if to tell her off for not giving him enough food.

Annie glanced back into the skip. Carefully, she picked up another food bag, but this one was empty. Then with a lurch of horror, she caught sight of the rat again. Or maybe it was another rat! Maybe this whole skip was teeming with them!

Help! She had to get out of here.

And that was when the idea sprang into her mind. It was one of those terrible ideas: the kind of idea which has too many problems, too many reasons why it might not work. So Annie acted quickly, instinctively, before she could talk herself out of it. She grabbed hold of the handle of the old spade lying in the skip.

Then she lunged for the rat, whimpering a little in horror . . . What if he ran up the spade handle?! On to her arms! She would faint. She really would.

But the big fat rat, heavier than she expected, was now on the spade.

Elena must have seen him because now she began to scream.

With a mighty effort, Annie swung the spade and launched the rat into the air. 'Grab the rolls!' she instructed Elena.

Meanwhile, Annie watched as the rat spun and twisted, its horrible tail flexing. She wasn't sure if it would splat and die on impact, but she scrambled for the fabric rolls close to her feet as she watched.

The rat landed and for a moment was very still.

Dead? she wondered.

No. The dog heard it land and, as Annie had wildly hoped, ran over towards it.

Now, exactly as she'd wanted, the rat raced off and the dog bounded after it.

'Quick!' she urged Elena.

The rat scurried under another skip a good 50 metres away and the dog, tail up in the air, stiff with excitement, began to bark and claw at the gap between the skip and the ground.

Now was definitely their chance. Annie heaved herself, her heels and her handbag over the rusty, flaky edge of the skip. She dangled for a moment, then let herself drop the two feet or so to the ground.

'Owww!'

She twisted her left ankle as she came down onto her heels. Next time she went out to source 'one-off' fabrics for a special collection she would wear a much, much more sensible outfit.

With shaking hands, Elena passed down the remaining rolls. Then, because Elena had maybe decided there was only one great big Brooklyn rat in that skip, she began rummaging deep down in search of more of the usable fabric.

These weren't big, supersized rolls. At a guess, there was somewhere between 15 to 20 metres of fabric on each one. Still, they'd now managed to find nine rolls: four navy, two grey and three a surprisingly nice bright magenta. How they were going to carry them out of the car park, even without the attentions of the guard dog, was another matter.

Elena scrambled down from the skip and stood breathlessly beside Annie, brushing her outfit down and looking about anxiously for the dog.

'He's very busy with the rat over there,' Annie said, 'I think we'll be OK.'

Elena bent down, tucked two rolls under one arm, three under the other and stood up. The weight was considerable. Annie loaded up with the remaining four rolls.

'OK?'

'Fine,' Elena answered, but she sounded shaky and close to tears. She really was very frightened of that dog.

'Don't run,' Annie instructed, 'just walk as calmly and quietly as you can.'

They were just a few metres from the gate when the dog looked up from his rat-worrying.

'Oh no! No!' Elena whimpered.

'Keep walking,' Annie hissed. She didn't look round, just kept marching towards the gate as quickly as she could.

For a moment, the dog stood still, watching them and figuring out what was happening. Then with an outraged yowl, he began to run towards them, his huge chain collar rattling from side to side with every bound.

Annie and Elena, still clutching their rolls of material, *dived* for the gate. As Elena slammed it shut, Annie shot the bolt just as the dog made a leap for them. He crunched into the metal rails, fell back, but was immediately on his feet snarling, barking and snapping his jaws ferociously.

That was when Annie saw the bright yellow 'Beware of the dog' sign on the gate. She had no idea how she'd missed it the first time.

But they were now in the road and the hound from hell was on the other side of the gate. Shaken, but strangely light-hearted now that the rat and dog horror was over, they shouldered their rolls and began to walk away from the scene of the crime.

'Now that,' Annie told Elena, 'is what I call a shopping adventure.

CHAPTER 15

Annie recovering:

Floral dressing gown (Elena's)
Hair conditioning masque (Paul Mitchell via
Elena)
Towel (also Elena's)
Plasters (drugstore)
Flat waffle slippers (hotel freebie)
Total est. cost: $3

'I'm sorry about the dog.'

Annie and Elena had tried to find a cab office, a cab rank or any trace of a cab at all. But to no avail. So, it was an exhausting thirty-minute walk, but together with their rolls, they finally made it to the subway station.

No one in the carriage gave a second glance to the two dirt-streaked females in stained dresses, holding several grubby rolls of fabric. In this part of Brooklyn, anything and anyone got onto the trains and it was best not to stare.

When Annie had recovered her breath and taken a full inventory of the damage she'd inflicted on herself and several cherished possessions – the shoes would never recover, she'd scratched the leather right off the side of the heel on the skip edge – she still looked over at Elena with a triumphant grin.

'We could have 180 metres of jersey here – about $4,000, maybe $5,000 worth. And we got it for free!'

'Yes!' Elena couldn't help smiling, 'but do you really think we can make good dresses out of it?'

'Of course!' Annie insisted.

'Is cotton jersey, is very different from silks and silk jersey we make first dresses from,' Elena pointed out.

'That will be the beauty of the dresses, though. Cotton, so wearer friendly. Beautiful design, beautiful fit and drape, but you can wear them all day long and chuck them in the washing machine.'

'We need nice buttons . . .'

'Yes,' Annie agreed, 'and lovely detailing. A little matching satin trim around the cuffs and the collars.'

'Yes! Sleeves draping or gathered with a bow. So elegant and beautiful, not too plain.'

'Are you OK?' Annie asked, 'I'm sorry about the dog.'

'I will be fine, but I rip hole in my dress and break two straps on my Gucci sandals.'

'That is bad,' Annie sympathized.

'No, not too bad. I get them at Designer Shoe Warehouse for $90.'

'You're going to have to tell me where that is.'

When Lana burst in through the apartment's front door face alight with the splendour of her library date and lunch with Taylor, she found Annie on the sofa bed: damp, in a dressing gown, with a towel on her head and bruises all over her shins.

Elena, also freshly showered, was at the Perfect Dress NYC nerve centre – the kitchen table – frantically tapping at her laptop.

'Mum, how come you aren't working?' Lana wanted to know. 'It's only four o'clock!'

'We've had a tiring day, believe me,' Annie told her. 'Anyway, I'm just regrouping and I needed to wash because my skin was crawling . . .'

She shuddered, still not able to shake the memory of the rat.

'I'll be back to work in about ten minutes, fresh as a daisy,' she insisted, 'but first of all . . . lunch went on a bit?! How was Taylor?'

'Yeah . . . well, no . . .' Lana stumbled and flushed a rosy pink, 'it was great. Really great. We toured round the library which is amazing and you totally have to go. Then we had lunch at this . . . restaurant!' She burst into giggles at the thought.

'A restaurant? So sophisticated,' Annie said.

'I hope you not be all British and pay for your meal,' was Elena's comment.

'No . . . well, I offered but he wouldn't let me.'
Lana couldn't help giggling again.

She was 'aglow', Annie thought. There was no
other word for it. But how incredibly amazing to
be almost 18 and in New York with a huge, massive
crush on a blond writer who took you on library
tours and out for lunch. Annie felt more than a
little jealous.

'Tell us all about everything, every little moment
. . .' Annie said, sitting up and patting the sofa
bed, 'but first of all, you have to look at our material and tell me what you think.'

Annie pointed at the rolls of fabric leaning up
against the kitchen sink. This was the only place
she'd found in the flat free enough of clutter to
have room for the nine rolls.

Lana walked over and looked carefully. Annie
was impressed at the serious attention she was
giving to the task; Lana realized how important
this was.

She peeled some fabric away from the roll, ran
her fingers over it and crumpled it up in her
hand.

'Sort of sweatshirty,' she said.

'Yeah.'

'Nice plain colours. I'm loving the magenta . . .
and the grey . . . and the navy too!'

'Simple colours to go with everything,' Elena
added, 'dress up dress down, very nice for New
York in winter with a coat and boots.'

'So a smart-casual sweatshirt dress?' Lana said,

getting the idea. 'I think it's going to be fantastic! Casual dresses. Smart shirtdresses but in cotton. Everyone is going to want one. I think you should make me one right now so I can wear it just as soon as it stops burning down at 30 degrees or whatever it is out there.'

'Long, long summer here. Sye say this is unusual,' Elena said, 'but long, long winter here too. Very cold, then you will miss the burning sun. This how is in Ukraine too.'

'The material's great, but doesn't it look a bit . . . dirty?' Lana asked tentatively. 'I hope you got some money off.'

At this, Annie began to laugh: 'We got it out of a skip, darlin'!'

'Out of a skip? Seriously?!'

'Seriously. Your mother like dis—' Elena tapped the side of her head in the universal sign for crazy person.

'We're going to wash it all at the launderette, which will hopefully kick start the worn-in, faded look,' Annie explained, 'then we'll get a US factory to run us up as many of our amazing new Perfect Dresses as we can afford. Once the money comes in from those, we can get all fancy and go back to stretchy silk and shiny satin. But maybe carry on the cotton if they do well.'

'This is the plan,' Elena reminded them. 'We don't know if this is going to happen yet. No factory has agreed to make dresses—'

'Yet,' Annie chipped in.

'And if these cotton dresses not good enough, existing orders might be cancelled,' Elena warned.

'The dresses will be good enough,' Annie insisted. 'C'mon Lana, fire up the coffee machine, tell us all about dreamy Taylor . . .'

'Muuuum!'

'Then we'll get started on a fresh round of calls.'

An hour later Lana had already gone out; a friend of Greta's, passing through New York, wanted to meet her for a pizza. So Annie was left in the apartment with an increasingly agitated Elena.

Elena was upset because Sye hadn't phoned her for two days and now a volley of his Venezuelan photographs had landed in her in-box.

'Look at this!' Elena turned the screen to Annie, who took in the lovely shot of a young, tanned vision of gorgeousness frolicking on the beach in the obligatory wet bikini. Her face was turned with deep and tantalizing eyes towards the camera.

'He's very good at his job,' Annie reassured her.

'He not phone me and I can't make connection with his phone.'

'He's on the beach in Venezuela,' Annie reminded her, 'the signal's probably not very strong. Please, calm down! The guy is crazy about you. I can see it, his friends we met the other night said it. He's probably just as desperate to speak to you as you are to speak to him.'

'When you are on trip with five models, why

170

you want to speak to girlfriend?' Elena snapped back.

'I promise you, there is no need to be jealous. Jealousy is one of the most horrible emotions you can waste time on. It's all bitter and destroying and in your case, based on absolutely nothing. What has he done to make you think he's not totally into you?'

'The only words with this photo are: "I am in love with this girl". I think he send it to me by mistake,' Elena declared angrily.

'Elena! "I'm in love with this girl" it's just photographer-speak. It's his job. You know it's his job. You knew he was a photographer when you first met him. I mean how incredibly flattering to have someone who takes pictures of some of the most beautiful faces in the world, be so in love with yours.'

'He has never said he loves me,' Elena snapped. Aha.

'Of course he's in love. You're both in love,' Annie assured her. 'Anyone can see that. It's oozing out of every pore when you two are together. Pure 100 per cent guaranteed in love. But yes, I understand, *saying* you're in love. That's hard. Maybe you're both waiting to see who says it first.'

'Maybe . . .'

'But don't be jealous. Not without any reason. Are you going out tonight?'

Elena shook her head, but then said: 'Maybe just to drugstore to buy some—'

Annie cut her off: 'Babes, have you looked in the bathroom lately?'

Elena glanced over at her in some surprise.

'You have your very own drugstore right there. Whatever it is you could possibly be looking for, you will find it in here.'

Annie pushed open the door to the small but perfectly formed bathroom. Just like in Elena's bedroom, every shelf, surface and available space was taken up with stuff. Although in here it was bathroom stuff: hair bottles, shower bottles, lotions, potions and make-up.

'I hate to say this,' Annie began gently, 'but I think there's about $2,000 worth of products in here.'

'No!' Elena protested.

'The buy one get one free habit can really mount up . . .'

When Annie saw Elena's shoulders slump and her hands move up to cover her face, she immediately regretted her words.

Rushing to Elena's side, she put an arm around her and said, 'You've been going through so many difficult things. You'll get through all this. Please stop worrying about Sye and . . . you'll get over the crazy shopping thing. I'll help you, if you'll let me.'

'The bedroom,' Elena said finally with a tragic sigh, 'maybe I could take you to the bedroom and we could just make one small corner tidy.'

Annie's face lit up at the thought. Back in her

172

personal shopper days, she'd subsidized her income with a home wardrobe makeover service and there was still almost nothing she liked more than being invited into the chaos of someone's cupboards to restore order.

Down there in the back of the wardrobe, the truth always came out. Whatever was going on in someone's life, it would be reflected in their cupboard: new lover, new lingerie; loveless marriage, really bad old knickers; unexpected pay rise, handbag splurge; financial disaster, worn-out suits and high street tops; ageing issues, inappropriate use of Topshop; and infidelity always caused wardrobe schizophrenia – boring suits and much red lace.

Annie could probably wander through a wardrobe and paint an exact picture of the woman who owned it without knowing anything else about her.

'I know there is problem here . . .' Elena admitted hesitantly, as they gazed into the room.

'Have you spoken to Sye about it?' Annie wondered.

Elena shook her head vigorously.

'But he must have noticed,' Annie pointed out. 'No one who's been in your room could help noticing the plastic bag mountain. Maybe he's trying to find the right moment to talk to you about it.'

'Maybe.'

As soon as they were crammed together in the

bedroom, Annie knew there wasn't going to be enough space here to sort things out, so she instructed Elena to bring a selection of carrier bags into the sitting room. There Annie opened out the sofa bed, so they would have somewhere to tackle the chaos of Elena's out of control shopping habit.

The first two bags Elena emptied contained entirely new clothes, labels still attached, receipt in the bag.

'What do you want to do with these?' Annie asked gently. 'Keep them? Give them away? You might even be able to take them back, the receipts are still there. I used to offer to sell things for my clients, but I don't have a US eBay account . . . maybe we could find a second-hand shop.'

Elena looked at the items with a mixture of confusion and surprise. 'I can't even remember buying them,' she told Annie. 'When I'm in a shop, I feel I have to have something, it's like a want that won't go away until I buy, then I feel better. Sometimes, I don't even look in the bags again.'

Annie put her arm around Elena's waist and squeezed: 'That's not good. And it's a very expensive problem to have, girl. But as soon as you start admitting these things to yourself, they start to get better by themselves. Honestly, I promise. Why don't we take back as much as we can? All the things you've bought in the last month. Then we'll try and sell the other things you don't want. We have to make a start on bringing that credit card bill down.'

During the next two hours, eighty-three plastic bags were upended – nearly one for every day Elena had been in New York – and the contents sorted out. Everything still within date and with receipts was sorted into one collection. Another pile of items to sell was created and then there was the much smaller collection of things which Elena actually wanted to keep.

Now that the clothes, shoes, bags and other accessories were lying in front of her on the sofa bed, not hanging tantalizingly from rails in a shop, Elena found there was surprisingly little that she really wanted.

'Maybe you should shop online, Elena,' Annie suggested, 'just stay away from the shops for a good long time if they make you feel like this. I hope you realize you've spent $24,000 on things that you've not even looked at again. Do you know what you could have bought with that money?'

It didn't take Annie long to do the fashion maths: 'Sixty pairs of Christian Louboutin shoes or fourteen Yves Saint Laurent tuxedos – yes fourteen! Or two handmade Hermès bags . . .'

She could have gone on, but Elena looked guilty enough.

'I remember going shopping with you when you first arrived in London,' Annie added. 'You were so excited and you bought soooo many things. I didn't realize how much trouble I was going to cause you in the future.'

'I know!' Elena said, but at least with a smile.

The bags of stuff to go were all piled right at the door of the apartment. Annie would help Elena to get rid of them as soon as she possibly could. Nothing worse than dead wardrobe wood hanging about once it had been efficiently pruned away.

Expert Annie soon had Elena's remaining clothes up on hangers, ordered into sections and neat piles. Clinically perfect stacks of tops were created and the drawers were neatly regimented.

Elena sat quietly on her bed and watched.

'OK, I'm going to put all your hangers backwards on the rail like this,' Annie explained, 'and every time you wear something you put it back on the rail facing the other way. Then in a few months' time, you'll be able to see everything that's never been worn at all and you can consider whether or not you want to keep it.'

'Clever,' Elena admitted.

'Less is more,' Annie promised. 'A few lovely pieces are always much better than piles of rubbish.'

When the wardrobe was as beautiful and organized as it could possibly be, Annie stepped back and admired her handiwork with pride.

'Life is going to be simple from now on. Just wear the lovely things you already have . . . and in the bathroom, use all the things you've already bought. Tidy up every day and enjoy your space.

Save your money, pay back your bills and you will, I absolutely promise, reach a place, not so long from now, when you'll be back on track. When you go into a shop to buy something you need that you've got the money for, you'll feel so much better.'

'Is this what you do?' Elena asked. 'Only go shopping for things you need with money you already have?'

Annie tried to keep a straight face:

'Well . . . no,' she admitted. 'Not exactly . . . but sometimes. Sometimes I manage it and it feels fantastic! In fact, sometimes I can't even bear to part with my hard-earned cash and I go away and buy something much cheaper instead.'

She sat on the bed next to Elena. 'It turns out, babes, it's much easier spending other people's money – like Mr Visa's – than spending your own.' Glancing at her watch, Annie suddenly leapt up. 'I have to call home!' But it was probably too late and she wondered now why Ed hadn't phoned her to say good-night.

They'd spoken on every evening of her New York trip so far and she'd assumed that was how it would go on. She needed to have the little chats, to hear how the day had gone at home. It helped her to feel less guilty about being away from everyone.

'I'm going out for a NY takeout and ur in bed,' she texted. 'I missed u. Speak ASAP. Let me know how everyone doing. Loads of love A xxx'

Now . . . one of those unbelievably good Chinese takeouts? Or was she going to be wholesome and saintly and go to Whole Foods Market for their dinner?

CHAPTER 16

The Manhattan Yummy Mummy:

Pink gingham shirt (J. Crew)
White skinny jeans (J Brand)
Teeny silver belt (Banana Republic)
Oversized sunglasses (Chanel)
Pink gingham sneakers (Keds)
White and tan drawstring bag (Dooney &
Bourke)
Total est. cost: $640

Not smiling, just frowning

It wasn't exactly easy to get into Central Park unnoticed. From the moment a tourist emerged from the subway closest to the park, there was a full-on hustlers alley to negotiate.

'Ice cream, ice cream.'

'No thanks.'

'Water, bottle of water?'

'No.'

'But you get thirsty in park.'

'No, thank you.'

'Umbrella, lady? It might rain?'

'No. Really.'

Even inside the gates of the park, there was a man in a low buttoned checked shirt insisting:

'Map, you must have map of Central Park. Only $2. Just $2.'

'No, thank you. I'm fine.'

Annie kept on walking just as quickly as she could, desperate for peace, quiet, greenery and calm – some of the things she'd been sent here by Lana to find.

After a whole morning of phoning factories and trying to phone Ed, she felt totally frazzled. Everything was bound to be fine. It was a Friday. He was in school. Yes, she'd tried to time her calls for his breaks, but maybe he was doing some extra tutoring.

She'd tried to speak to Dinah, who would be with the twins today, but the home phone just rang out and Dinah's mobile was infuriatingly off.

But she was sure they were fine. Everyone was fine, she kept telling herself. Otherwise someone would have told her. She would know by now if something was wrong.

She kept walking at a brisk pace until, fifteen minutes later, she found herself at the boating pond. This was where Lana had told her to go.

'Go and watch the water, admire the gorgeous apartment blocks all around and just relax, Mum. You need to relax . . . hire a boat,' she'd suggested.

Annie found a bench that wasn't occupied and took a seat.

She watched the water a little bit, she gawped at the apartment blocks overlooking the park, and she also became very absorbed watching the colourful people of NYC strolling past. It was a sunny day, though not as fiercely hot as it had been, and the park was busy. Nannies and mommies were pushing babies about in very top of the range buggies.

It was easy to tell the nannies from the mommies: the nannies were typically black or Hispanic, sometimes in uniform, and their charges were as white as white. The mommies wore high fashion or athletic gear, carried little hipster water bottles and jogged as they pushed their prams.

Sooooo New York.

Annie leaned her head back to get a better view of the swaggeringly grand apartment blocks around the edge of the park. These were surely the swankiest, priciest blocks in the entire city. She watched a helicopter land on the roof of one of the buildings.

Soooo New York.

It was the kind of city where she could be in the park, totally jealous of the people who were living in the blocks, but the people in the blocks were probably totally jealous of the guy in the penthouse who had the helicopter.

And maybe the guy with the helicopter was jealous of the guy with the jet and the mansion out of town. That's how it was in this city, she was coming to understand. Everyone, everywhere was hustling, on the make, trying to get another rung up the ladder.

'What's Perfect Dress going to do for us?' she'd been asked so many times on her round of factory calls. 'Is it getting good promotion. Is it high end? Will it bring us more clients? How many orders are you going to place in the future?'

Annie's phone began to ring. She snatched it up and saw Ed's name flashing across the screen.

'FINALLY!' she shouted down the line as soon as she'd answered.

'Annie, how are you doing?'

'Much, much better for hearing you, babes, how's it going?'

'It's going great . . .' he sounded as if he was trying not to laugh.

'What's so funny?'

'Nothing. Everything is fine. I promise. Where are you?'

'In Central Park and it's gorgeous. So there!'

'Fantastic . . . where in Central Park? Paint me a picture.'

This time, she could paint him the full picture; this time she had nothing to hide.

'I'm sitting on a bench at the foot of the boating pond. I'm looking across the water at the gorgeous little boating hut and there's a restaurant on the water's edge too. I remember it from *Sex and the City*. I think this is where Carrie fell into the pond and ruined her shoes.'

'Oh dear . . .' There was still a throaty giggle to his voice.

'C'mon, what's so funny?'

'Nothing, honest, go on.'

'It's lovely. It's so peaceful, but it's impressive too. It's not the countryside, it's nothing like the countryside, it's the big, show-off garden right in the heart of this city, which is the most fabulous city I've ever been to, by the way . . .'

She wondered if it was too early to tell him how much she'd love to move them all over here . . . eventually. Somehow. Even if it was just for a year or two.

But then the line went dead.

'Ed? *Ed?*' she asked her phone, but there was no response.

She was about to dial his number and try again when she felt a tap on her shoulder. Startled, she turned round and was astonished to see who was standing behind her.

'ED!!' she shrieked, causing several nannies and mommies to turn in concern.

For several moments, she could only stare, making strange 'whhhh . . . whhhh . . . whhhh . . .' noises.

But finally, she broke out with a great rush of questions: 'What are you doing here?! How did you get here? Where are the babies? Is everyone OK?'

Despite the delighted grin on Ed's face, she couldn't help feeling a little panicky. Surely he could only be here if something was wrong?

'Annie, it's fine. Everything's fine. This is a surprise. *Surprise!*' he repeated and bent down to kiss her on the mouth.

It felt very nice to be kissed. Now that she was kissing Ed again, it felt like it had been a very long time.

But she still had so many questions for him, she had to break the kiss off early and ask again, 'But how are they going to manage without you?'

'Everyone is fine,' he replied. 'Dinah's going to take the babies for the three nights I'm here and Owen is staying at Milo's when school ends today. The dog's with Mrs B next door.'

'So . . . why are you here? How did you get here? I can't believe you! What about school?'

'I know, I know . . . I didn't mean to give you such a shock. Poor you.'

He moved round to sit on the bench beside Annie and wrapped her up in his arms: 'You won't believe this, but Owen bought me the flight for my birthday.'

'Owen!!'

She hugged him back and let herself be kissed on the cheek.

'I know. I think he got a great deal, but still. And then we all got a bit carried away with the idea of it being a surprise.'

'Lana sent me to the boating pond!' Annie was working it out now, 'so she knew.'

Ed nodded: 'My partner in crime.'

'You're not planning on staying at the flat, though, are you? It's the size of a stamp.'

184

Ed shook his head and smiled at her: 'No. I've booked us a hotel . . .'

'A hotel? A real, live hotel? Where I'll be able to sleep in a non-sofa bed and order room service?'

She was almost starting to relax and enjoy this surprise now.

'It's not far from your flat. It's nothing flashy, but hopefully nice. Birthday treat,' Ed said and kissed her again.

'Three nights?' Annie asked, pulling away from him once again, 'is that all?'

'I'm afraid so. Better take advantage.'

He'd taken a transatlantic flight for a weekend with her. That was romantic, that truly was romantic.

She slipped her hands around his neck and looked into his face. Despite the travel and the jet lag, he looked well.

'How was the plane?' she asked.

'No idea. I got on at Heathrow, put in the earplugs, woke up at JFK. Best sleep I've had since the twins were born. Do you know, this is the first time I've been away from them?'

'No!'

Annie felt shocked. She'd regularly been away, ever since the twins were tiny, on trips for the TV show. How had she let Ed go for almost a year without a single night away?

'You *deserve* your New York birthday treat,' she said. Moving her lips against his ear, she promised, 'I'm going to make sure you have a very good time. Really.'

'Really?'

'Oh yes . . . but what am I going to do about the birthday treat I've organized to arrive at the house on Sunday?'

'Cancel,' Ed said. 'just phone, email, whatever. I'm here . . . this is the best! Remember the last time we were in New York?'

'Oh yes. I definitely remember . . .' For a moment, a little vision of their very first long weekend together filled her mind, but then like a pin pricking a bubble, the troubling question returned: 'Ed, how did Owen get the money? I mean . . . he sells second-hand CDs and DVDs. How can he just drop £200 on an airline ticket for you? That seems too generous. And did you know that he lent Lana £600 spending money to bring over here?'

'Stop worrying,' Ed said, 'Owen is fine. He really is perfectly fine. I've seen him at his stall and he's good. He's a natural salesman, which I would never have suspected when I first met him.'

'But I knew there was this bubbly, funny person in there all the time just dying to get out.'

Annie had to kiss him properly now, because Ed had been one of the most important people to help Owen transform from shy boy to market stall trader.

'Mmmmm . . . you taste good,' he told her. 'Do you want to hire a boat? We're snogging on a bench, when we could be snogging in a boat.'

'This is how it begins. Next you'll only want to

snog on a yacht . . . then only a private jet will do. It's the New York one-upmanship thing. Don't you have luggage?' she wondered.

'It's at the hotel. I tried to see Lana, but she was heading out.'

'Ah yes . . . Lana has met this *Vogue* writer guy and she has it bad.'

'*Vogue* writer?'

Annie loved the way Ed's hackles were rising, just like Lana's real dad's would have.

'No, I know, you're thinking old, suave and sophisticated . . . but he's a student, doing work experience at *Vogue*. He seems OK . . . bit full of himself. Bit big-headed, but she really likes him and I am trying to step back.'

Ed gave a wince. 'Big bad scary New York boys, though. Is she ready for that?'

'I think you mean: are we ready for that? C'mon let's go and get into a boat. I bet you can row, can't you? It's going to be another of your many schoolboyish talents, to go with your schoolboyish charm.'

'Oh yeah, I can row, baby. Somewhere in the bottom of my sock drawer, I even have a rusty old medal to prove it.'

He stood up and offered her his arm.

As they walked together in the direction of the boating hut, Annie finally grinned at him with a stunned excitement. 'I'm so chuffed you're here.'

'Are you sure? You looked a little appalled back there.'

'I'm still shocked. But I'm very pleased to see you. It's getting a bit intense with the dress thing. It's all still very up in the air. We may have a factory, we may not . . . they may do the dresses in time, they may not.'

'Inner calm,' Ed suggested.

'Inner Valium, more like.'

Annie watched Ed row with giggly admiration.

'Ooooh, what broad shoulders you have,' she teased, 'oooh what strong arms.'

It was so strange to see him here and to see him without at least one baby in his hands. It was re kindling all sorts of tingly romantic thoughts.

A hunk in a college letter sweater streaked past them, rowing so hard he was pink with effort.

'Harvard rowing team?' Ed asked. 'You've got to get the practice in.'

The water smelled clean and green as they floated over it. On the rocks beside the shore small turtles were basking in the sunlight.

'This is so nice. Why didn't we do this the last time we were here?' Annie wondered.

'We were too busy exploring other important new areas.'

'We were.'

Almost all the sightseeing on their last visit had been done inside their locked hotel room.

'Have you flown all the way over here expecting the same again?' she asked with a smile.

'Well . . . *hoping* for *some* of the same,' Ed

answered. 'If you can fit me into the hectic schedule, obviously.' He pointed to her bag where her phone was now ringing.

'Hi?' Annie answered.

Elena was on the other end of the line: 'The factory we like, the one in Connecticut. The owner wants me to meet him there, this afternoon. Annie, you have to come with me.'

CHAPTER 17

Business Elena:

Grey silk shirtdress (Perfect Dress sample)
Snakeskin courts (Ferragamos via Svetlana)
Large purple tote (Marc Jacobs via Century 21)
Total est. cost: $160

'We long way from Manhattan now.'

As Elena stood in the hallway urging Annie to hurry up because otherwise they would miss the train, Annie explained at speed to Lana that Ed was in the café downstairs working his way through the muffin menu.

'He's expecting you to go and join him. I've told him to wait there for you. Then you have to look after him until I get back. He's flown all this way!' Annie was flooded with guilt: 'Now I have to go off for the afternoon.'

She really didn't want to be in a factory for

possibly four or five of the precious hours that Ed was here on his surprise visit. But Elena needed her and Annie was going to have to put business first. It was the reason she was here. They would all just have to get on and deal with it.

'We'll have a wonderful evening . . . and the whole of Saturday and Sunday. And he'll enjoy being with you today,' she added, to try and calm her guilt. 'He's in the café,' she repeated.

Lana, freshly showered – it was a teen thing, teens had showers whatever the time of day, maybe because they had no routine – stood holding her towel about her, hair dripping into a little pool on the floor. She knew that when her mother was this wound up it was best to just stand and listen, nodding frequently.

Then, all of a sudden, Lana's towel slipped and Annie found herself faced with a full frontal view of her daughter's full frontal waxing.

She gasped, and it was hard to recover the conversation from there.

'Probably on his fifth muffin . . .' Annie attempted, but then she just had to blurt out: 'A *Brazilian*? Have you seriously had a *Brazilian*? Here? In New York?'

All the things that this meant whirled around Annie's head. You didn't have a Brazilian just for yourself, you had a full frontal scalping to show off to someone else, that much was fact.

'Lana, you've not known this guy for very long,' Annie said gently. 'Really I should sit you down

191

on the sofa and we should talk right now . . . but I have to get into a cab with Elena.'

'You're talking all New York,' Lana said with a smile.

'You're *looking* all New York,' Annie replied, pointing low.

'Muuuuum, you'll have to step back a little and leave this to me. I know you want me to look after myself and I will. Now go. Go!' Lana insisted, 'I'll look after Dad for you, even though he probably has a map in his wallet of all the music shops he wants to visit now that you're out of the way.'

'Probably.'

Annie kissed her daughter on the forehead. Even in her heels, she had to reach up to do that now. 'See you later.'

Pittsfield, Connecticut was not Manhattan. This was obvious as soon as the cab had pulled away from the station and Annie and Elena, along with their fabric rolls, were being driven through a suburban landscape of long streets, grocery stores and houses hidden behind gardens and fences.

'Those cute little mailboxes with flags,' Annie heard herself pointing out.

'Ya,' Elena was intrigued by this different scene too, 'we long way from Manhattan now.'

The factory was a low brick building right on the outskirts of the small town. A row of cars sat in the joyless car park. Peeling paint and faded signs showed that there had almost certainly been better days at Fashion Parade Inc.

Elena paid the taxi fare and then the two hauled their fabric towards the reception.

The man at the door didn't exactly scream 'fashion'. In his baggy checked shirt, faded beige cords and small gold-rimmed glasses, 'Grampa' was the word more likely to jump to mind.

But Brad Barrington seemed pleased to see them at first. He shook their hands, ushered them into his neat office and made some small talk.

But when they lifted the fabric up onto Brad's big table, along with the design sketches and thin paper patterns that Elena took out of her bag, he didn't look quite so enthusiastic.

'Making up these patterns in stretchy jersey will be difficult,' he pointed out. 'Take the gathered sleeve there, with the bow at the end. I don't know if we can do that, for example.'

'Maybe you could give it a try?' Annie asked encouragingly.

'I'd rather not. We've got a very narrow time frame here.'

'We have to have the sleeves like this,' Elena insisted. 'It is supposed to look like upmarket and chic, but in sweatshirt material. This is the style.'

Brad Barrington scratched the back of his head and took a long, appraising look at the sketches.

Silence. One of those silences when clearly no one wanted to back down.

Annie and Elena stole a little glance at one

another. They weren't going to give in. If Brad here wanted their business he would have to give the dress sleeves a go.

'All right . . .' he said finally, 'I'll give them my best shot, but I can't promise they'll come out OK. Could we have that in the contract? If they don't work, then we'll put something simple on there, a button cuff maybe?'

'Yes,' Elena said, 'but tight button cuff, then much looser sleeve gathered into it.'

Annie was impressed with the way that Elena was so on top of all the details.

'Well, if you ladies would like to get comfortable in the waiting room, drink a coffee or two, I'll take some of your fabric and your paper patterns and we'll go make you a dress right now so you can see what it's like.'

'Now? Really?'

Annie couldn't believe it would be so quick.

'Yes, really. Settle in over there, read through your contract with us and I'll come back with the first finished product. Have you brought labels for us to sew into the dresses?'

Elena snapped open her bag and handed over an envelope.

It was not even twenty minutes later when Brad returned with the dress.

Annie jumped up from her chair and headed towards him, desperate to take a look.

Turning the hanger this way and that, she showed

the dress to Elena. 'Look at the seams, so straight, so cleverly done. Ooh, I love the way the skirt flares out.' Although it was a straightforward shirtdress, the panels of the skirt were cut diagonally to give plenty of flippy movement.

'How are the sleeves?' Elena asked, her deep voice still solemn.

Brad held them out for her to inspect. 'They didn't go as badly as I'd thought. In fact we got very close to your original design here, we've just shortened the ties a little to make it a bit easier to handle.'

'And this you can do on all the other ones?' Elena asked.

'Yes . . . yes, I think so.'

'Good.' Elena didn't go over the top with her approval. She was touchingly businesslike.

'Try it on,' Annie urged her, 'just slip it on over your dress and we'll get an idea of what it's like.'

Elena stood up and slipped her arms into the grey sleeves. She buttoned up the front and did a twirl for Annie and Brad.

Annie could see now how genius these dresses were going to be. She loved the chic, uptown colourful, silky numbers that Perfect Dress had been producing so far, but this was the fantastic downtown version. A slouchy, casual but totally pulled together look which everyone was going to love. Heels, a belt and a beret, it could do the school run, even the office at a push. Leggings, flats and a slouchy bag, and it was totally sexy weekend.

'I love it!' Annie said. 'Isn't it cool?' she asked Brad, but she sensed the term was slightly lost on him. This was a man in a checked shirt and saggy cardigan.

'It's a nice design,' Brad said professionally, 'your designer's really thought the pattern through. It works. Apart from the sleeve, it's all very simple.'

The contracts were signed, the delivery dates were agreed and as they climbed into the taxi, Annie felt truly optimistic about the dresses for the first time since she'd touched down at JFK.

'I hope you're pleased,' she told Elena. 'I really think this is going to work, *and* he's promised to get everything to us in time for the first due dates!'

'I have to go and show the new dresses to the clients, make sure they still want these dresses, even though they are different from the ones they ordered.'

'But they will,' Annie enthused, 'I've worked in fashion for years and I know that these dresses are absolutely perfect for right now. They're really going to sell.'

Elena still didn't look especially happy and Annie wondered if it was to do with Sye. To Annie's knowledge Sye had barely been in touch from his model shoot. But he was due back in town tomorrow, so surely the lovely couple would be able to make up then.

They sat silently for a while, then Elena's phone

began to ring. She looked at the screen and issued a totally Svetlana-like 'Tschaaa' of disapproval.

Sweeping her hair out of the way, she pressed the phone to her ear.

'Sye, yes, hello. How are you?'

Annie tried not to listen, but she was in the back of a cab with not much choice. Well, especially as the conversation now took an unexpected turn.

'I am very busy, Sye,' Elena began. 'I don't think I have time to see you this weekend. I don't know when I'm going to have time to see you . . . no not next week. Sye . . . maybe not ever.'

There was a pause, which Annie assumed must be Sye objecting. But to her amazement all Elena said in reply was 'No, I don't think so, Sye. No. Goodbye.'

With that, she hung up, stuffed the phone quickly into her handbag . . . and burst into tears.

CHAPTER 18

Lana's dinner date:

Dark blue boob tube (J. Crew sale rail)
Black harem trousers (discount warehouse)
Blue suede three-inch heels (on loan from Elena)
Silver clutch (Macy's)
Packet of condoms (Duane Reade)
Cloud of perfume (duty-free sample)
Total est. cost: $125

'Just coffee!'

As Annie slid the plastic card into the hotel room lock, Ed called from the other side of the door. 'Annie?'

'Oh yes,' she said pushing the door open, 'it's me and I've made it back from the wilds of Connecticut.'

Ed, wet-haired and wearing a fresh shirt and pair of trousers, was lying on top of the bed. He patted the empty space beside him.

'Lie down, enjoy the soothing breeze of the air conditioning and tell me all about it.'

198

It was the best offer Annie had heard for hours.

She dumped her bags and flopped down onto the cool white sheets. This bed was so soft and springy compared with the sofa bed. 'Heaven . . .' she told him.

'I know: just you, me, a locked hotel room.'

'Was sightseeing fun?' she asked, turning to put her arm over his waist.

'Yes, but I have even more fun in mind,' he said and moved in to kiss her on the lips.

'Mmmmm . . . smooching, it's been too long,' she agreed.

But right on cue, her mobile began to ring.

'Leave it?' Ed suggested.

'I can't,' Annie replied, already up, reaching for the phone, 'it might be Lana, it might be home . . . someone might really need me.'

'But I really need you,' Ed complained.

'Hello . . . hello?' There was no sound at the other end, but Annie immediately knew who it was. 'Mum, is that you, are you there?'

Ed sat up.

'Mum, it's Annie here. Did you mean to phone me? Isn't it very late at home?'

'Annie, I can't sleep and I just wanted a little chat,' Fern began.

Annie noticed how tired her mother's voice sounded. 'How are you doing?' she asked soothingly.

'Oh not too bad. Not too bad at all. But I can't sleep and I thought you might still be up.'

'I'm in New York, Mum,' Annie reminded her.

'You're in New York? What? Now?' Her mother sounded astonished, as if this couldn't possibly be right.

'Yes. I'm here for a few weeks.'

'All the way over in New York? Why didn't you tell me?'

'Well, I did, Mum, but it must have just . . . gone to the back of the queue, you know.'

This was their code phrase, because any mention of 'forgotten' or 'forgetful' made Fern upset.

'Oh no, dear, I wouldn't let a thing like that go to the back of the queue.'

'I wouldn't come all the way over here and not tell you, would I, Mum?'

'Well . . . I don't know,' she said, 'you do always like to rush off here, there and everywhere.'

'Mum, you're phoning me, all the way to New York on my mobile. I think you should put the phone down and I'll call you right back.'

'Good grief,' Fern exclaimed and put the receiver down without another word.

'Would it be cheaper to call her back on the mobile or the hotel phone?' Annie asked Ed.

'I have no idea.'

He leaned over and selected a magazine from the bedside table. He had a feeling this was going to take some time.

'I just want to settle her down. Make sure she knows everything's OK.'

'That's fine . . . of course.'

'Are you sulking?'

'Just a bit. I'll get over it. We're supposed to be meeting Lana for dinner in . . .' he glanced at his watch: 'twenty-five minutes. You don't have to miss that, do you?'

'Of course not. She's going to try and bring Taylor along. I'm not missing that.'

'If you phone your mum back, the romance window will have to close.'

'I have to phone Mum back.'

'I know. Pity.'

'Well, they managed to stay for a respectable two courses,' Annie said, looking over at the two empty seats at the other side of the restaurant table.

'I don't think Lana ate much though, she was too excited about him and too nervous about us,' Ed pointed out.

'*She* was nervous? I was terrified. For 20, he is quite scary. How often did he mention the words "career plan" and "resumé"? I have no idea why he's hanging out with Lana and not trying to date an heiress or at least the boss's daughter.'

Ed smiled. 'I know, but don't be too harsh. I deal with guys like him all the time at St Vincent's. Their parents are rich and important and all that self-confidence and sense of entitlement rubs off on their kids too. I know sixteen-year-olds even more bullish than him. Please, let's not fret too much. This is their first week of dating. Lana's on holiday over here, it's not as if we're discussing her future husband.'

201

Annie gave a little shriek of terror at the very thought. Then she noticed Lana's empty glass. 'He topped up her wine glass more than once . . . do you think she's OK?'

'She was when she left,' Ed reassured her. 'Taylor said he was going to buy her a coffee and see her back to the apartment. I'm sure everything will be fine. She has a phone if there are any problems. "Just coffee!" she said.'

'I've told her he's not allowed back to the apartment with her. I'm sorry if that's a bit Victorian but I'm with you, Elena's probably out, and Lana's only known this guy for a few days. Way too soon.'

'For unsupervised access,' Ed added, trying not to smile.

'Bloody right.'

He reached across and took her hand in his. 'What about us? Are we tired?'

'Yes.'

'But are we going to have a coffee? A little dessert? Try to rally?'

She slipped her hand over his: 'Two double espressos and a chocolate mousse might do the trick.'

'Here's hoping.'

Over the chocolate mousse and coffee, they sent a couple of texts to Dinah and Owen to make sure everything was fine at home, then finally the bill was paid and Ed and Annie made the short walk back to their hotel.

'I hope you're thinking what I'm thinking?' Annie asked Ed as he unlocked the door to their hotel room.

'Oh yeah,' Ed replied.

Inside the room, Ed took off his jacket, landed his wallet and keys on the table, then threw himself into the depths of the deep cushions and fluffy duvet on the white bed. 'Hours and hours of sex.'

Annie sat on the edge of the bed and unbuckled her shoes, rubbing her hands over the marks the straps had made on the skin.

'Hours and hours of sleep,' she told him, smiling fondly at him.

'Technically, this is our honeymoon, have you thought about that?' he said, reaching to stroke her back.

'This is our honeymoon?! Three nights in a budget hotel worrying about who our daughter's with? Does it get more romantic?'

'Annie, just phone her if you're worried.'

'Ed, they said they were going to a place three streets from the apartment. Then he was going to drop her at the door. I'm almost totally convinced that she's safe. But if I dial, she won't pick up because it's embarrassing getting phoned by your mum, so then I'll spend the next hour worrying myself into a frenzy.'

'Which would be a shame,' he said, moving closer, 'because you could spend the next hour doing something much better.'

'You are dangerously cute,' she told him, but her arm was reaching out across the bed. This bed was so big . . . it was so soft. She'd spent night after night sharing a sofa bed with Lana and this really was going to be heaven.

'Take your clothes off,' Ed whispered against her ear.

'Just what have you got planned?'

'Massage?' he offered.

'Ooooh baby, yes . . . yes!'

She unbuttoned her dress and flung it over the back of a chair, then she unhooked the straps of her bra and let herself fall face down on the bed. She sank into crisp white cotton and fluffiest down duvet.

Bliss.

Ed's warm fingers were at the nape of her neck. He began circling with his thumbs, easing away the knots of tension there.

Annie murmured in approval. 'Do you have any idea how good this feels?' she whispered.

'You used to say that about some of my other moves too.'

'Keep going, just keep going and I may perk up enough for some of those other moves too,' she said, although now that her shoulders were loosening, it was becoming very, very hard to keep her eyelids from drooping.

Ed lay beside her and began to trace his finger lightly down her spine. 'Hey . . .' he said gently, tenderly against her ear.

But Annie's eyes were closed.

Ed leaned down a little closer. There was no mistaking the sound. It was quite a small and quite a low sound, but it was definitely Annie snoring.

CHAPTER 19

Ed in New York:

Light blue linen shirt (Boden, present from Annie)
White chinos (Hackett, present from Annie)
Blue flip-flops (market stall)
Sunglasses (dodgy knock-offs borrowed from Owen)
Factor 30 suncream (Boots)
Total est. cost: $210

'It feels like a date.'

'Mustard or onions?'

'Both!' Ed replied with a grin, 'I'm in New York, I need to have the full experience.'

Annie got the hot dog salesman to load up their buns with onion and mustard. Then, hand in hand, they walked towards one of the benches on Museum Mile to eat and to watch New York go by.

'I've not made you go to too many museums?'

Ed wondered, his mouth now full of hot dog and onions.

'Four museums in one day is a lot, but I came prepared,' she said, pointing to her unusually sensible shoes. 'I loved MOMA and the Folk Art Museum,' she added through her second mouthful, 'the presidents' heads? Remember?'

'Oh yes,' Ed laughed, 'by the barber, who'd carved them in his shop over the years, in all the spare time between customers.'

'Thank you for taking me,' Annie told him, leaning against his arm. 'Sometimes I forget how much I like museums and proper art . . . sometimes I'm maybe a little too caught up in the art of . . .'

'Shopping?!'

'Fashion,' she corrected him, 'it's fashion, *never* just call it shopping!'

'I know, sorry, how could I forget.'

'There's all this incredibly creative stuff going in fashion. It's an art form all of its own.'

'OK . . . art student,' he teased.

'Music buff,' she teased straight back.

'Are you glad I came all the way to see you?'

'Of course! Of course I'm glad you came. This has been one of the nicest days we've had together for . . . ages.'

'It feels like a date,' he said, carefully wiping his hand with a napkin, then reaching over to hold hers. Sweet.

'I know. I can't get over how much time there

is in a day when we don't have the twins with us. I feel like we've been out for hours and hours and it's still only 4p.m. We have the whole evening ahead of us. Unbelievable!'

'What are we going to do tonight?' Ed asked.

'Tonight? Tonight is all about going back to the hotel room early to bounce the headboard off the wall,' she said and shot him a wink.

'Really? It's not going to end like last night? Me massaging, you snoring.'

'I do not snore!' Annie protested. 'Look over there, other side of the road. Could that couple *be* more Upper East Side?'

Ed followed her gaze to a middle-aged man in a gold-buttoned navy blazer accessorized with cravat and cigar. Walking alongside him was a younger, very thin woman in a pink shift dress and huge sunglasses leading a minuscule fluffy dog on a pink lead.

'Look how thin her arms are,' Annie whispered. 'How does she lift up that vast gold bracelet?'

'Wiry but tough, these New York girls.'

'Don't you love it?' Annie asked, leaning back against the bench, turning her face to the late, late summer sun. 'All human life is here. When I wake up in Manhattan, I feel that anything could happen. Absolutely anything!'

Ed leaned over and kissed her on her slightly mustardy lips.

'This sounds a little bit like longing,' he said.

'I know. I've got a big, big crush. Huge. If I

didn't have any attachments, then I might consider it. A move stateside. My own postage-stamp-sized apartment, eating pancakes in the diner for breakfast every morning . . . having a New York adventure every day. But I love every single one of my attachments,' she added quickly.

'Are you sure?'

'Of course! You know I do. Please, let's not start talking about the children, or I'm going to feel very homesick and sad.'

Four storeys below Ed and Annie's hotel room, a cab was honking impatiently. On the other side of the street, a rowdy, open-windowed party was in full swing. Every half an hour or so, hotel guests would wander up and down the corridor; one even tried to open their door with his key-card.

But still Annie and Ed remained very soundly, very deeply asleep. They were lost to the sleep of exhausted parents, over-toured tourists and deeply satisfied, reconnected lovers.

The headboard had been well and truly bounced. The household routine, the children's timetables, all the stresses and strains of running a family together had been completely obliterated by fifty-eight minutes of increasingly free and abandoned lovemaking.

They had been with each other fully, with their absolute attention, absorbed in all the ways of making one another thrill without any distractions.

Now they were fast asleep: skin salty with dried

sweat, hair messed and limbs thrown out, carelessly entangled, across the bed.

Until the sound of Annie's phone tore through the room, forcing her to surface from her deep, deep sleep. She snatched it up.

'Hi,' she said in a whisper, just awake enough to register that the phone hadn't woken Ed.

'Mum, it's me,' Lana said and burst into a volley of sobs.

'What's the matter? Are you OK?' Annie asked, now as awake as if she'd been doused with cold water.

'No! No, I'm not OK.'

Lana sounded almost hysterical.

'Lana, where are you?' Annie asked, getting out of bed and hurrying to the bathroom. She closed the door, turned on the lights and tried not to panic.

'I'm at Elena's. And he's gone. He's gone for good. I'm never going to see him again . . .' Lana couldn't say any more because she was so overcome with sobs.

'Sit tight, babes, just sit right where you are. I'll be there in ten minutes. OK?'

'No. No, it's OK, I just wanted to—'

'Don't be silly,' Annie interrupted, 'I'm coming over. Of course I'm coming. You've got to have someone to put the kettle on. And I'll bring hankies. I don't think there are any in the flat. You can't blow your nose on toilet paper darlin', it makes it all red.'

For a moment, Annie could hear snuffling and gulping down the other end of the line.

But then Lana managed, 'Thanks, Mum.'

As quietly as she could, Annie tiptoed into the bedroom. By the light shining from the half-open bathroom door, she rummaged through the overnight bag she'd packed in haste for the hotel, found tomorrow's 'sightseeing in Manhattan' outfit and slipped into it, then slid into her sensible tourist pumps.

She scribbled Ed a bedside note: 'Had to go comfort Lana in middle of night. I was right about Taylor – creep! Sleep baby, call me when you're ready for breakfast and I'll join you. Love A xx'

Then as quietly as she could, she closed the hotel door behind her and slipped out of the lobby and into the street.

On the side streets, all was peaceful, just a couple or two heading home after a night out. But out on Fifth, it was still busy. Yellow cabs nose to tail, looking for that big fare from a nightclubber with a long journey back.

On Elena's street, Annie stepped into the brightly lit glare of an all-night grocery store and bought Kleenex, those strange Lipton's teabags which everyone seemed to think were so English, and an industrial-sized bar of chocolate, although she already knew that American chocolate just wasn't the same.

As soon as Annie exited the lift she heard the

apartment door unlocking and there stood Lana, in skimpy pyjamas, looking totally fraught.

Annie held out her arms and hugged her.

'You were right,' Lana moaned into her ear, 'everything you said about him was right. He's a terrible arrogant selfish guy, but that doesn't make it hurt any less. It hurts . . . it really hurts.'

Annie steered Lana back into the apartment and sat her down on the sofa bed, arm tightly around her daughter, to hear the very raw, very worst of it.

Lana had really liked him, really trusted him. Over the past two days, they'd been having sex. Annie felt her toes curl at this news, but she didn't say anything, just let Lana carry on.

When Elena had come back to the apartment at 2a.m. or so tonight, Taylor had woken up and got dressed. Lana had asked him if they were going to see each other tomorrow, and he'd shrugged, said he was pretty busy and anyway, she was going back to London soon . . .

'What's the point? He asked me, w-w-what's the p-p-point?' Lana's shoulders heaved with sobs as she said this.

'That's very cruel and very unkind,' Annie said rubbing her hand soothingly up and down her daughter's back. In her head, Annie was silently raging: *You slept with him?! You slept with that arrogant prat?! How could you?!! I told you . . . I warned you to go home alone until you knew him better!*

Annie didn't think Lana had slept with anyone

212

else before. There had been close encounters of the teenage kind, but now she'd gone and actually slept with this . . . this specimen.

And the first time was after drinking wine her mother had paid for! It just got worse and worse.

'I shouldn't have let you go out with him after dinner yesterday,' Annie complained, 'I knew you'd had wine . . . but he said it was just coffee and then he'd walk you back.'

'I liked him so much though, Mum. It wasn't the wine, and you wouldn't have been able to change my mind.'

'I know baby, I know,' Annie said, but still she was kicking herself. How could she have let her daughter be hurt like this? Anyone older than 25 would have been able to spot what a *tosser* he was. Ed hadn't wanted her to be too harsh, but Ed had been wrong too.

Annie's thoughts were jam-packed with plans of revenge. How could she organize for Taylor to wake up one morning with the words 'I am a jerk' tattooed on his forehead? How could she have him walk down Fifth Avenue naked? There must be a way.

Annie broke open the teabags, the tissues and the chocolate: all the ingredients a romantic crisis of this magnitude required.

When Lana had drunk half a cup, her sobs subsided a little; from frantic, racking bursts, to small, tearful, hiccuping sobs.

'How come we've not woken Elena?' Lana asked quietly.

'If she only went to bed at 2a.m., she's probably deeply asleep – just like we should be.'

But even when they'd snuggled down into the sofa bed – Annie trying not to mind too much that Ed was sleeping with utter abandon in king-sized bliss – they found they were both too awake to sleep and Lana wanted to talk anyway.

'Who was the first person you ever slept with, Mum?' she asked in a small voice out of the darkness. 'Was it my real dad?'

Annie smiled to herself, she liked the way Owen and Lana now called Ed 'Dad', totally naturally as if they'd been doing it all their lives, and Roddy was given the honorary title of 'my real Dad'.

Annie and her children had lost Roddy many years ago now. 'Lost' didn't feel like the right word. It wasn't that they'd misplaced him carelessly. He hadn't casually wandered off never to be seen again, the way some dads do . . . Annie's for instance.

No. They'd lost Roddy after a tragic accident. In a small, calm hospital room, with a view of the hospital car park and the busy ring road beyond, life support had been switched off, disconnected, unplugged and wheeled away.

Life support.

That's just what Annie was trying to give Lana now.

She'd been unable to give life support to Lana's father, but she was damn well going to be here for every moment Lana needed her. Just the way Roddy would have been.

Annie considered the question carefully: '*Who was the first person you ever slept with, Mum? Was it my real Dad?*'

It would have been romantic to answer: 'Yes.' To say that Roddy had been her first love and the very first person she'd made love with.

But it wasn't the truth.

Maybe for Lana's sake, it was lucky it wasn't the truth. Maybe Lana would feel a little comforted to hear that her mum had gone through something not so entirely different to this.

'Your dad was the third person I slept with,' Annie broke the news gently, 'there was someone first who I was totally crazy about and it lasted about a year or so. He was at Art College with me, but he dropped out and moved away. When we broke up, I thought I was going to die of a broken heart. I really did. I thought I was going to cry myself to death. It was awful.' Annie reached over to stroke Lana's hair.

'And then?' Lana asked, her back still turned, but obviously interested in what her mum was going to say next.

'Well then, I was all numb and traumatized and I didn't care about anything, so the class Romeo just scooped me up for a wild fortnight. I was crazy about him too, but when that ended it didn't hurt at all, because I was still too upset about the first guy. And just at that point . . . that's when I bumped into a very attractive, dark-haired, blue-eyed actor.'

'My real Dad?'

'Yeah. Just when you're heartbroken and not really looking, that's when you meet the really, really good guys. So you'll need to keep a sharp lookout from here on in.'

Lana gave a half-hearted laugh but then in a choked voice, added, 'I thought he was a really good guy. I did, Mum.'

A forehead tattoo wouldn't do for Taylor, it really wouldn't. Annie's mind ran through all the other possibilities: running him over, booby-trapping his camera so it blew off his head, hiring a hit man . . . This was New York: how hard could it be to find a hit man?

CHAPTER 20

The rose seller:

Red shirt with ruffles (Flamenco! Flamenco!)
Black jeans (Old Navy sale)
Black pointed shoes (stolen from cousin)
Amla hair oil (Dabur)
Total est. cost: $65

'I think you both movieee starrrrs.'

When Annie crept back towards the sofa bed after an early morning bathroom visit, Lana woke up and immediately burst into tears. 'Oh, it's all true, isn't it?' she asked mournfully as she pulled the sheet over her face.

Annie sat beside her and stroked her back. 'Why don't you come back to the hotel with me? Have breakfast with us. You'll feel much better once you've washed your face and had something to eat.'

'But what will Dad say?'

'About what?'

'About the whole Taylor thing. I mean, we were just having dinner with you on Friday night. It's only Sunday morning and I'm already dumped,' she wailed.

'Ed will only say nice things. You know he will. He'll feel very sorry for you and want to cheer you up. So c'mon, wash face, nice outfit and we'll go and have a lovely breakfast.'

This was Ed's last day in New York as he was leaving very early on Monday morning. There were many special things he'd planned to do on his last day: a music museum visit, the Empire State Building at sunset once again, a candlelit dinner in a tiny Jewish restaurant. But now all these plans came with a terribly sad teenager in tow.

Ed and Annie totally wanted Lana to come with them. They were hoping to cheer her up and could never have left her weeping by herself in the apartment. But the day wasn't as either of them had imagined. Lana was a sighing, tear-stained presence. She tried very hard not to cry all over the sparkling city views, but letting her drink a cocktail turned out to be a vast mistake.

Finally, right in the middle of dinner, she declared a terrible headache and Annie and Ed found themselves gulping down the remains of their meal so they could hurry her back to Elena's.

★ ★ ★

'Do you want me to stay with you, my darlin'?' Annie asked with as much big-heartedness as she could muster at the apartment door.

Fortunately Elena was there to intervene. She put her arms around Lana and insisted that she would be in charge of her for the night.

'I don't think Lana wants to go out,' Annie warned.

'No. I stay in too,' Elena replied, 'but you two must go out. Lana and I look after each other. Single girls have to stick together. You two lovers go off and enjoy Ed's last night in New York.'

'Are you honestly single?' Annie asked Elena, 'have you not made up with—'

Elena shook her head vigorously and waved away any further questions about Sye.

'But . . .' Annie tried to protest.

'Go out!' Lana told her. 'Or I'm going to feel even worse.'

As Annie stepped out of the building's front door, her hand in Ed's, the great burst of energy that was New York at night took hold of her.

Lights were bright; cars were honking, sirens still blaring up and down the nearest avenue. People were out and dressed up big even though this was Sunday, the very last gasp of the weekend.

'How tired are you?' she asked Ed.

'Hardly tired at all,' he replied, although when he turned to grin at her, his eye bags told an entirely different story.

'Shall we go out? You know, just go out without a plan – like we used to. Well, no,' she remembered, 'we never used to because I've always had children, but do you remember, way back, going out and not knowing where you were going or how long you'd be out for? Can we do that? Just for once?'

'Yes!' Ed agreed with a grin, 'that's what we'll do. Go have a New York adventure!'

First of all, they bar-hopped in the streets off Union Square. Sipping long, icy cocktails, they chatted but also could not help listening in on the loud and totally New York conversations going on all around them.

'Poor Morty, I kept telling him to go to the dawcta's. I'd say "go to the dawcta's Morty, it might be serious." But no, he just kept taking the tablets, hoping it would go away. And he's dead now. Let that be a lesson to us all. If something's not right, you've got to go to the dawcta's.'

'What kind of a wedding is this going to be, already? They're not going to use Schwartz's for the flowers? Why not? Everybody knows if you want the best flowers, you gotta go to Schwartz's. And have you seen the size of her ring? Microscopic. Really. Barely half a carat. She's throwing herself away.'

'My date? My date was terrible. Truly. He had alopecia and eczema and, oh my God, he grew up in Queens!'

'Yeah, well my therapist wants me to think about

220

Freddie and how this is affecting him. But I'm thirty-seven, it's time to think about me and ask: whaddo I want?'

Ed drained the last of his drink and leaned back in his chair: 'He's dead now, let that be a lesson to us all,' he repeated, making Annie laugh.

'What would you like to do tonight?' he asked, 'what's your idea of New York big night out heaven? Do you want to go and queue for a nightclub? Walk across the Brooklyn Bridge?'

Before Annie could answer, a small, sharp-faced man in a pinstriped waistcoat and vibrant red, ruffled shirt appeared at their table.

'You are a very beeeeeauwtiful couple,' he said in a heavy accent Annie couldn't place. 'Famous? I think I know your faces from somewhere.'

Ed shook his head and laughed.

'Yeeeeees. I think you both movieee starrrrs, but trying to keep it quiet, no?'

'No,' Annie assured him.

As if by magic a large bunch of roses was revealed.

'Ah, roses for sale.' Ed understood the flattery now.

'It has been so long since we were offered roses for sale!' Annie exclaimed.

'I'll take three red ones,' Ed volunteered without hesitation.

'Thirty dollar,' the man said, without blinking.

'Fifteen,' Annie offered.

'Twenty,' the man agreed.

221

'The romance,' said Ed, extracting a $20 note from his pocket.

Annie took the three roses and unpeeled them from their tragic cellophane wrappers. 'Thank you, you're very sweet,' she told Ed, holding the slightly droopy flowers up to her face.

'So where would you like to go?' he asked again.

'What do you think about a ride round Central Park in one of those horse-drawn carriages? Do you think that's just tooooo cheesy?'

'Your wish, my darling, is my command,' Ed promised. He led her out of the bar and into the street, where they hailed a cab for Central Park.

There was a queue at the rank for the horse-drawn cabs, but it didn't take much longer than half an hour to get to the front.

In the back of the carriage, it was a little breezier and bumpier than Annie had expected. But she snuggled up against Ed for warmth and watched the glittering lights of the buildings on Fifth Avenue go by.

'Is this as romantic as you were hoping?' Ed asked.

'Yes, definitely,' she insisted. Although really, she hadn't expected the horses to break quite so much wind. Then there was the whole business of the rubber sheet at the back of the horse which caught the droppings – noisily. That wasn't quite so picturesque or romantic either.

But still, she snuggled up under Ed's arm and

told him: 'This is beautiful. I think I'm falling in love.'

'Well, that's good, what with us being married and everything.'

'I'm in love with you already, babes. But I'm falling in love with this city. Deep, deep, deeply in love.'

CHAPTER 21

The Bloomingdale's secretary:

*Black and white wrap dress (Diane von
Furstenberg)
Purple suede heeled pumps (Cole Haan)
Diamond engagement ring (Tiffany's)
Total est. cost: $2,750*

'She only has a few minutes.'

'Hi, I'm Annie Valentine, I'm calling you from Perfect Dress . . .'

'Hello, my name is Lana, I'm a representative with Perfect Dress . . .'

'This is Elena Wisneski I wish to speak with you about your Perfect Dress order . . .'

Monday morning and the Perfect Dress team were back in business at the tiny apartment table, using every available phone.

Everyone who'd already placed a dress order needed to know when those dresses were arriving, and that there were going to be some changes in

224

the fabric and the design for the initial consignment of dresses.

'Just the first fifty dresses will be like this. We wanted to do something especially fresh and now for the first consignment, and you are going to love it, absolutely love it. I've worked in fashion for a long time and I am 100 per cent confident you will not be disappointed.' Annie was trying to sound breezy with the prickly woman on the other end of her line.

Annie glanced over at Lana, who seemed to be doing fine on her phone call. Annie wanted Lana to stay busy because when Lana was busy she didn't sob, which was definitely a positive.

They were in New York for another two weeks and Annie needed to make sure all was absolutely fine with Perfect Dress before she left.

Part of her was desperate to go home, because saying goodbye to Ed as he'd boarded the bus to the airport had felt very hard. He was going back to their lovely home and all the people she missed very much: Owen, Micky and Min, her sister, her mum.

'No! You can't cancel, please don't cancel the order.' Elena was clearly dealing with a tricky customer. Annie and Lana exchanged a worried glance. Quickly, Lana scribbled something down on a piece of paper and slid it over to Elena. 'Pass her on to your style consultant!'

Elena looked at the paper and frowned.

Lana pointed at herself.

225

'I'm just going to pass you on to our style consultant,' Elena said obediently.

'Hi,' Lana took the phone with a burst of confidence, 'would you like me to send you over some images? We have photos of our in-house model in the grey dress. I'll get those over to you right now and I think you're going to love it.'

When she hung up, both Elena and Annie stared at her in surprise.

'That was good,' Annie said, 'but we don't have any photos.'

'No worries, we'll get Elena to put the dress on and we'll take some.'

'No,' Elena said, 'you put on dress Lana, I take your picture. You're going to look *vonderful* in this dress.'

This made them all laugh as 'vonderrrrrful' had always been Svetlana's catchphrase.

Lana slipped into the sample dress, and then Annie couldn't help styling her a little. She added high brown boots and a shiny blue belt, borrowed from Elena's beautifully reorganized wardrobe. Then she brushed out Lana's long dark hair, tied it into a 'very now' messy plait, and added a chic blue beret. A slick of berry-coloured lip gloss, and Annie pronounced Lana camera ready.

'I'll take the pictures,' Annie said, getting out the camera she'd brought for this trip but had not used once since the very first day at the top of the Empire State, 'but really, we should have some professional shots . . . Maybe you should speak to that very, very nice photographer you know, Elena . . .'

Elena gave her trademark 'tscha' and immediately turned back to her laptop.

'Elena, you can't break up with him just because he's a photographer who happens to take pictures of beautiful girls!'

Quickly Elena picked up the phone to avoid any further conversation.

Annie sighed and redirected her attention to Lana. 'C'mon my lovely model, let's try and find a clear space for you to be photographed in. Stand beside the café table there, with the light behind you – perfect.'

Once Annie had pictures she was happy with, she sat down at her computer and began to download them. She emailed them across to Elena, and she also sent one to Ed.

'What do you think of our model girl in our brand new dress? Hope you like. Call me when you get home, I want to hear how you coped with back to school and jet lag. A xx'

Elena was looking at her computer screen with intense concentration. A little furrow was biting deep between her eyebrows.

'What is it?' Annie asked.

Elena's fingers pulled at her lip anxiously: 'Email from Bloomingdale's,' she replied, 'they cancel the whole order of dresses. Our biggest single order.'

The doorbell and Annie's mobile began to ring

at the same time, before they could even react to this disaster.

'Connor!' Annie exclaimed, seeing his name on the screen, 'now's not exactly the perfect moment.'

'Oh yes it is, my princess. I have found the Gawain!' Connor announced joyfully, 'I am coming to New York to train with Gawain.'

'Really? You're coming here?' Annie asked in total surprise, as Lana went to open the door. 'When?'

'Very soon,' Connor replied.

'It's like Piccadilly bloomin' circus. Lana's here, Elena's here, Ed's been over – and now you!'

'But I have found Gawain,' Connor repeated.

'Who?'

'Gawain my green knight. I have found him. He's living in Williamsburg and working in a SoHo gym.'

'Who is this Gawain? Is he a boyfriend I don't know about?'

'No! I wish. I told you – he's the personal trainer. The one and only. The body shaper. He's not known as Mr Spanx for nothing.'

'You are flying to New York for some personal training sessions?'

'Yes. It's cheaper over there anyway. Plus, I'm going to beg him to come back to London. Plus, have I told you, I'm going to be on *Strictly*!'

'*Strictly Come Dancing?*'

'Yes! Is that not the most career-revitalizing news you have heard in a long time? Connor is back, this time in dancing pants and very, very shiny shoes.'

'Perfect,' Annie had to admit, 'but I thought you wanted to be an action hero?'

'Still on the cards, doll,' he assured her, 'and talking of career-reviving moves . . . have you heard any—'

'Not a peep,' she interrupted him, 'not a whisper, not one iota of news of any kind at all.'

'Sit tight, baby. This too shall pass.'

'I would love to see you in New York. I'm in total love with New York. I'm trying to work out how I can get my family to move over here.'

'Really?'

'Well, sort of . . . fantasy really.'

'TV is very, very hard to get into over there. Especially if you're carrying just a teeny little bit of excess . . .'

She burst out laughing: 'You're very sweet. But I think what you are trying to say is if you're a thirty-something who's not had a brow-lift and zeroed down to a lollipop stick, we can probably forget it.'

'But you never know, baby, maybe they need a bit of reality TV. Maybe they need some Annie love. As soon as I get there, we will go out. Prepare to party. There are some people I met in a Florida sauna who I'm meeting up with again.'

'Just when I thought I'd heard all the lurid gay sex tales I'd ever wanted to hear.'

'I've told Gawain about you. He can do crisis

management too, baby. Crisis management. That's what you need.'

Annie glanced up to see a delivery man struggling in with the biggest pink and blue bouquet of loveliness she had ever seen. She saw Lana's face turn to the delivery man with just a glimmer of hope.

Annie hoped it too.

Maybe this was Taylor apologizing. Maybe Annie could call off the hit man . . . well, not that she'd arranged one, but the thought, the thought was still well and truly there.

'Delivery for Wis-net-ski?' he stumbled over the name.

'Oh yeah, she's just here,' Lana said brightly.

But Annie had seen her face fall.

'So. Exciting, huh?' Connor asked. 'I'll be there very, very soon. Not telling you when. Surprise!'

Before Annie could ask another question, he hung up. Infuriating!

'Tscha!' Elena exclaimed, ripping open the card, then tossing it to the floor, 'Sye. So Annie, what we do about Bloomingdale's?'

'You'll just have to go, Elena. In person. Looking totally 'vonderrrrrful' and carrying the beautiful, purple dress with you. If anyone can get Mrs Bloomingdale to change her mind – it's you!'

Somehow, Annie had made it sound easy.

So Elena had, as calmly as she could, phoned

230

Bloomingdale's and asked to speak to the head women's fashion buyer, Mrs Westhoven.

Although the thought of actually speaking to Mrs Westhoven had made Elena's heart hammer painfully, because Mrs Westhoven also happened to be Sye's mother.

Elena had told Mrs Westhoven's secretary that she would be coming to Bloomingdale's today, and would Mrs Westhoven be available for a very quick meeting? After a long and agonizing pause, the secretary had come back on the line to tell Elena that Mrs Westhoven would be delighted to meet with her at 4p.m.

This was why Elena was now surfacing from the subway station exit and making her way nervously towards the Bloomingdale's staff entrance.

There followed a long, nervous wait in a large, minimally furnished room, in which she busied herself nibbling at the skin around her nails.

Sye's mother and the first Bloomingdale's dress order had been crucial to the fledgling Perfect Dress business. The first release of dresses over Spring and Summer had sold well through Bloomingdale's and new orders had been placed almost immediately. Although Elena and Sye had been a couple for almost six months, somehow the opportunity to meet Mrs Westhoven had never come about. She was too busy, Sye was too nervous, Elena was too scared . . . many reasons.

Had the dress order been cancelled because

she'd broken off with Sye? Elena bit deep into the side of her nail at this thought.

She'd thought breaking off with Sye would bring her some sort of peace from the relentless jealousy, the constant worry about where he was, who he was with, whether he'd met someone he liked better than her. But, in fact, now that she'd told him it was over, she seemed to worry about him ten times more.

Yes, of course, when she and Sye had been together Elena had indulged in a little daydream of meeting his parents. But she'd never imagined it would happen like this, with Elena in a waiting room, expecting a formal summons any minute, and an argument about a cancelled dress order.

'Miss Wisneski?'

The secretary was at the door.

'She'll see you now, but she only has a few minutes.'

Elena picked up the briefcase, into which she'd carefully folded the tissue-wrapped purple Perfect Dress, and followed her down the corridor.

She was shown into a light, airy room with a small but magnificent, 100 per cent Manhattan view. But all of Elena's attention was focused on the woman sitting behind a tiny laptop at the otherwise empty desk.

Hello Elena,' Mrs Westhoven said, standing up and leaning over to shake Elena's hand, 'it's lovely, just lovely to meet you. I've been *dying* to meet you, to tell the truth.'

'Hello, nice to meet you too,' Elena said, smiling broadly and shaking hands.

Mrs Westhoven did not look nearly as 'fashion' as Elena had expected. But then Annie had warned her that buyers were like fashion editors – they almost always wore very expensive black clothes in classic shapes because they didn't like to risk getting caught out. Wearing something too high fashion the nano second it was 'over' was career suicide.

Mrs Westhoven was a small, sinewy lady in an expensive-looking navy blue jersey dress. Maybe Gucci, Elena guessed, taking in the golden touches. She had a highly blonde bob and eyes – almost exactly like Sye's – that looked piercingly acute.

'Sit down, tell me all your woes,' she began in a crisp, cultivated New York accent.

Elena felt at sea. Did she mean breaking up with Sye? Did she mean the dresses? What woes? Elena was not here to talk about her woes.

Because Elena hesitated, Mrs Westhoven went on: 'You've obviously had big production problems. You've had to change the fabric *completely*, you've had to change your factory, you've even messed around with delivery dates.'

Before Elena could open her mouth to defend herself, Mrs Westhoven was tapping at her computer. She called up a spreadsheet and turned it towards Elena so that she could take a look too.

'The last dresses we bought from you sold . . . reasonably. Not so amazingly well that I'm desperate to buy them in again, especially if they're not going to be as well made as the first run. We've other lines that are doing better. So try not to take it too personally, but I think Bloomingdale's can live without the "Perfect Dress".'

She made little quote marks with her fingers in the air as she said Perfect Dress.

'There have been some small problems,' Elena said, finally finding her voice and taking extra care with her English 'but this has only led us to create a much, much better product.'

'Oh. Really?' Mrs Westhoven sounded entirely unconvinced.

'I've brought one of the new dresses with me, I'm sure you'd like to see it.'

'Well . . . OK then.'

Elena leaned over to unzip her briefcase and realized that her hands were shaking slightly. Nevertheless, she took out the dress and stood up so she could spread it out over Mrs Westhoven's desk.

As she smoothed out the magenta jersey creation, she felt a rush of pride in it. It was beautifully cut, beautifully made, and it was a really clever idea. She pointed to the satin-covered buttons and the gorgeous ribbon tie sleeves. She couldn't think of anyone who wouldn't want such a useful Autumn/Winter dress as this. Who wouldn't look better, more pulled together, wearing this?

Mrs Westhoven put on a pair of swanky, be-jewelled reading glasses and bent over the dress. She picked up a sleeve and inspected it closely, running the fabric between her fingers.

'Sweatshirt material? With Lycra or without?'

'Stretch jersey with Lycra.'

'This is nothing special, you could pick it up in any warehouse anywhere in the city.'

Or any skip, Elena thought.

'No, but we make a special dress out of ordinary fabric. This is our selling point. It is a dressed up, pulled together casual dress. You could wear this with diamonds and heels to look very bohemian at a party. But it is also wonderful with boots and a jacket, looking very, very casual.'

Mrs Westhoven didn't even pause to consider. 'No, I don't think this is what a Bloomingdale's customer is looking for. I think this dress is tonally confused. It's not one thing or the other. It's all wrong, Elena. Not for us.'

Mrs Westhoven was definitely not 'tonally confused'. The way Mrs Westhoven said this, it sounded final.

Elena decided not to argue. She wanted to fold up the dress and get out just as quickly as she possibly could. Yes, it was an order of ninety dresses – their biggest single order – but somehow she would just sell those ninety dresses to someone else. She would certainly not humiliate herself pleading with Mrs Westhoven.

As she packed the dress back into her briefcase,

Elena met Mrs Westhoven's piercing eyes. 'Is this because I'm not with Sye any more?' she asked, surprising herself. The question just bubbled up out of nowhere.

'No. I'm delighted that you're not with Sye any more,' Mrs Westhoven replied coolly, taking off her glasses and setting them down on her desk. 'When I heard your story . . . well, I just knew it was going to lead to trouble: the poor girl from the Ukraine moving to America for love. I thought you'd be engaged for a permanent visa within months, and it would all end in divorce before anyone could say "starter marriage". No, I don't need any of that and neither does Sye. I told him to get rid of you and I'm delighted he has done so.'

Elena was so stung, she didn't know which slight to argue first.

She zipped up her briefcase, hands trembling with rage. 'I'm very sorry you are missing out on our dresses, Mrs Westhoven. I think you're wrong, I think they are going to be the must-have item this season. The number one go-to piece.'

Elena tried to leave it there. But then, she found she couldn't.

'I am not a poor girl from the Ukraine, I have an engineering degree and a Business Master's. My mother and business partner is very . . . a very wealthy woman. I have no need of marrying Sye, not even for a visa.'

Elena stretched herself to her full height, displaying her lean, athletic body to best advantage.

With the most condescending face she could pull, she added, 'And Sye did not finish with me, he still trying to call me ten times a day. I finish with him. Thank you for your time to see me.'

She turned on her heel and swept out of the door, thudding it shut behind her.

In the corridor, Elena kept on walking very briskly, blinking back hot humiliated tears. Ninety dresses . . . how on earth was she going to find orders in a fortnight for ninety dresses?

When she was out in the street once again, Elena looked around and tried to get her bearings. There was the subway station. Good yes, she could get on a train and get back home, just as soon as she had calmed the huge, bubbling tension building up inside her.

She needed to be nice to herself. She needed to do something caring and generous for herself. She needed to buy something. Right now. As soon as possible.

She began racing down the sidewalk in search of a shop which could help. A drugstore wouldn't do. Shampoo, even bottles and bottles of discounted shampoo, would not be enough. Elena *needed* clothing. Nice shiny new clothing, with the tags still on, double-wrapped in carrier bags, with all the shiny promise of newness, of exciting, good times ahead. She needed something lovely, a treat to make herself feel better.

But it had to be cheap, special offer, sale

purchase. Only if she was sure she wasn't paying full price could she be happy.

She soon came across a red poster in a window promising 'Special purchase – this week only.' Here were racks and racks hung with all the summer clothes the store was trying to offload at the tail end of September. Skimpy dresses, shorts, frilly T-shirts, everything that had hung out all summer long and not been chosen.

Expertly Elena began to flick through the rails looking for her size. There was a concentrated zeal to her pursuit. This had nothing to do with buying something nice or something needed: it was about buying to fulfil a hungry urge.

Flick, flick, flick . . . the multi-coloured halter-neck tops were rejected; then she moved on to silky, tie-dyed T-shirts. She liked these, liked them enough to buy them anyway. She picked out a pink one and a turquoise blue.

Then she moved on to skirts. The simple linen skirts were nice. She would take the white one and maybe the blue too. To go with the T-shirt. All her size, all looked about right.

Elena didn't feel satisfied yet. She looked around the shop desperately, grasping the T-shirts and skirts tightly by their hangers. Over here were scarves, necklaces and shiny handbags. Like a magpie, she assessed and then swooped. One pink and white checked cotton scarf; two ropes of pastel glass beads and a shimmery pink clutch bag.

Now that Elena had a hold of all these items,

the panic subsided a little. She gathered up her hoard and went to the till, where the cashier smiled at her pleasantly. 'Hi there and how are you today? We have a fitting room if you'd like to try these on?'

'No, no, is fine. I'm in a hurry and I need them for . . .'

Elena paused.

In her hand was her credit card all ready to hand over. All ready to add a few more hundred dollars to the vast, out of control landslide of debt she'd already built up.

Plus, she couldn't finish her sentence. What exactly *did* she need these things for? Not to wear. She would never wear them. She would never even take them out of the shopping bag. She would just put them into a corner of her clean and tidied, calmly ordered bedroom and begin to build up her mountain of unwanted items all over again.

'I'm sorry,' Elena blushed and retreated from the till, 'I think I make mistake, I come back later.'

'Sure, no problem, would you like me to put these to the side for you? We can hold for twenty-four hours,' came the friendly response.

'No, is fine . . . is fine, thank you,' Elena said as she backed towards the door.

Out on the sidewalk again, blinking against the sunshine, Elena felt shaky, still panicky, but there was a tiny glow of accomplishment building up inside her. This had been a very difficult afternoon, but somehow she'd managed to back away from her usual stress relief.

The store just a few doors down from the clothes place was a small chocolatier's. Elena stepped inside and stood in the air-conditioned coolness inhaling the rich aroma and trying to calm herself.

Personally, she had no interest in chocolate. She'd never been given chocolate when she was a child so it had none of the comforting associations that it seemed to have for so many women.

But she wanted to buy something small. A present. She wanted to simultaneously scratch the buying itch and do something generous for the woman who had helped her understand it a little bit better.

With cash, not credit, Elena went to the counter and picked out a bespoke selection of chocolates and candies, had them wrapped in a pink box and tied with an exuberant flourish of pink and white ribbon.

Once it was in the shiny plastic bag and Elena had it in her hands, she felt her panic subside, just as easily as if she'd just splashed out $300 on discount summer clothes. This was good. This was definitely progress.

She beamed at the cashier as she left, stepped out of the store, and walked right into Sye.

'Elena . . .' he began, but then he just held open his arms and wrapped them around her as she fell against him.

'Sye!' she exclaimed, 'Sye.'

For several moments, they just remained tightly entwined, feeling each other's hearts thud terrifyingly fast and loud.

Then Elena felt his hand stroke the back of her neck and she was suddenly crying against his shoulder.

'I'm sorry,' she blurted out. Whatever thoughts she might have had about trying to end this relationship had vanished as soon as she'd set eyes on him.

'I don't think Mom will change her mind, even if you are very nice to me,' he said gently.

'No,' Elena said against his shoulder.

'She told me you were coming to see her, so I rushed over as fast as I could. I had to see you and . . . well, you haven't been easy to see lately.'

'No,' she said again, wanting the tears to stop, but they came thick and fast, creating a stain on his shirt.

He still held her tightly.

'Have you followed me from Bloomingdale's?' Elena asked, lifting her head and scanning his face anxiously.

Sye smiled and nodded.

'So . . . did you see me in the clothes store?' she asked, wondering why he was still holding her and not speed-dialling a psychiatrist.

Sye nodded again.

'I had a crazy moment.'

'No . . . you had a sane moment,' he told her.

'You *didn't* buy another double shopping bag with a double knot on top.'

She searched his eyes. He was smiling, but he also looked concerned, sympathetic.

'Did you know?'

'About the compulsive shopping bag thing? Elena, anyone who's been in your bedroom knows.'

She rested her head against his shoulder and had the most wonderful feeling that from now on, everything had a very real chance of turning out OK.

Sye kissed her on the forehead then told her: 'You're worth full price, baby. Try to remember that.'

CHAPTER 22

Connor in town:

Tight black T-shirt (Diesel)
Purple chinos (Jermyn Street)
Black ballet pumps (Freed)
Black messenger bag (Mulberry)
Total est. cost: $570

'Time for another cocktail.'

'Flatiron-slash-Union Square is like the best neighbourhood. Seriously . . .'

Connor's New Best Friend Freddie, cocktail in hand, was holding forth.

Connor had only stepped off the plane a few hours ago, but already he was hunkered down in the bar of the nanosecond, surrounded by beautiful people, looking utterly at home.

Was Freddie's hair real, or fake? Real? Fake? Annie wondered. It was hard to tell. Especially after a second martini. He was light black – were you allowed to say light black? But his hair was bleach blond, very straight and either made of plastic or totally covered in some heavy-duty hair product.

Still, real or fake hair aside, this was Annie, out in another achingly cool New York bar. Again. At home, she hadn't had a night out in months. Here it was routine. You ate out, you went out, you didn't even make breakfast at home, and she had the great gaping hole in her bank account to prove it.

'My famous NBF lives round there,' Freddie added.

'So who's that?' Connor asked.

'Emily Wilmington.'

'Emily Wilmington?' Annie repeated 'No way.'

'Yes way. Waaaaay yes.'

'I've seen her. She lives on Elena's street,' Lana chipped in. 'That's where we're staying.'

'Are you on 16th? Get outta here.'

'Do you know Emily Wilmington?' Annie asked.

'Of course I know her, she's my NBF.'

'Would you give her one of our dresses?'

'Mum!! That's a brilliant idea!' Lana exclaimed.

'Well . . . yeah . . . if I like your dress enough, then I will pass it on to her. She gets a lot of stuff and, believe me, most of it is . . .' Freddie pulled a face, 'sooooo tacky.'

'Our dresses are definitely not tacky,' Lana said sternly.

'Lana . . .' Annie turned to her daughter, 'has

Elena told you? She wants to have a fashion show, so that all our potential customers can see just how amazing the new dresses are.'

'A fashion show? Genius!' Lana agreed.

'A fashion show?' Freddie clapped his hands gleefully. 'Waaaaaay exciting. I know this hotel. Soooo cool. My friend's the manager, I'm sure we could do a deal.'

'Will you invite Emily to our fashion show?' Lana asked quickly.

'I will ask her but her schedule . . .' Freddie rolled his eyes, 'impossible!'

Annie couldn't help smiling at Connor's NBF, Freddie, who was also Emily's NBF. It was a complex web of relationships.

'Having a lovely time, Annie?' Connor asked, moving his arm around her, 'or missing home?'

'You know, sort of both. If I don't think about home, I am having the best time ever. But as soon as I stop for a moment to think about the babies, I miss them very much.'

'Time for another cocktail.'

'Maybe. What do you think of Lana, by the way?' Annie asked in a whisper. 'Don't you think she's turning out so beautiful?'

Connor turned and took a long appraising look at Annie's daughter, who was currently deep in conversation with personal trainer Gawain. In true personal trainer mode, Gawain was drinking a grassy green pure vegetable and wheatgrass concoction.

'Roddy's looks and your brains,' Connor said cheekily, 'a totally winning combination. She is going to go very far.'

Annie smacked his arm: 'Roddy's looks? Don't I have any looks left?'

'Nah, not really. You're a saggy mum now. That is your USP.'

When Connor saw how much this made Annie's face fall, he promptly called Gawain over.

Gawain, the buffest, trimmest man Annie had ever set eyes upon, positively skipped across to sit beside them. He was so dainty and light on his feet, Annie was convinced that he must once have been a ballet dancer. His muscles were firm and tight but tiny in the way she'd seen on the occasional dancer body she'd helped to dress in her days at The Store.

'Hi there, I'm Gawain, professional body re-sculptor, proprietor of Train with Gawain, *trademark*,' he said and held out his hand for her to shake.

She took his hand and shook it, although he'd done this only thirty minutes or so before when he'd come in and met her the first time. Maybe it was a self-promotion thing. He aimed to tell you his name and his profession so often that you always remembered him.

'Gawain, my darling,' Connor began, 'Annie and I were talking about her physique. She's on television in Britain, you know.'

Annie could have done with slightly less of the appalled surprise in Gawain's, '*Really?*'

'Yes and, just like me, she could do with a little shape-up, don't you think?'

'Stand up,' Gawain instructed Annie.

Annie really did not want to stand up in some hipper-than-hot Manhattan bar and be professionally appraised by a body re-sculptor. But Connor prodded her and she got to her feet.

Now everyone at the two tables they'd occupied was looking at her.

'Yeah . . . I'm getting it,' Gawain said, 'and turn.'

Annie shuffled round in the tight space, trying to ensure that her well-padded derrière didn't deal a death blow to any of the astronomically expensive cocktails.

Gawain leaned over and prodded a surprisingly sharp index finger into her lower buttock. When she wheeled about in surprise, the finger went into the rounded bulge of flab around her tummy.

'I'm checking out the muscle structure,' he told her.

Muscle structure? Well in that case, she really didn't think he would find what he was looking for.

'Have you ever been in shape?'

Annie, still standing, not sure if she was allowed to sit down again or not, considered this question. She'd spent a lot of her adult life running after small children, running up and down stairs and walking very fast along London pavements in high heels. All this activity had kept her relatively slim in the past. But since the arrival of the twins, there had been much less walking, much more snacking, and the weight/food/activity equilibrium had been shot to bits.

But gyms . . . workouts, sit-ups, weights and all that stuff. Dinah was into all that. Not Annie. Not at all. She'd set foot in a gym once or twice, but so long ago she couldn't even remember much about it.

'Well . . . I walk a lot,' Annie replied, defensively.

Gawain laughed and shook his head. 'You walk?! Walking is not exercise. Walking is how you get to the gym.'

'So?' Connor broke in. 'What should she do? Where should she get started? I know you can help, because you work miracles.'

'Getting people who've been in shape back into shape is hard work but it can be done. Getting people who've never been in shape into any kind of shape at all is kinda tough,' Gawain declared. 'They've got no muscles, they've got no aerobic function, and they don't know what hard gym work is all about. Plus their mental attitude usually sucks.'

'Oh, and there I was thinking you weren't going to be nice about me,' Annie said, her face reddening.

'If you've never been fit before, lady, it is going to be really, really tough to get fit. And that is the absolutely honest truth. You're going to have to want to be fit with every fibre of your being. You're going to have to want to work out every single day way past the point of throwing up with pain.'

248

'Lovely.'

'This is my card.' He handed it over to her. 'We could have one introductory session, I can assess you, I can give you a basic plan and you can see if you're going to be able to tough it out.'

Before she could get out the words, 'No thanks', Connor butted in with, 'If I buy it for her, Gawain, how much? Mates rates?'

Gawain blessed Connor with a perfectly white-toothed smile: 'For you, Connor McCabe, only $400.'

'Deal,' Connor said.

Annie gasped in horror. Not just at the phenomenal price but at the fact that Connor was buying it for her. If he bought it, he might even make her go!

'I'll add it to your bill,' Gawain told Connor, then brought out his phone, flipped through to the diary and asked Annie when she could fit the session into her schedule.

Annie felt like a bunny in the headlights.

'Ummm . . . the next few days are very hectic,' she stalled, 'we're preparing for this fashion show.'

Now Lana was leaning in, getting up to speed with the conversation.

'Are you going to "Train with Gawain – trademark"?' she asked, trying not to giggle. 'That is so cool, Mum. I can't believe you're going to do that. He's really, really good. He was just telling me about his special squats, guaranteed to lift your butt by at least two inches – "trademark".'

'I don't know. We'll be so busy with the show.'

'Squeeze it in, Mum,' Lana urged. 'C'mon, early one morning, maybe?'

'That would be perfect,' Gawain confirmed. 'I have a 5.30a.m. slot. The gym does get really busy after 6.30 with my trader clients who need to be at their desks by 8a.m.'

'5.30a.m.??'

Annie wasn't sure if she'd heard properly.

Yes, jet lag might have been working for her on the first few days in town, allowing for some outrageously early mornings, but now she stayed out late and lay in bed till 8.30.am. just like all the other fashionistas in her apartment.

'5.30a.m. on Friday?' Gawain asked, nail poised over his phone.

'Fine,' Annie replied, completely confident that something would come up and she would be able to back out of this torment.

CHAPTER 23

Tiffany's assistant:

White shirt (Gap)
Black suit (Uniform)
Comfortable black trainers (Geox)
Diamond earring (Tiffany's with staff discount)
Watch (Tiffany's with discount)
Total est. cost: $620

'. . . always very happy to talk . . .'

It was 8.30p.m. and growing dark when Annie managed to extricate herself from the 'Connor comes to NYC' reunion party. Both Elena and Lana tried to persuade her to stay on, but Annie needed to get away from Gawain's critical gaze and dieting suggestions.

She'd been in New York for nearly three weeks and there were still so many places that she hadn't seen. With Ed, she'd chalked off a few museums, so she wasn't going to worry about that too much, but there were still so many unvisited shops!

She hadn't yet set foot inside a Coach handbag store, although Coach was the bag every second New Yorker she passed was carrying. She still hadn't been into a typically US jeans warehouse, or to Century 21, Bergdorf Goodman, Dooney & Bourke, Brooks Brothers or to any of the famous New York names she'd promised herself she would at least browse around.

Hurrying towards the top of Fifth Avenue, she was delighted to see that she still had a good hour or so before the shops closed.

And here was Tiffany's – the fabulously famous Fifth Avenue jewellers.

Right here.

She couldn't possibly walk past the windows, thinking of Audrey Hepburn, without going in to take a little look.

Inside the store, it was cool and glittery and much bigger than she had expected: a vast ground floor, then elevators at the back leading to even more dazzling goodies. Smart and sophisticated sales staff stood behind the glass cases where Tiffany's jewelled delights were beautifully displayed. Annie walked slowly past key-shaped pendants encrusted with diamonds.

'Good evening, ma'am and how are you today?' the salesman behind a counter began with a fresh and friendly smile, although he must have asked the question hundreds of times today.

'I'm great, thanks, but I think I'll keep on walking . . . there are too many diamonds here for me.'

'I'm always very happy to talk, if you need me,' he added with direct eye contact and another smile. Whoa . . . now that was service.

As she rounded a cabinet studded with some of the most graceful diamond necklaces she had ever seen, her phone began to ring. She was delighted to hear the deep and melodious tones of her favourite multi millionairess on the other end of the line.

'Annnnnaaaah,' Svetlana began, 'what is the news from New York?'

'Svetlana, hello!'

Eyes widening at the price tag on the diamond pendant she'd been admiring, Annie added: 'I'm in Tiffany's . . . I was just thinking of you.'

'Tscha, Tiffany's for tourists, go to Harry Winston or Cartier, if you like to buy something nice.'

'I wasn't really buying. I was looking.'

'Buy!' Svetlana instructed, 'you have some money now and your jewellery is all . . .'

Annie waited for the killer blow. How would Svetlana, usually dripping in hundreds of thousands of pounds' worth of jewels dismiss Annie's jewellery, which was usually an impulse buy from Accessorize?

'*Unimpressive.*'

Ouch! That was understated yet harsh. *Unimpressive.*

'Well, we didn't all marry money,' Annie snapped, unable to stop herself.

'Big mistake,' came the tart reply, 'but I not

phone to talk about this. Tell me about the new dresses, the orders and the show you are organizing. I hear from Elena, of course, but I like to know what you think. Is it vorrrrking?' she asked.

'The dresses look brilliant. We used cheap jersey material but made them very stylish,' Annie began with the positive, 'but the orders are not so good, which is why we are holding the show. We've invited everyone who made an order to come and take a look at the dresses in the nicest setting we can find for $1,800.

'Oh, and Bloomingdale's has cancelled. You know that?'

'Ya. Is very, very upsetting. But this to do with Elena finishing with Sye. Like I tell her to.'

'You told her to finish?' Annie bent down low to look at the cabinet in front of her. The Tiffany keys. She loved them. She wanted all of them. The slim gold key-shaped pendant on a delicate, sliver of a gold chain – would that be impressive enough for Svetlana? No, Svetlana would treat herself to the huge platinum one, smothered in diamonds, with the five-figure price tag.

'Ya,' Svetlana replied casually.

'And she did that for you?'

Annie decided she would keep the information that Elena and Sye were totally back together to herself, for now.

'Ya, I tell her not to waste time on some photographer whose mother work in clothes store. This is waste of her beautiful talents.'

'She should be marrying rich?'

'Of courrrrrse, just like her mama.'

Now Annie felt tetchy enough to remind Svetlana: 'The rich men did not make you very happy.'

'No. But divorce settlements did.'

'Only the last one. And remember how he tried to get away with leaving you nothing.'

'All forgotten now I have my millions and my Harry.'

It had, in the end, worked out very nicely for Svetlana, Annie had to admit. And it was no use griping that she hadn't worked hard to get where she was today.

Being a millionaire's wife was one very, very high maintenance career choice. It explained why Svetlana had 'settled' for just a 'very wealthy' man for husband number five. Harry loved her just the way she was, apparently.

Just the way Svetlana was involved a daily personal trainer, a live-in maid, quarterly Botox, anti-ageing laser treatments, jewels, furs, and purely designer clothes and accessories.

This explained why Svetlana, believed to be in her late forties, looked like most women did in their mid-twenties.

'Where is the show? Has Elena picked good place?'

'It's a lovely hotel with an old-fashioned Russian émigré theme. It's chandeliers, marble and leather but with a cool edge. Dark blue walls, very moody.

She's calling it the Eastern Bloc Party. A DJ friend is doing the music, lots of S—'

Ooops, Annie had nearly said 'Sye's friends'.

'Lots of very cool people are coming,' she corrected herself, 'I think it will do wonders for sales.'

'Press?' Sveltana asked immediately. 'No good even breathing in a Perfect Dress if no press around.'

'Some photographers are coming, so hopefully we'll get something into the press.'

'Ha. I know how we will get a fabulous front page story. I am going to come to the fashion show and I bring a very special friend.'

Annie turned away from the latest glass case she'd been peering into. 'You're going to come . . . from London?'

'Ya. I have decided. I arrive just in time for lunch with my especial friend, then we come together for show. Tell the photographers they are getting surprise.'

'Are you going to tell me who it is?'

'Of course not!'

'Why not?'

'I like surprises. Also, tell everyone you invite that I am giving out goodie bags. Very special goodie bags. Everyone come for a good freebie. I've found some money I can spend, Annah. I sell some boring old watch – I forget who give it to me – and I put $15,000 more into this show to make it more special.'

'Fantastic . . .' Annie said, although it would

256

have been nice to have known about that before they entered the marathon price negotiating session with the owner of the hotel. Both Elena and Lana had been working like slaves trying to get everything for nothing for this show-on-a-shoestring.

Still, $15,000 now would make a huge difference and yes, plenty of extra guests would come for Svetlana's idea of a goodie bag.

'How is your family, Annah? I not hear anything about them yet.'

Annie was now standing in front of a display of tactile round golden pendants on black silk cords. They were beautiful. She wondered if Svetlana would be impressed. Probably not. Probably nothing short of a rope full of diamond bling would cause Svet to even look twice.

'The babies are fine. I'm missing them much more than I think they're missing me,' Annie replied. 'Owen is good, Lana is *loving* New York. I'm worried that I won't be able to get her to come home. Ed is somehow managing without me.'

'If this run of dresses sells big, Annah, you should move to New York, like I tell you to, and work for us,' Svetlana said, just as casually as if she was inviting Annie for lunch. 'Why not?'

CHAPTER 24

The boutique buyer:

Grey pencil skirt (Ralph Lauren)
Silver taffeta blouse (Vera Wang)
Brooch (Christian Dior)
Black heels (Salvatore Ferragamo)
Total est. cost (but spread out over years): $1,650

'Not too madly expensive.'

Annie fiddled with the canapé arrangements until the glares from the huge Russian waiter behind the bar told her that she was to leave everything alone now.

The room where the show was to be held – terrifyingly soon – looked perfect and so serious with its deep, dark blue walls, shiny black woodwork, black floor and heady white magnolia flowers set out in black vases.

A catwalk of blue carpet curved through the room. The plan was to seat the guests at the black lacquered tables, where they could sip at their

Russian cocktails and watch the three models walk past in Perfect Dresses styled for every occasion.

Annie had thought she would be backstage, helping the models to rush in and out of the outfits which she, Elena and Lana had so carefully put together: Perfect Dress with diamonds, pearls and heels. Perfect Dress with boots and cardigan. Perfect Dress with whichever appropriate accessories could be found in Elena's, Annie's and Lana's wardrobe.

Annie had even lent out the precious sea-green bag. But only to the one model she could totally trust with it: Lana.

Yes, in just twenty minutes or so, Lana was going to be holding her own with two professional catalogue models. (Catalogue models because they were cheaper, shorter and wouldn't tower over Lana too much.) Elena had insisted on Lana modelling. She thought Lana in ballet pumps, a knitted scarf and a beret was the *face* of the Perfect Dress casual line.

Elena had designated Annie to front of house, so she would be chatting to guests, telling them about dresses, prices, availability, and generally using her abilities to sell, sell, sell.

Elena suddenly appeared from the room which was serving as the backstage area. 'Is anyone here yet?' she asked, glancing at her dainty watch.

'No. Not a soul, we should at least have got Sye and some friends to come round early and fill the space up a bit.'

At the mention of Sye's name, Elena's face softened into a smile. As Elena hadn't been in her own room for almost a whole week, Annie could safely assume all was very well on the Sye and Elena bliss front.

'Sye doesn't think it's good for him to come . . . because his mother has decided to be here,' Elena revealed.

'His mother? The wicked witch from Bloomingdale's? In person? She's not just going to send some minion in her place?'

Elena nodded, then said: 'Maybe she hear about gift bags?'

'Aha!'

The pale blue, specially commissioned Tiffany's gift bags were currently locked up in the hotel's safe. Each one contained a silver Tiffany key ring, a discount voucher, an invitation to an exclusive jewellery preview event, a mini bottle of Taittinger and a pot of finest Beluga caviare.

Word of the gift bags had been spread to all the invited guests.

'Why is Mrs Bloomingdale's coming?' Annie wondered. 'Does she know you and Sye are back together?'

'I don't know . . . and my mother coming too. It is going to be hell. Absolute hell.'

Before they could wind their pre-show nerves into any more of a frenzy, a small knot of people began to approach the room.

But not before Annie realized that an urgent

ringing sound was coming from her tiny clutch bag. 'One second,' she promised Elena.

Elena set her face to smile and began to approach the new arrivals.

'Hi it's Annie here,' Annie began, not recognizing the incoming number.

'Annie, it's Tamsin. I'm so sorry, it's been weeks and weeks, but drop everything you're doing. We have movement! I'm meeting someone to talk about you this afternoon and I'd like you to come along for the final part of the meet.'

'Really!' Annie gasped and wondered just how Tamsin was going to take the news that she couldn't possibly drop everything and be in central London for this afternoon. 'That is so fantastic. Brilliant. Absolutely brilliant news.'

'I know. It's Gregor Forman from Channel Five, and we're meeting at the—'

'Tamsin, I can't be there. I would absolutely love to be there . . . but I'm in New York right now.'

There was silence.

Annie looked up to see more and more guests streaming into the room and Elena glaring at her, urging her to finish the call and help meet and greet.

'You're in New York?' Tamsin asked. 'Why did I not know about this? I've told him you'll be there. When can you get back?'

'I don't know . . . as soon as I possibly can,' Annie said, but she didn't know if this was true. She wanted to be here. She wanted to make sure everything was working out with the dresses before she left. And she felt truly torn. Between a career she'd thought she'd loved and this exciting new fashion business which dazzled her with all its possibilities.

'This is so extremely rude of me, I know, Tamsin, when you're working so hard for me. But I'm in the middle of something big. I'm going to have to go but I'll call you back just as soon as I can.'

'Right, fine,' Tamsin said and hung up without another word.

Annie put away her phone and tried to file away all her fears about this call. Just like Elena, she set her face to smile and began to head towards the nearest group of guests.

'Hi, how are you? Welcome,' Annie began, trying to sound as transatlantic as she could, 'what can our Russian barman fix up for you? A White Russian, perhaps? A little chilled vodka cocktail? Maybe keep it simple with a glass of champagne? Can I just say, that is one fabulous brooch.'

The woman she had adopted, because she looked chic and formidable and just totally fashion, broke the smallest of smiles. The upper corners of her mouth twitched a fraction. It might have been the Botox effect, Annie wasn't sure.

'Christian Dior,' the woman said proudly.

'Oh, I love the Dior jewels. Love. Love. Love.'

'And not too madly expensive. My store just got a wonderful new delivery.' With that the woman handed over her card and tipped Annie a tiny wink.

'I hope you're going to love our new dresses.'

'Yes. Looking forward to your show. Now where is my White Russian, and – ah! Louise . . .' she recognized another new arrival and rushed over to do the air kissey, kissey thing.

Annie smiled to herself. It was sooooo fashion.

She did miss TV. Yes, she did, she decided. But would designing, making and selling dresses be even more rewarding? Especially if it was in New York. If enough dresses were sold on this Autumn/Winter run, maybe Elena really could think about having another US partner once again.

Yes, Elena could think about it . . . and Annie could dream about it . . . but what about Ed, Lana and the rest of her family? They might not know quite what to make of this new idea.

Whatever smile might have been playing round the corners of Annie's un-Botoxed mouth was wiped away almost immediately by the sight of Elena's cool friends arriving in a knot. Right there, out in front, tossing blond hair back with his hand was . . . Taylor.

Annie gave a little gasp. What was he doing here? Had Elena actually invited him? Did he know Lana was going to be here? Even more importantly, had he not realized that Lana's rampagingly furious *mom* was going to be here?

But the room was filling up, there were important people to meet and greet and steer towards select reserved tables. Even when Annie was deep in charming hostess mode, she kept trying to locate Taylor, catch his eye and shoot a withering, evil look which would send him running from the room.

But no such luck. He was installed with the cool friends at a table close to the end of the catwalk. If he'd spotted Annie there, he didn't seem too worried about it.

What Annie really worried about was Lana spotting him and stumbling or tripping mid-walk at the sight of him. No matter how important Annie's job here at the front of house was, she owed Lana at least a warning about Taylor being in the audience, especially as he was obviously going to be right there on the edge of the catwalk, drawing full attention to himself.

Past the canapés and the growing fashion crowd she went, edging towards the backstage area.

'Annah? Have you seen my mother yet?' Elena was suddenly at her side, tapping at her watch.

'No . . .'

'Why she not here yet? She make late entrance, huh? Just like the celebrity she think she is.'

'Do you know who her mystery guest is?' Annie asked, but this was a mistake. Elena's face immediately clouded over.

'She is bringing someone? Who is she bringing?'

'Well, I don't know . . . she told me it was someone important, someone who'd land Perfect Dress on the front pages.'

'Oh no!' Elena's hand covered her mouth. 'Is always about her!' she hissed, 'never about the dresses, always about her.'

'Maybe it will help,' Annie told her soothingly, 'maybe it really will help to get us noticed. And let's face it, right now we need all the help we can get. Emily Wilmington isn't coming, by the way. She texted her NBF this afternoon to let him know.'

'Oh!'

Elena looked upset now. Too upset for Annie to tell her that Connor and his little NYC entourage weren't going to come either.

'You'll manage without us, won't you? We'd just get drunk and be noisy,' he'd said, also by text, earlier in the day.

Flipping fair-weather friend flake.

'Where are you going?' Elena asked.

'I have to tell Lana something . . . backstage'

'No, you can't,' Elena hissed. 'Sye's mother, Mrs Westhoven is here and she is walking towards us.'

'Elena, so nice to see you,' said an icy voice behind Annie's shoulder.

Mrs Westhoven flicked her eyes over Annie in such a haughtily disapproving way that Annie had to wonder if she'd put her bra on over her blouse, sprouted spinach between her teeth or committed some other unforgivable faux pas.

'This is Annah Valentine from London,' said Elena, keeping her cool. 'She is helping us in the business, we are very lucky to have her, she works in television and she was with The Store for years.'

'The Store, yes, I know The Store. Which department did you buy for?' Mrs Westhoven asked, pushing her enormous sunglasses to the top of her head.

She was wearing Chanel, Annie saw immediately. Funny how all the stringy mean women seemed to be drawn to Chanel. But only the stringy could wear skirts and boxy jackets cut from thick tweed bouclé. Who else needed all that extra bulk from their clothes?

'I wasn't a buyer . . .' Annie began. She could have pretended just this once, and probably have got away with it, but she didn't care. 'I was the personal shopper there.'

Mrs W seemed to physically recoil. She'd been talking to staff from the shop floor! And no one had even warned her.

'Where am I to sit?' she asked Elena, turning her shoulder to cut Annie from the conversation completely.

'I have a lovely front row table just for you,' Elena said as graciously as she possibly could. 'Let me take you over.'

Elena settled Mrs Westhoven into her chair, but just as she was about to walk away, she couldn't resist imparting a little nugget of information in her ear: 'I'm seeing Sye again. It's all going very well, very well indeed.'

Mrs Westhoven seemed to snort on the mouthful of champagne she'd just taken. There must have been plenty she would have liked to say to Elena at that moment. In fact, Mrs W might even have walked out of the show. But just then, the lights dimmed and an overhead spotlight snapped on to illuminate the start of the runway.

Annie, as close to the backstage entrance as she'd managed to get in several frantic seconds, whispered frantically to whoever was there, 'Tell Lana, Taylor's here . . . just so she knows in advance.' But there was no reply and she couldn't be sure anyone had heard.

Meanwhile the room had fallen silent in interested anticipation – which was exactly why Svetlana chose this moment to make her late, *great* entry.

Sweeping in through the door, a white ermine fur coat swishing at her ankles, spectacular diamonds blinking in the pale available light, great blonde beehive hair making her appear about six foot five, she announced in her deep, husky voice, 'Oh darrrrlink, we are just on time. Look they wait for us and here is our seat, right at the front.'

Heads all around the room craned as Svetlana, coat, diamonds and beehive picked their way through the tables and chairs to the prime seat right at the top of the runway.

Svetlana's arm was tightly gripped by her old

friend and the richest New York male she could lay her hands on at short notice – Donald Trump. His hair, tan and diamond-studded tie clip glittered and shimmered in the spotlight just as much as Svetlana did.

As the pair sat down, they began to sip elegantly at the glasses of champagne which appeared as if by magic in their hands.

'My mother,' Elena breathed into Annie's ear: 'it's always all about her.'

CHAPTER 25

Svetlana at show-time:

Pink, white and green wrap dress (Missoni)
Pink strappy heels (Manolo Blahnik – personally)
3-carat diamond and emerald ring
(Cartier via 3rd husband)
Diamond drop earrings (Harry Winston
via 2nd husband)
Diamond-studded watch (Chopard, no husband
required)
Breathtaking diamond and emerald necklace
(can't even remember)
Floor-length white ermine coat (Fendi)
Total est. cost: $270,000

'From Mayfair, London'

For the next half an hour, Annie couldn't worry about Svetlana and Elena. She couldn't even think about Svetlana and Elena. She was totally focused on her daughter. Could Lana handle being the model in a show where the boy who had dumped her so cruelly and callously, was sitting in the audience?

The music began and, one by one, the girls strode out: Lana at the back, but snaking her hips and strutting just as competently as the others.

The dresses were fantastic and Annie thought her daughter looked almost unrecognizably good; the long fringe gone, swept up into a quiff and carefully pinned under the beret so that all her delicate pale features were on display. What startling big blue eyes she had! During the years of fringe, Annie had almost forgotten their impact.

Annie's eyes flicked to Taylor, and she held her breath as Lana strode down the catwalk. As she turned at the bottom to a volley of camera flashes, Annie thought Lana paused for just a little too long.

But if Lana had seen Taylor, she didn't let it put her off her stride. When she came back up the blue carpet, her walk was as confident and purposeful as before and her face didn't give any hint of fluster.

'That's my girl,' Annie couldn't help saying under her breath as she watched Lana turn the corner to backstage and no doubt race to have her outfit restyled.

When the next models came out, the dresses were 'evening' with chandelier earrings, buttons undone low, lacy slips peeking from underneath and highest heels.

It worked, it really did work. Annie dared to look

at the audience now to make sure people were watching and noticing how cleverly these dresses had been made. There had to be orders! Otherwise Elena's tiny apartment would very soon be filled with way too many dresses with no homes to go to. She, Lana and probably even Elena would have to move out to make room.

After another two outings in an assortment of dresses and colourful accessories, the models returned to take a bow. Then the lights were raised, the music turned down and the girls stepped out to walk amongst the guests. This way everyone could look at and even feel the dresses in detail.

Annie hurried through the crowd, determined to speak to, charm and chat up just as many buyers as she possibly could.

That was when she saw Lana sashay past Taylor quite deliberately. He smiled at her and seemed to say hello, but Lana just swished on straight past him. This was good, Annie thought, though not nearly as much revenge as she wanted to see dished out to the boy. Enforced tattooing, red hot pokers . . . something like that would be much better.

Now Annie's attention was caught by the proximity of Svetlana to Mrs Westhoven. If that conversation was going to happen, she felt she should get over there to make sure nothing went too drastically wrong.

By the time Annie had made it to the table, Mrs Westhoven had approached Svetlana.

'Hello, I'm Sylvia Westhoven, head buyer at Bloomingdale's. I don't believe we've met before, although Donald, I'm sure you remember me,' Mrs Westhoven gushed, reaching over to take Donald Trump's hand. 'My husband is Sam Westhoven. He's one of the partners at Brinks, Westhoven and Shipman.'

'Of course, Mrs Westhoven,' the world-famous billionaire replied, smiling politely but without much sign of recognition.

'So what brings you here today, Donald? Is there a personal connection?' Mrs Westhoven had to ask.

'I'm here with my friend Svetlana Wisneski. This is her dress label.'

'Oh . . .'

Momentarily Mrs Westhoven seemed lost for words, so Annie stepped in.

'Mrs Westhoven, please meet Svetlana, Elena's business partner in Perfect Dress who also happens to be Elena's mother.'

'I see,' Mrs Westhoven managed and held out her hand.

Svetlana had a way of presenting her hand, jaw-dropping diamonds first, before she turned it elegantly for the shake.

Mrs Westhoven held out her diamonds and gold watch too and there was almost a clatter of jewels as the two formidable madams made their hand-shake.

'You are Elena's mother?' Mrs Westhoven

seemed torn between conflicting emotions. She'd clearly decided to disapprove of Elena but now, seeing Svetlana's obvious wealth and status, she seemed to be having second thoughts. 'From the Ukraine?' Mrs Westhoven went on, making this sound as sniffy and dismissive as she possibly could.

'From Mayfair, London,' Svetlana said with a gracious smile. 'Ukraine is such a long time ago. Vonderrrrrful childhood memories,' she gushed, untruthfully.

'So you've started up this little dress business?' Mrs Westhoven said with just as much of a sneer as she could get away with. She clearly felt she had the upper hand.

'Yes, is little hobby for me . . .' Svetlana gave a tiny shrug of ermine-covered shoulder, as if to imply that she had far too much money to need to worry about making any. 'I love clothes. But this is important for Elena. She wants to run business and take over the world. She is very smart girl.'

'I see.'

'And why have you come to the show, Mrs Westhoven?'

'I am the head buyer with Bloomingdale's.'

Annie could see the answer registering with Svetlana, and her sharp mind working it out. She knew about Bloomingdale's, she knew about Mrs Westhoven and she definitely knew about Sye.

'Sye Westhoven . . .' Svetlana began.

'Indeed,' Mrs Westhoven said, drawing herself to her full, Chanel-clad height.

'So, how you enjoy your . . . *job*?' Svetlana said, giving an unmistakable little sneer of her own on the word 'job'.

'I love it. I can't imagine being a lady who just . . . lunches,' came the icy reply.

Svetlana made a tinkling and obviously false laugh. Then she threw in, with a significant stroke of her glittering necklace: 'Oh, life is verrrry, verrry interesting when you have enough money.'

'Indeed.' Mrs Westhoven's eyes narrowed. She looked furiously angry.

'So our children are dating again,' Svetlana purred, before adding the killer. 'Of course, I do not approve.'

Now, the kid-skin gloves were off. Annie's heart hammered. Where would they go from here?

'If you think I approve . . .' Mrs Westhoven hissed: 'how can I possibly approve of Sye taking up with some unwanted Eastern European *love child* brought up by *relatives*, who didn't meet her own mother until she turned twenty?'

Svetlana froze. This woman knew far too much.

'This is mine, give it to me,' Svetlana said and grabbed at the Tiffany's goodie bag which Mrs Westhoven was holding.

'I beg your pardon, it's mine,' Mrs Westhoven said, snatching the bag back. For a brief moment, both women were involved in an undignified tug of war over the goodie bag, which held up admirably under the pressure.

'Ladies,' Donald Trump intervened with a genial smile, 'why don't we settle this over another bottle of champagne?'

'Never!' Mrs Westhoven declared, and with that she let go of the bag, turned on her heel and began to march to the door.

Elena, who had been watching this disaster from a safe distance, did not dare to approach Mrs W on her way out. But Annie decided maybe she would give it just one desperate try. This was, after all, the woman behind the biggest single dress order.

'Mrs Westhoven, I'm sorry, Svetlana is a unique and colourful character. She often says things she doesn't mean . . .' Annie began apologetically. 'I hope the dresses at least spoke for themselves.'

'Don't waste your time,' Mrs Westhoven said, not even turning to look at Annie as she continued her march to the door, but she raised her voice so that as many of the guests as possible could hear her. 'Your dresses are unoriginal and cheap. The Bloomingdale's order remains withdrawn.'

CHAPTER 26

Sye ready to mother-meet:

Thick white shirt (Brooks Brothers)
Beige combat trousers (Patagonia)
Hiking boots (same)
Digital camera (Nikon)
Woven wrist bracelets (Bolivia)
Total est. cost: $680

'There's another side.'

The post-show party was not intended to be a big event but it was nevertheless one of the most glamorous get-togethers Annie had ever been to, because it was in Svetlana's room at the Carlyle Hotel on Madison Avenue.

Even Svetlana didn't splash out on a suite at the Carlyle, so this was an intimate and cosy party based around Svetlana's king-sized bed and the vast sofa at the foot of it. But it was still perfectly glamorous in every way and with views from eleven floors up right over Manhattan.

Sculptural orchids on every available side table? Check. Impressive white marble fireplace? Check. Bowls of too perfect to eat fruit? Check. Luxurious furnishings and fabrics? Swathes of silk and satin? Check and check.

Still, Svetlana had spread her ermine coat over her king-sized bed, just to make it that touch more luxurious.

Now the little handful of guests – well, in fact, it was just Svetlana, Annie, Connor and Lana – were drinking wine or fizzy water and picking from the silver trays of food brought up by room service.

Annie and Lana were on the sofa, while Svetlana and Connor were draped across the ermine and the bed. Annie wondered why her two friends had only met so briefly in the past. The two divas seemed perfectly suited to one another.

'I can't believe you didn't come to the show. I still can't believe you didn't come,' Annie complained to Connor.

'I'm sorry. I didn't want to take the spotlight away from anyone,' he said with such pomposity that Annie had a fit of the giggles.

'No, of course not,' she managed, 'because you are soooooo famous in New York, I don't know how you manage to get out the door in the morning without being mobbed by your fans and the paparazzi.'

'Have some more champagne, darrrling,' Svetlana said, dangling the bottle over Connor's glass. 'This the worst day in my business life so far. We have to celebrate.'

'You need a marketing strategy,' Connor offered, already sounding sozzled.

'Shut up,' Annie told him, 'no one's talking about marketing strategies tonight. We're just going to enjoy being in a room at the Carlyle. For me, this is a once in a lifetime event. Well . . . unless Tamsin gets me a job starring in the next blockbuster, obviously.'

'Too fat,' Connor informed her.

'Shut up!' Annie repeated, filling up her own glass. 'Anyway I'm training with Gawain, *trademark* tomorrow. So look out, Hollywood.'

'If you are training with Gawain tomorrow,' Connor said, sitting up to look at her, 'you better put that glass down right now. You have no idea how much pain he is going to inflict. You can't have a hangover as well. It will kill you.'

'I will fight the pain with champagne, *trademark*,' Annie insisted and downed another mouthful.

There was a tap on the door and as Svetlana called out, 'Come in!' Elena and Sye, hand in hand, strolled into the room.

'Oh hello.' At the sight of another so obviously handsome man, Svetlana automatically patted her hair, adjusted her cleavage and sat up on her bed. Then she extended her diamond-encrusted hand. 'Wonderful to meet you properly,' she said graciously, then spoiled it slightly by adding, 'Your mother is total beeeeetch.'

'Well, Mrs Wisneski,' Sye began, sounding relaxed, 'I guess you wouldn't be the first person to think that. But maybe you need to get to know her better. There's another side. A very charming side.'

'Hmmm, I don't know if there is going to be much getting to know this woman better. But you, Sye, Elena thinks I need to know you a little better, so sit on bed here, have a drink and talk to me.'

Annie thought it was a good thing that Elena sat right down beside Sye to protect him, because Svetlana looked dangerously like she might eat him all up in one gulp.

'How are you, baby?' Annie asked her daughter, who was sitting quietly on the sofa, sipping at mineral water and watching all the lavish Svetlana antics with wide eyes.

'I'm fine.'

'Did you like modelling?'

'Not much. Another fantasy fulfilled, which turns out to be not as much fun as you'd thought.'

'Ooooh so young and so world-weary,' Annie teased. 'You did see . . . you-know-who, didn't you?'

'Mmmm,' Lana confirmed with a little nod.

'You seemed to handle it very well. Just a cool and casual dismissal. So classy. Much better than I could ever have managed. I'd have wanted to throw glasses, shriek and cause a scene.'

'I'm very glad you didn't!'

'No, I meant if I'd been you. But I'm so obviously not you. You're very much your own person – and I just wanted to say that you handled him so well, I was proud of you. I bet he felt about two inches tall.'

Lana's smile broke out now: 'Do you think?'

'Yeah, definitely. You were the ice queen. He saw you on the catwalk, looking amazing and he realized just what he'd let get away there.'

'Good!'

'Because obviously you'd never have him back?' Annie just wanted to check.

'Never!' Lana agreed. 'How's home?' she asked, 'I thought I might even try and speak to them today.'

'Big of you.' Annie winked. 'Let's get my phone out . . . ah, but it's already 6p.m., midnight at home . . . we'll text, see if Ed's awake.'

Within moments, Annie was reading the reply:

Just going to sleep. Too tired to talk. Will spk tomorrow promise. Ed xx

Which was fine, of course. She'd left it so late.

But . . . just the slightest little but . . . they'd not spoken for two whole days now. That was a long time. Just a little inkling crossed her mind that maybe not everything was OK.

The alarm bleeped at 5a.m. Annie groaned, smacked it off and rolled over again.

'What's that for?' Lana asked groggily.

'Nothing,' Annie said, pulling the sheet over her head against the early morning light.

'It's the gym, isn't it?' Lana sat up, remembering just where her mum was supposed to be at 5.30 this morning.

Annie groaned in reply. She felt terrible. Just exactly how many White Russians, or Black Vodkas or Vodkatinis, or whatever else had she drunk last night? Her stomach churned and her head throbbed in reply.

If it was now 5.05a.m., then she'd only managed about four hours of sleep. And now she was supposed to go and *Train with Gawain* . . . trademark?

'I can't go,' she mumbled, 'I'll have to phone in sick.'

'You can't phone in sick!' Lana exclaimed and gave her mum a poke in the ribs. 'Connor would lose all his money! And who knows, Train with Gawain might never speak to him again. He might be like *totally* humiliated,' she added in finest New York accent.

'Train with Gawain – huh – more like Gawain the pain,' Annie huffed from her side of the sofa bed.

'Get up, Mum and go to the gym,' Lana instructed her.

'I've got nothing to wear . . .' Annie whined, trying out a new line of defence.

'Are you serious?' Lana asked with some amazement. This was just not something her mum ever said. No matter what the event, Annie could put together a killer outfit for it.

'You mean you've booked in for a session with New York's number one personal trainer at one of New York's swankiest gyms and you've not even thought about getting a pair of gym shoes?'

'Well, I have trainers . . .' Annie mumbled from underneath the pillow.

'So you bought trainers?'

'No . . . I brought them from home.'

'Why? You last wore trainers in the . . . nineties?' Lana guessed.

Annie didn't want to tell Lana about the little daydream she'd had back in London of jogging effortlessly round the Central Park reservoir, like all the other fit New Yorkers. Somehow she'd thought if she came over to New York, the will to be fit and slim would just transplant itself into her brain, along with the will to drink Cosmopolitans and shop daily on Fifth Avenue.

'OK.' Lana, despite her puffy eyes and sleep-deprived head, was getting out of bed and rummaging through her bag. 'I have short socks, I have leggings . . . you could use one of my big sleep T-shirts, but I haven't got anything that will help you in the way of a sports bra.'

'Oh, don't worry. I'll just wear two bras.'

'Two bras?'

'Old school trick.'

Annie sat up gingerly. She couldn't believe she was actually getting out of bed. But yes: despite the four hours of sleep and the hangover, she suddenly seemed to be washing, brushing her teeth and climbing into the leggings and T-shirt offered by her slightly too eager daughter. Just one look in the mirror told Annie that she really was not fit to brave a New York gym. She should be wearing fashionable fitness clothes, not her teen daughter's pyjamas.

She should do her hair and apply at least a light coating of waterproof make-up. This was *Train with Gawain*, for goodness' sake. Gawain was probably used to looking at SJP first thing in the morning, not VPL.

'Is there something I could use as a headband?' Annie asked, beginning to feel slightly panicked by her reflection.

'Why?' Lana said, warily.

'Headbands . . . people wear headbands in the gym, don't they?'

'No. Well, maybe they did like last century.'

'OK, no headband, then. Can I go like this now?' Annie asked her daughter, hoping, really truly hoping, that she would say no.

'Yes, and you need to go right now. You'll have to find a cab to get there on time. It's in SoHo. That's So-hip-it-hurts-Ho.'

'Thanks. I'm feeling better already.'

The cab dropped Annie off on a corner where two wide streets of low warehouse conversions crossed. There was hardly anyone about: she could see clear down to the Hudson River, golden in the early morning light. Black fire escapes zigzagged up every one of the impressive four- and five-storey brick buildings and Annie felt weirdly energized.

Yes! She could go to the gym at 5.30a.m. Yes! She could learn some moves from Train with Gawain 'trademark' and she *would* join the crowds of svelte fashionistas marching up and down the avenues in slinky clothes. Annie walked towards the large glass doors which she guessed must be number 17. No number was attached to the doors, but there was a number 15 on one side, and a number 19 on the other. She looked all around for a bell, a buzzer, a button of any kind: but there was nothing, just a small black box with a tiny green light at the corner.

Was she supposed to talk to it?

'Hello? Is this the gym?' she tried. No reply.

She looked at her watch. It was 5.27a.m. Surely Gawain would already be here? Wouldn't he be looking out for her, since there was no obvious way of getting inside?

'Hello?' she said to the box again.

Just then the tallest, thinnest, blondest girl Annie had ever set eyes on, away from a catwalk, strode up to the door. As she was dressed in tightest vest, tightest capris, a pink hoodie and trainers with soles as thick as mattresses, it was obvious where she was headed. Annie gave her a friendly, we're-all-in-this-together kind of smile and stood aside hoping the girl knew how to get in the door.

The girl, in turn, gave her an icy up-and-down, whipped out a set of keys with a little grey electronic tag attached and waved them at the black box. Immediately the green light turned orange and the glass door sprang open.

The girl went through and attempted to close the door in Annie's face.

'But I'm going to the gym too!' Annie protested, 'I'm supposed to see Train with Gawain and I don't know how to get in.'

'The rule is no tailgating,' the girl replied.

'Please!' Annie whimpered, 'or can you at least tell someone up there I'm here and to open the door?'

With a sigh, the girl relented. Annie followed her into a tiny elevator where they stood facing each other, the duck and the stork, saying nothing. The lift stopped on the second floor and the girl got out: 'This is the gym,' she told Annie, then with a bounce of perfectly pert arse she was gone, leaving Annie in a criminally, minimally chic waiting area.

She gazed at the tall, black, shiny counter, dazzlingly white walls and floor-to-ceiling Manhattan view. Oh, and framed, signed photos of the gym's clients, of course: Julia Roberts, Tina Fey . . . No, Annie wasn't intimidated. Nooooo, no. Why on earth should she feel intimidated, standing in a place like this in fifteen-year-old trainers and her daughter's pyjamas?

As she contemplated getting back in the lift, a perfectly proportioned, perfectly tanned, perfectly blond man in a tight black T-shirt bounded up and slid behind the counter.

'Good morning,' he said with a way too perky for 5.30a.m. smile.

'Good morning,' Annie replied.

'And you must be Pam, our new cleaner, in bright and early.'

Annie looked at him in horror and felt the blood rush to her cheeks. 'No,' she squeaked, 'I'm Annie, I have an appointment with Gawain.'

Now it was the blond's turn to look surprised: *'Really?'* he said with a little too much astonishment, 'Gawain?' Then came the killer: 'Are you *sure?*'

'Yes, I'm sure. Could you just tell him I'm here, please?'

The guy pressed some numbers on the phone in front of him and there was a brief buzzing sound. Moments later, Gawain appeared in the reception area.

He was already in a white vest top, looking slighty sweaty. Either he'd been doing a workout, or his first client of the day had already been and gone.

'Hi Annie, how're you doing?'

Gawain held out his hand and didn't look entirely unfriendly.

'Hi,' Annie said, shaking it and trying not to faint, die or throw up with fear.

But Gawain was already striding off. 'Follow me.'

She was shown to another bright white and black room where Gawain served her a shot of wheatgrass juice. 'Bitter but beautiful,' he promised, handing her a questionnaire.

More like bile and bleuuuuuurghh, she thought as she took just the one gulp and filled in her answers.

Gawain watched over her shoulder and as she neared the end, he came to his conclusion: 'Unfit but not unwell. Good. We can work with that, girl. We're going to work hard with that.'

He smiled encouragingly as he opened the door to the gym, and Annie, dazzled by the bulging biceps and the bright white smile began to fall in under the Train with Gawain spell.

'You are going to feel pain with Gawain. But you will gain with Gawain. Every single day that you train with Gawain, you will gain with Gawain,' he began to chant at Annie as she hauled her great lardy bum onto the seated bike.

After a minute or two of sedate cycling, she decided this was OK, she could do this. But that was when Gawain gave her the bad news.

'OK Miss Annie, that was the warm-up.'

As she tried to crank up the pedals, Gawain encouraged her with all kinds of visualizations: 'You're about to win gold at the Olympics . . . there's someone right on your tail, at your shoulder now, come on, girl, race, race! You want to take gold!' Panting hard, Annie just focused on the bike's timer. *Hideous* – only 25 seconds had gone past. How could this be when her heart was hammering and her lungs were heaving in and out like bellows? 35 . . . 42 . . . time seemed to have ground to a halt. 41?? It was going backwards. Her breath rattled in her chest and she wondered if she was about to die.

'Come on, you can do this . . .' Gawain urged.

When she looked again: 58, 59 . . . 60. She'd made it! Gawain told her to pedal 'nice and easy' for a minute.

He also looked at her with some concern.

'I'm not used to dealing with someone who's so out of shape,' he admitted, but before Annie got too downhearted, he helpfully added: 'So it's a learning experience for both of us.'

Before she knew it, Annie was pedalling her heart out again. The beautiful gym with its arched windows and state of the art machines was almost empty, apart from skinny girl who was in the corner on some upright machine which looked like the modern version of a medieval rack.

'Water,' Annie gasped, 'I need water.'

'Yes, you're right, we are going to re-hydrate in just 16–15–14–13 seconds. C'mon, pedal. PEDAL! Faster. Faster!'

As they repeated the 'one minute fast, one minute easy' routine on every machine in the room, Annie's state of mind seemed to hover between, 'I'm going to die, right now, and never see my lovely children again' and – when Gawain's voice was right in her

288

ear, urging her on – 'I can do this. I can get fit, I can shift the weight. I really can!'

It was almost as intense as childbirth. Almost as much pain too. As she slid off each machine, Annie clung to Gawain's arm, needing his support. There was no way she could ever work this hard in a gym without Gawain right beside her

'You're already fitter and you're already stronger,' he told her, so convincingly that she almost believed him. 'The aerobic part is almost over, Annie girl, then we're gonna tone.'

Tone. Tone? What could it mean? She felt so hot it was like delirium, so sore it was like death.

Skinny girl was finished on the machine in the corner, and patting at her ever so slightly shiny face with a towel, then sipping from a chic lilac water bottle. Two guys and another supermodel-like being had also appeared now. But Annie was in too much pain to care.

Gawain was strapping her into the torture device in the corner of the room. Her feet were being fixed into weird strappy pedals, and grips were being placed in her hands.

'This is like a cross trainer, but much more effective. We can tilt and wobble you while you work. We can hit every muscle. Muscles you didn't even know you had are going to hurt you so bad tomorrow.'

She couldn't wait.

Annie tried to pump her arms and legs the way Gawain was demonstrating, but she felt as if she was trapped in treacle. Nothing moved.

'Right . . . OK there, I'll just move those weights down a notch.'

Finally she started. Shuffling her legs forward, pumping her arms.

'Now out to the sides. *Raise*, and lower,' Gawain urged, again demonstrating. Leg out to the side, arm out to the side. Was he serious?

Annie scanned the gym, searching hopelessly for some sort of help. She now took a proper look at the guy pounding furiously on the treadmill in front of the window. His face was in profile, tilted slightly away from her, but his bright blond hair and broad shoulders gave him away.

It was Taylor! It had to be – right there on the treadmill, just feet away from her!

Now Annie found the strength to pound. She began to punch her arms forward as hard as she could, imagining she was pummelling Taylor in the face with every move.

Smack! Smack! Punch! Wallop!

'Whoa . . .' Gawain ordered, 'hold on now, I need to put the weights up again.'

But Annie couldn't wait. She had Taylor in her sights and blind fury said she wasn't going to stop.

As Gawain loosened one of the elastic straps, Annie let fly with a left hook.

Ping!

The elastic strap shot out of its mooring and a small metal clip flew across the gym.

As if in slow motion, Annie watched as it made

straight for Taylor, and caught him on the cheek-bone, just below the eye.

'What-the-f—?' His hand shot up to his cheek and when he felt blood he paused in surprise.

Pausing on a treadmill going at full throttle is always a mistake. Taylor's feet were whipped out from under him and then he was stumbling, tripping, falling and flailing for anything to break his fall. With a horrible bumping, grinding crunch, he was thrown backwards off the machine.

Gawain leapt forward to press the treadmill's emergency stop, stepping hard on the super-model's water bottle and sending jets of water in every direction.

Annie, one arm free of her machine, pulled at what she hoped was a release lever, but suddenly found her legs whipped up into the air by their elasticated straps. Now she was dangling like a trussed chicken.

'Heeeeee-lp!' she squawked. But no one paid her any attention because they were all crowded round Taylor.

He sat up and put a hand to his cheek again.

'Can you move your ankles, man?' Gawain asked.

'You better hope so,' Taylor snarled, 'or I am going to make trouble.'

Everyone backed away from him a little.

He got up carefully, circling his ankles and wrists, feeling himself over for damage. And as he looked around the room at each of them in turn, Annie saw that it wasn't in fact Taylor. Ah.

This man was older and he looked angry and threatening. His accusing eyes fell on Annie, who was dangling helplessly on the machine, but thankfully Gawain stepped in just in time, full of charm.

'This is my fault,' he told the man. 'Fortunately you seem to be OK. But I think I should offer you a month's free membership and a personal training session to make up for this accident.'

The man grunted his agreement. Then he dusted himself down and got back onto the treadmill, leaving Gawain to rescue Annie from the machine.

'Now don't worry,' Gawain assured her, when their session was finally over, 'I'm going to give you your specially designed programme for month one. Then you log on to my website, pay your membership fee and get your second programme.'

'But it won't be the same,' Annie protested. 'I'm not sure I can do this without you, Gawain.'

What had Train with Gawain done to her? Annie wondered. She, the gym-hater, the gym-aphobic, was already trying to work out how she could fit in a session tomorrow. He'd made her believe that even she could shape up.

'You can also download this week's "Playin' with Gawain" gym music, with my special words of encouragement.'

'Really? You're speaking on it?'

'I'm speaking just to you, girl, listen to me and move! The next time you come to New York, we'll meet again and I am gonna marvel at how wonderful you look and how amazing you feel.'

Now she understood why Connor had crossed the Atlantic just for this man.

'You should be on TV,' Annie told him, as she headed to the lift. And at that she pulled up sharp and spun back to face him.

Would Gawain want to be on TV? Could he come over to Britain and be on TV . . . with her? Wouldn't it make for a great show? She needed to phone Tamsin and pitch the idea!

'I'd love to be on TV, hasn't happened yet though,' Gawain laughed. 'See you soon, Annie,' he said, clasping her hand, looking deeply and sincerely into her eyes. Then he was gone and she was in the elevator.

As she left the building, Annie understood why there was an electronic lock on the door. It was for Gawain's protection from his adoring fans.

Wandering forlornly down the street, Annie saw a café. Inside she ordered a freshly squeezed carrot and apple juice, not because she was now a health freak but because even the thought of coffee and a muffin, after the punishment she'd just given her body, was making her nauseous.

At the table, waiting for her juice, she decided to phone Dinah. Her sister was a gym bunny, a fitness fanatic, she would want to hear every last detail of Annie's pain with Gawain, trademark.

She dialled her own home number first,

wondering if Dinah and the babies would be there. It only took a couple of rings before Annie heard her sister's voice on the other end of the line.

'Helloooo, it's me! Guess where I've just been?'

'Tiffany's?'

'No.'

'Ermm . . . Macy's?

'No.'

'I don't know, Annie. I give up. I don't know the names of all the fancy shops out there. I've never even been once.'

'Dinah, babes, it's not even 7a.m. over here. I'm not shopping, I'm recovering from my session at the *gym* with Connor's trainer Gawain.'

'You are not! You have not! *Really?*'

'Really!'

'Annie, I am so impressed. This is really, really good news.'

See, that was Dinah; totally sweet, wishing her well, wanting her to succeed on the treadmill.

'It was amazing, I will tell you everything, but first you have to tell me about home. How is everyone? How are my babies? And Owen? Has he sold off the entire contents of the house down the market yet? And Ed? All I've had from Ed in two days is texts!'

'Everyone's fine. Well, the children, yes, don't worry about any one of them for a second. Min's had a tiny little cold, but she's already perking up.'

'Oh, my little love.'

'But Annie . . . something is up with Ed. I was

going to phone you as soon as I thought you'd be up. Something isn't right. He's so quiet. He seems worried. It started the day before yesterday and . . . he left at 8.15 this morning, but he didn't take his briefcase. I honestly don't know if he's gone to school or not. To be honest, I'm quite worried.'

Annie didn't like the sound of this at all; now she wished she had coffee. Very strong, black coffee. Not this wimpy do-gooder drink in front of her.

They said their goodbyes and Annie quickly dialled Ed's mobile number. 'Could I have an espresso over here?' she called over to the waitress as she waited for him to answer.

'Ed!' She felt a rush of relief as she heard him pick up, 'Ed, you're there. Thank goodness! We're all so worried about you. Are you OK?'

'Ye-es . . . I think I'm OK,' he replied. But she knew him so well that she immediately knew he wasn't telling the truth.

'Of course you're not OK. This is me, Ed. Please, don't think you need to tell me anything that isn't true. I love you. You're my best guy, babes. What is it? I'm panicking over here. Take a breath and just tell me.'

Ed gave a long, deep sigh.

'It's OK. We can handle it,' Annie assured him.

'I've been suspended from school, Annie. There's porn all over the school's internal computer system and somehow . . . I have no idea,

Annie, I really have no idea at all . . . but it's all been linked to me.'

Annie clutched at the table in front of her. Not for the first time that morning, she thought she was going to faint.

CHAPTER 27

Business Elena:

Navy jersey dress (Perfect Dress free sample)
Gold earrings (gift from Svetlana)
Gold ballet pumps (Old Navy stores)
Total est. cost: $15

'Hello, Mrs Westhoven'

Annie listened as computer keys tapped frantically in the background.

'Ma'am . . . I could offer you one flight tomorrow afternoon, at a re-booking fee of $350. But I can't transfer both passengers.'

Annie paused to consider, taking a sip of her espresso. She and Lana were due to fly home in five days' time. She was of course going to spend the $350 to come home early, but did she need to pay for Lana to cut her trip short too? Wouldn't she be OK on her own for a while? And what about Perfect Dress? Annie had solved some of the problems she'd flown over to handle, but there weren't nearly enough orders in place for her to go home with a clear conscience.

But Ed . . . Ed was on suspension while terrible allegations were being investigated. He needed her to be at home with him. He'd told her not to leave early and cut short her New York adventure, but it wasn't just about what he needed. She needed to be with him too.

'Yes, I'll take the flight tomorrow,' Annie said, making up her mind, and taking out her credit card.

As she hurried down the street towards the subway entrance, Annie glanced at the three newspaper vending machines chained to the railings. Nothing unusual about that, this was how newspapers were sold all over New York.

But on the front page of one paper was a paparazzo shot of the actor Josh Hartnett. Nothing unusual about that either. He lived in New York and seemed to pop up all over every newspaper and magazine.

But Josh Hartnett was holding the hand of the *Vanity Fair* writer Emily Wilmington. And . . .

Annie bent low to make sure she had seen this right . . . Emily Wilmington was wearing, along with a blue felt trilby and brown boots, the blue jersey Perfect Dress which Annie and Elena had sent her.

Annie shrieked. She couldn't help herself. Fumbling in her purse, she found quarters and jammed them into the slot. Snatching up her newspaper, she scanned the headline over the photo: 'Who's that girl with Josh?' Underneath, the photo caption read: 'Josh Hartnett takes a walk in the park with Emily Wilmington. She's that girl, but more importantly, where do we buy that dress?'

Annie shrieked again, to the surprise of the passers-by scurrying to get to the subway entrance. She put all the quarters she could find into the vending machine and bought five more newspapers.

Forgetting for a second the horrible news from home, Annie couldn't help feeling an enormous burst of triumph. This was the best thing that could have happened to Perfect Dress.

'LANA!!' she shouted excitedly into her phone, 'we've had the most amazing break! Get out into the street, tell Elena, and buy a copy of the *New York Post*. Emily from *Vanity Fair*'s on the cover in her Perfect Dress! Seriously! I'm on my way back, we have to use this in every way we can.'

Annie knew she would have to tell Lana about Ed and about her flight home tomorrow, but that could wait for a little while. Just until they'd done as much as they could to make this good news really work for them.

When Annie arrived back at the apartment, both Lana and Elena were already on the case.

Elena, phone glued to her ear, was talking to the

New York Post feature desk: 'Ya, Emily Wilmington, on the cover of your paper today. She is wearing the dress by my company, Perfect Dress . . .'

Lana was busy compiling the press release about to be emailed to as many newspapers, feature pages and fashion editors as she could think of. She was also pasting the photo, properly captioned with names and the Perfect Dress label, onto as many fashion websites as she could think of.

It wasn't even 8a.m. yet and so much had happened!

Annie made coffee, sat down at the tiny table and thought hard. How else? How else could she use her last day in New York to make this incredible stroke of luck work even harder for them?

Obviously, she would phone every customer who'd ever placed a dress order, ever thought about placing a dress order, or even cancelled a dress order.

She had another idea too, born of her days at The Store. Just as soon as the shops were open, all three of them would make as many calls as possible in as many different voices as possible. They would all pretend to be customers looking for that dress.

In particular, they would make a point of phoning Bloomingdale's . . . a lot.

For the next few hours, the small apartment sounded more like a call centre than a fashion headquarters.

'Hi, I'm looking for the label Perfect Dress? Yes, I saw a dress in the *New York Post* this morning. Do you stock the label? Do you think you will? Is there any way I could make a reservation?'

'Five thousand and fourteen hits on the Perfect Dress website just this morning,' Elena reported, 'we've posted up that the dresses will be here in a week and we've allowed people to pre-order.'

'Have you spoken to Brad at the factory? Can he do us another run if we need him to?'

Elena nodded, then added with a little smile, 'Maybe we go to a warehouse and *buy* the fabric this time?'

'Yes,' Annie agreed, 'that might be easier.'

Elena's phone began to ring. 'Good afternoon, this is Elena Wisneski of Perfect Dress.'

Elena coloured up slightly when she heard the reply. Annie looked away, but couldn't help listening in keenly.

'Hello Mrs Westhoven, how are you?'

For a stricken moment, Annie wondered if all the calls they'd made to Bloomingdale's this afternoon had been traced to the flat and to their mobiles. Maybe the terrifying Mrs Westhoven had found out just what they were up to.

'Yes, I'm very well too, thank you,' Elena said, sounding admirably calm and civil. 'Yes . . . OK . . . no problem . . .'

Now Annie was desperate to know what this was about.

'All ninety dresses. Yes . . .' Elena looked over at

Annie and gave her a huge grin. 'Reinstate the order, and possibly order more. Yes, that is no problem. But we would have to take a deposit from you . . . because of the previous cancellation.'

Annie almost gasped at Elena's nerve.

'OK, yes. If you email me a confirmation, I'll start to process your order right away. Delivery of the dresses? You're looking at one week from now, but we'll try our best to bring that forward. Yes, we can provide full publicity material. We're going to buy usage of the Josh Hartnett and Emily Wilmington photo.'

When Elena clicked off the call, she gave a little shriek of glee, sprang up and began a victory dance around the room.

Lana and Annie had to join in.

'This is so exciting!' Lana said. 'I can't wait, I can't wait to see all our dresses arriving and then hanging up in the shops!'

Annie realized she would now have to break the news about Ed and tell Lana and Elena that she wouldn't be here when the dresses arrived.

She would be back in London.

CHAPTER 28

The handsome Asian home-comer:

White T-shirt (Gap)
Light blue cashmere sweater (J. Crew)
Beige chinos (same)
White sneakers (Converse)
Total est. cost: $390

Too busy hugging and being hugged . . .

Annie watched the luggage going round on the carousel through eyes puffed and bleary from the flight. Flying to New York with Lana had been so exciting that the cramped hours had passed quickly. But flying home, Annie had fretted and worried about Ed and his suspension all night long, only managing short snatches of sleep.

That bag was hers. She hurried over to the carousel and heaved off the large holdall. New York shopping had resulted in two extra holdalls; Lana was going to bring one and Annie was in charge of this one.

When Ed realized she really was going to come home early just for him and there was nothing he could do to persuade her otherwise, he'd offered to pick her up at the airport but she'd told him no, she would be fine. She'd take the train to Paddington and a cab from there.

Now, wheeling along her trolley loaded with two heavy bags, the beautiful green Mulberry bag over her shoulder, Annie wasn't so sure about the train idea. Carrying both bags at the same time was torture – almost as much torture as training with Gawain.

As she wheeled her trolley through the exit, she was caught up for a little moment in the glamour and emotion of the arrivals hall. A chauffeur in a shiny peaked cap was holding up a sign for 'Mr Bendell', and a large Asian family, including Gran, Grandad, plus toddlers and babies, were all falling over a handsome young man . . . maybe home for a holiday from his exciting US job.

Annie's eyes were drawn to the other cardboard signs bearing titles or company names. There was even one that read, 'My lovely wife'. Oh, how sweet was that?

Then with a gasp of surprise, she realized it was being held up by Ed.

'What are you doing here?' she screeched, hurrying her trolley in his direction, her eyes suddenly prickly with tears.

'Do you always have to greet me like that?' he asked jokily.

But then they were caught up in a hug. A great big, who cares if anyone is looking or what anyone might be thinking hug. Their arms were tightly around each other, holding on for dear life, the hug as supporting as it was supportive.

'I'm so sorry,' Annie said into his shoulder.

He patted her soothingly on the back, the way he patted the babies. 'It's not been good,' he said.

She pulled away from his shoulder so she could look at his face. 'It's going to be OK,' she told him, 'it really is going to be OK. I'm back. I'm going to look after you and we'll sort this all out.'

He pulled her in and kissed her on the top of her head.

He seemed so quiet, so tense and so needy that she felt a surge of worry. 'It is going to be all right, Ed? There's nothing . . .' she paused, suddenly unsure what to say. It had never for one moment occurred to her to think anything but the best of Ed. 'There's nothing we need to talk about first?' she asked, feeling a tight knot in her throat.

'No, no. Of course not,' he replied, shaking his head, 'but the stuff is on my school computer. This is some sort of set-up. I just don't know who would do this to me – or how.'

His eyes darted away from her face and for a fleeting second she wondered if she should read anything into that. But no, she brushed it away. If he'd told her there was nothing, then she had no reason to doubt him.

'Do you want to get a coffee?' he asked.

She shook her head. 'No, I'm desperate to get home and see everyone. They will all be there, won't they?'

'Dinah and babies, yes, unless they've gone off to the toddler group. Owen is obviously at . . . school.' The word came out with difficulty.

'Ed, you'll be back there ASAP,' she soothed, 'and they'll have to take out a billboard to make an apology big enough for my liking.'

Once they were in the car and heading towards north London, Annie began trying to piece together just what was going on with Ed and St Vincent's.

'Where is this investigation at, though? Right now?' she wanted to know. 'What are they doing for you today?'

Hands on the steering wheel, Ed shrugged. 'It's being investigated, that's all I know. They'll contact me when they have more information.'

'But what are they doing? Who's doing the investigating? And are they on the case today, or is it just sitting in the headmaster's in-tray until he decides he can find some time to deal with it?'

Ed shrugged again.

'I can't believe you didn't tell me sooner. I'd have been over here. I'd have been helping you to sort this out.'

'I didn't want you to come back for this,' Ed said, his knuckles tight on the steering wheel. 'I just want this to be over, and as soon as possible.

I want them to realize it's all a mistake and for everything to go back to how it was.'

'Do you want me to get in touch with Harry?' Annie asked, 'Svetlana's husband. He's a QC, remember? He could give you some legal advice.'

'I don't want to blow this up into something it's not. I've not done anything. This is nothing to do with me! This is a computer glitch.'

'But you've been suspended. It looks terrible! People will be talking. You're a music teacher . . . you take private tuition!'

The traffic lights ahead were at red, long enough for Ed to turn his face and look at her.

'Don't you think I don't know that?' he asked, voice barely above a whisper.

'We have to do something,' she protested, 'I think we should phone Harry.'

'No.'

'But why not?'

'If I have a lawyer, then I immediately look guilty!' Ed exclaimed, suddenly sounding very upset.

'I don't think so,' Annie said, trying to stay calm. 'It's to protect you. Maybe if you had a lawyer, you wouldn't have been suspended. People think if you're on suspension, there must be a reason. But if Harry was involved, he'd probably have you back at school tomorrow.'

'Annie, I don't want him to get involved. Just give it some time.'

'Please, Ed, all I want to do is to help you. Harry

really is very good. He got Svetlana an amazing divorce deal. He got her children back when Igor tried to abduct them . . .'

'He's a QC, Annie. What makes you think we can afford someone like that? I'm a suspended music teacher and you're an out-of-work TV presenter. We're in serious trouble.'

'I don't think he'd charge us anything,' Annie said quietly. 'He's Svetlana's husband and we've helped Svetlana out enough. I've just been working in New York for free, turning her dress business around completely.'

Silence.

Ed wasn't agreeing with the idea and Annie didn't want to push it. 'Why don't we talk about New York?' she said into the silence, in the most cheerful tone she could muster.

Looking out of the window at the low, ugly, brick buildings sitting squat in the gloom of an overcast morning, she already missed Manhattan.

After a fifty-minute battle through the congested arteries which ran from west London to north, Ed pulled the car up in front of their beautiful old house in Highgate. It had once belonged to Ed's parents, but was now Ed and Annie's family home, the inside all slick and twenty-first century.

Whatever anxieties Annie might have been feeling about Ed's predicament were forgotten, at least temporarily, by the rush of excitement she felt at seeing her family again.

The big double buggy was parked by the front door, so she knew that Dinah couldn't have gone out with the twins. Leaving Ed to deal with the bags, Annie sprang out and rushed towards the front door. She didn't even want to waste precious moments trying to find her house keys, so she rang the bell and peered in through the glass, desperate for her first glimpse of the twins.

For a moment, all she could hear was the manic barking of Dave, the family dog. It was so lovely to be back home that she thought she might even feel quite pleased to see Dave again.

Then Dinah threw open the door and while they hugged each other tightly, Annie looking over her shoulder for the babies, Dave bounced up and down against her leg, dangerously close to shredding her tights.

'Hello, hello darlin', how are you? How are my babies?'

'Come into the sitting room and see,' Dinah urged.

Annie rushed into the room and practically fell on to her youngest children. She squeezed first Minnie and then Micky right up against her and suddenly couldn't believe that she'd managed to exist for a whole four weeks without them. They were so much bigger than she'd remembered! And so gorgeous, so perfect and totally adorable.

'Hello, hello, Mummy's back!' she kept repeating like a demented person.

The babies accepted several cuddles but then wanted to be freed so they could go back to the button-pressing and drooling that they were busy with this morning.

'Have they been OK?' Annie asked her sister.

'They've been perfect,' Dinah replied, 'but you know how it is; you'll get it in the neck now. Every time you leave the room, they'll squawk for you.'

'I'm never leaving the room though, so that's OK,' Annie said, lying on her side across the play mat and letting her twins crawl and drool affectionately all over her.

Ed was bringing bags into the hallway. 'Shall I take these upstairs?' he called.

'Yeah,' she replied so that as soon as he was out of earshot she could whisper to Dinah: 'He's so upset. Has he been like this ever since it began?'

Dinah nodded.

'I want him to phone Harry, you know Svetlana's husband, the QC. He could at least give him some advice.'

'Good idea.'

'Yeah, except he won't.'

The door opened and Ed was standing in front of them.

Annie immediately smiled brightly. 'Presents!' she said, jumping up from the play mat, 'I have to get everyone's presents.'

Sure enough, as soon as she stepped out of the room, the twins began to squawk in unison.

CHAPTER 29

Owen by day:

White school shirt (Asda)
Black school trousers (same)
Black school socks (same)
School tie (St Vincent's uniform store)
Hair clay (Brylcreem)
Total est. cost: £30

'Just a weeny corner?'

I t was 4.30 in the morning, but Annie was jet-lagged and so wide awake that she'd had to give up lying in bed.

For the past half an hour she'd been in the tiny room which served as her office space and the overflow of her wardrobe. Here she was soothing herself with one of her favourite occupations: a mini-wardrobe cleanse.

Tomorrow was the first day of October, officially time to lay her Spring/Summer wardrobe to rest. She was sorting through a rail of clothes, with the aim of dividing things up into store, sell, give away or keep out for autumn wear.

Annie loved clothes. Yes, she loved shopping, but she really loved clothes. There was a difference. People who loved shopping often didn't wear their purchases more than a few times before they hid them in the back of the cupboard and went out shopping again. Annie couldn't imagine committing such a waste.

She shopped with great care and attention, mindful of the things she needed, mindful of the seasons and the up and coming events. Yes, of course, like everyone who loved clothes, she was often seduced by the treasures and once in a lifetime finds which threw themselves at her when she was looking for something else. But most of the clothes in her wardrobe were regularly worn.

Well . . . that's how it had been in the past. Now, she had to accept that there was a large selection of things which she was either going to have to fit back into or move on out.

A large pink storage box was open on the floor. Tenderly taking out of her wardrobe a selection of light dresses she hadn't worn once this summer because of waistband issues, she decided that she would store them just for this winter. If by next April the Gawain magic hadn't worked and she couldn't get back into them, then she would have to pass them on.

Folding hundreds and hundreds of pounds' worth of clothes into the box, she realized how expensive it was to gain weight. Her whole philosophy of buying nice things and keeping them for years would have to change. She would either have to have far, far fewer expensive clothes, if she was going to have to size up every few years, or she'd have to find more bargains.

The weight was costing her. And she didn't like it. Not one little bit.

Annie had desperately wanted to seduce her unhappy husband tonight. But she hadn't been able to. He'd been so down, he'd just curled up in bed, accepting only hugs and pleading with her to understand that he just wasn't in the mood.

Much as she wanted to believe this was all about the school problem, she couldn't help asking herself: if she'd been foxier and fitter, maybe she'd have been able to banish thoughts of it from his mind for at least a little bit.

He hadn't even cheered up much at her gifts. The lovely Brooks Brothers shirt and tie had been admired in the packet, then put to the side.

Annie's attention turned to her summer shoe and handbag collection. Now, here was happiness. Here were the items which loved you right back no matter how many pounds you put on.

Was she going to be one of those ladies, though? Dressed from head to toe in stretchy and forgiving black, but wearing Gucci shoes and carrying a stunningly expensive bag as a sort of charm to ward off evil looks? It would be like turning into one of the Arabian princesses Annie had often dressed in The Store. They had priceless shoes, handbags and jewels but in between they were just swathed in draping black. It seemed such a shame.

She cleaned the summer sandals gently with a damp cloth and dried them, before returning them to their boxes. The shoeboxes were then placed into the storage chest.

The best thing about putting items away like this was that when spring came around again next year, it would feel like her birthday when she opened the boxes filled with all these treasures once again.

She checked the handbags for stray contents and found a strip of passport photos of Owen.

Ha! Owen!

Now, he had been delighted with his New York presents. 'Mum! What a total star!' he'd exclaimed, fanning out all the DVDs she'd found for him in her one harried trip to Bleecker Bob's. He'd immediately grabbed the NYC Police Department T-shirt and put it on over his school shirt and tie. 'Loving it, totally loving it!'

Then, because he was still her little boy, no matter how endlessly long his arms, legs and feet seemed to grow, she'd presented him with Reese's Pieces, Hershey's Kisses, multi-flavoured jelly beans and a bag of personalized M&Ms.

'Mum! I love you!' he'd yelled, wrapping his gangly arms around her and immediately breaking into the jelly beans and offering them all around.

'No, no the babies can't have them!' she'd told him off.

'Maybe just a weeny corner of Reese's?' he'd suggested.

Good old Owen. Annie smiled at the passport photos. She remembered the day they went to get them done. He'd hated them because his hair was too flat, insisting on ruffling up his mop and going into the booth again, while Annie had slipped the rejected photos into her bag.

She'd liked the pictures because when his hair was flat like this, he looked just slightly younger and smaller. Funny how when your children were tiny, you so looked forward to each new stage and each new accomplishment – baby's first word, baby's first step, baby's first shoes . . . But then round about age 10, they began to grow too fast, they began to look too big, seemed too independent and suddenly you wanted to halt time, put bricks on their heads, feed them shrinking powder and keep them small.

It seemed like suddenly time had sped up and rushed by. Look at Lana. She was now grown up enough to be staying in New York all on her own.

Annie went back to the wardrobe and pulled out the next piece waiting on the rail for her assessment: a lovely, classic trench coat by the British label, Aquascutum, as worn by Cary Grant, Humphrey Bogart, Sophia Loren, even HM the Queen. This coat had accommodated her extra inches without the slightest protest. For that reason alone, she put it back on the rail.

There was still hours of sorting to be done in here. Once she'd packed away all the summer things, she would take her winter boxes out, draw up a list of Most Needed items and plan for the season ahead.

Plan for the season ahead . . . Tucking up a little Marc Jacobs clutch into its soft cloth bag . . . Annie wondered what the season ahead would bring.

She had managed to talk to Tamsin earlier in the day to explain that she was back in London. Tamsin hadn't sold the programme to Channel Five and was still annoyed that Annie hadn't made it to the meeting.

'What do you think about a celebrity fitness show?' Annie had suggested. 'I met this amazing trainer out in New York. He's unbelievable. He's got me working out. ME!'

Tamsin had taken down a few details, not sounding convinced.

But Annie had to get back into the TV game, or else where would she be? Back sorting out other people's wardrobes, as well as her own, she thought gloomily.

Suddenly she felt far too tired to tackle the winter boxes. She decided to go back to bed. She would try and get some sleep, then set about sorting all kinds of things out in the morning.

★ ★ ★

Annie had only been asleep for a few minutes when she was woken by Dave's fierce barks.

'What's up?' she asked, feeling blurry and confused with tiredness. 'Ed, what's up?' She nudged him in the back.

Now she could hear the doorbell ringing as Dave's barking grew more and more frantic.

Several long rings were followed by a shout which had both Ed and Annie leaping from the bed.

'POLICE!'

CHAPTER 30

Owen by night:

Blue and white PJ bottoms (vintage M&S)
Red T-shirt (vintage Next)
Touch of spot cream (Clearasil)
Total est. cost: £15

'*The guys dropped it round.*'

'Lights! Turn on the lights!' Annie leapt down the stairs, well ahead of Ed who was struggling with dressing gown, slippers and trying to shake off deep sleep.

'I'm here, it's OK, I'm opening the door,' she called at the top of her voice and hit the light switch in the hallway. Heart racing, she threw back the locks and flung open the door to find herself face to face with four uniformed police officers.

The first one introduced himself as Inspector Williams and explained that he and his officers had a search warrant. Then they stepped into the house.

This could not be happening. How could this be happening?

Two officers had gone straight up the stairs and one was making for the sitting room before she could even get her first shocked words out.

'There's been a mistake. There must be some mistake,' she blurted. 'This is a family home . . . no one here's ever broken the law.'

'I'm very sorry, but we have a warrant to search this address. Now, please stay here,' Inspector Williams told her in a firm-but-fair, polite-but-in-charge voice. 'My officers will hold other members of the household in separate rooms. We don't want any conferring.'

Hold. Separate rooms?

'My kids are upstairs,' Annie began. 'My son's asleep in his attic room and the babies . . .' Before she could get the words out, she felt a sob push up between her shoulder blades.

The inspector looked at her with some concern. 'I'll escort you upstairs to the babies. You can wait with them in their room if you like.'

So Annie sat on the floor of Minnie and Micky's room while she listened to police carry out a systematic search of her house.

'What is this about?' she heard Ed ask in confusion from the bedroom. 'Surely you have to tell me?'

'Yes, once we have everything we need, we'll explain. Computers, sir? Where will we find all the computers in the house?'

As Ed began to list the locations, a horrible thought sprang up in Annie's mind. Computers?! This must be to do with Ed's suspension. The school had called in the police! And they'd not even warned Ed. Not given him a chance to plead his total innocence. Was this going to be in the newspapers? Would Ed have to go to court? Annie's head sank into her hands. This was a nightmare: *Posh school's music teacher's porn shame.* She felt as if she was going to be sick. But this was Ed. This was the man she loved and trusted absolutely. He was completely innocent. She had to do everything she could for him – and that included not falling apart. Not even for one second.

She could hear the police officers in her little office next door, probably raking through the Spring/Summer treasures she'd so carefully put away earlier tonight.

'Up here,' came a call from the attic.

The attic? *Owen!!*

Annie went to stand at the door. She'd been told not to leave the room where the babies were somehow managing to sleep through this, but she had to try to work out what was going on.

All the policemen now seemed to be upstairs. Dave was still barking like a mad thing downstairs. Ed looked out through the opened bedroom door and saw Annie standing there. There was blank dismay on both their faces.

'What is this?' she mouthed.

'No idea,' he mouthed back, shaking his head.

Ed looked as if he might cry. With everything else going on this was too much for him, the final straw. He kept pushing his hands through his wild hair and Annie wanted to run over and put her arms around him.

'What's going on?' she anxiously asked the policeman who was standing by the stairs. 'Why has everyone gone up to my son's room? He's only fourteen. I need to go up there. He doesn't deserve to be woken up like this.'

'Is your son Owen Valentine?' the policeman asked.

'Yes.'

'And he's only fourteen?'

'Yes!'

'Are you sure?'

'Don't be daft, of course I'm sure!'

'Well, OK, I think you better go up.'

Annie raced up the little attic stairs. Owen was sitting up in bed. His hair was on end and his face one great 'O' of surprise.

'Hey Owen,' Annie said gently.

'If you could just stay right where you are,' came the sharp instruction.

Annie stood on the threshold.

The officers were moving very complex looking computer equipment around the room. They seemed to be unearthing it from various corners and collecting it in a heap at the door.

This stuff did not look as if it had anything to

do with the old computer, bought at a school auction, which Owen used for his homework.

'What is this?' Annie asked her son in astonishment.

She saw the pile of jelly beans and chocolates carefully stacked at the side of his bed. This was her boy. Why on earth were police officers moving sophisticated computer equipment around his room?

'I was supposed to look after it. The guys dropped it round a few weeks ago.'

'Which guys?' one of the officers asked sharply.

Owen shrank back against his headboard.

'The ones I work with on the stall.'

'And you are Owen Valentine?' the inspector asked.

'Yes . . .' Owen sounded very scared.

Annie didn't care what she'd just been told, she moved over to his bed to sit beside him and no one stopped her.

'We've got a warrant to search your address because we've reason to believe that on your market stall at Elephant and Castle you're selling pirated DVDs, CDs and X-rated DVDs which you are making here on this equipment.'

Owen's mouth fell open.

'Owen's just fourteen,' Annie interrupted. 'Doesn't he have some protection from . . . from all this?'

'I just help to sell it . . .' Owen protested, 'I don't make any of it.'

'There's a stall at Elephant and Castle registered in your name,' the officer went on.

'He's fourteen!' Annie repeated. 'How can he have a stall registered in his name?'

The inspector seemed to soften a little.

'Well, son . . . where has all this stuff come from?' He pointed to the equipment heaped in the middle of the room.

'From the other guys on the stall. They run everything. I just help with the selling.'

'Do you sell the X-rated stuff?'

'Not usually . . .' Owen said, turning his eyes down.

'Have your market stall friends been working on their computers in your house?' was the next question.

Annie saw a hideously guilty look steal over Owen's face.

'Well . . . they were moving flats and they brought this stuff here, to keep it safe . . . and they may have done a bit of work up here . . . just a couple of afternoons . . . It wasn't much.'

Much as Annie felt flooded with fear, anger and terrible anxiety about her son, a growing ray of understanding was filtering through her mind.

Copying porn . . . If someone had been in this house *copying porn* . . . if they'd used Owen and Ed's computer . . . if they'd somehow got into the school system . . . this might explain everything.

'Look, I know it's early,' the inspector began, 'but we've got a lot of questions for you, Owen.

So I think it would be best if you and one of your parents could come down to the station with us. If you're lucky, we'll buy you breakfast. The canteen isn't half as bad as everyone makes out.'

This raised a small laugh from the two other officers in the room.

'You want us to come to the police station *now*?' Annie asked, not sure she could quite believe what was happening.

'Yes, my officers here are going to take the equipment,' Inspector Williams explained, 'then if Owen and you or his dad could come with us to help with inquiries, I hope that will be the quickest way of getting things sorted out. If Owen here's been selling pirated goods, then I'm afraid he's still in a lot of trouble.'

CHAPTER 31

QC Harry in action:

Bespoke blue shirt (Curtis and Dyer)
Bespoke blue suit (Gieves & Hawkes)
Gold cufflinks (Svetlana)
Black Oxford shoes (Church's)
Total est. cost: £4,300

'Splendid to meet you.'

Annie travelled to the station in the back of a police car with her son, both of them wearing crazed, jumbled outfits made up of whatever they'd been able to find in a hurry.

Ed stayed behind with the twins. Annie decided not to tell him her porn suspicions yet, because she wanted to be certain. She didn't want to give him the false hope that it would all be solved, until she knew much more.

'Owen's market stall's been selling pirated DVDs, he has to go to the station to tell them everything he knows about it,' Annie had explained as she'd been led down to the bedroom to change.

'Pirated? I thought everything was second-hand! And anyway, did they really need to send round four policemen in the middle of the night?' Ed had exclaimed.

In the back of the police car now, Annie was desperate to ask Owen all sorts of questions, but she felt the heavy presence of the officers in the car and thought it would be better if she didn't say anything just yet.

She tried to be a comforting presence for him, rubbing his shoulder and saying reassuring things like: 'It's going to be OK' and 'Don't worry.' Meanwhile, she felt very worried.

But with a start, she remembered Svetlana's Harry. That was who she needed to call immediately for advice. She took out her phone, checked it was OK with the officers then dared to dial Svetlana's home phone number at 6.15 in the morning.

It rang for a long time. By the seventh ring, Annie had almost lost her nerve. She imagined an irate Svetlana on the other end of the line berating her about lost beauty sleep.

Instead a sleepy, heavily accented voice answered and Annie realized at once that it was Maria, Svetlana's maid.

'Hello Maria, this is Annie Valentine, Svetlana's friend . . .'

Maria didn't say anything.

'I need to speak to Harry, if it's possible.'

'Miss Valentina, is very, very early,' Maria pointed out.

'I know, but it's an emergency, my son is in trouble . . . with the police.' As Annie said this, she heard the dangerous wobble in her voice.

'The police? They have your son?' Maria had grasped the important elements.

'Yes!' Annie confirmed, 'please, if I could speak to Harry, just on the phone. I need to get some advice. I need to know what we should do.'

'I go and knock on their door. I find out if he can come to the phone,' Maria said.

There was a long wait. Annie gripped the phone to her ear, crossing her fingers. If she could just hear Harry's reassuring voice on the other end of the line, she would feel much better.

'Annie?'

There he was!

'Harry, I'm so, so sorry to wake you up like this but I'm in a police car. They're taking Owen to the station . . .'

'Don't mention it, really. Delighted you thought of me. It's absolutely no trouble at all,' he assured her in his distantly-related-to-Royalty plummy voice. 'Which police station is it?'

As soon as she told him, he said: 'OK, I'll meet you both there.'

'Are you sure?' she asked, but she was smiling at Owen now, a wave of relief washing over her.

'Of course, no trouble at all. Now, just tell your boy not to say much to those chaps until I get there. On my way. Toodle pip.'

Now when Annie turned to Owen and said 'It's going to be OK', she was much more convinced of it.

Annie hadn't been inside a police station before. Well, not past the reception area. This station was very brightly lit with fluorescent strip lights in long rows along the ceiling. With Inspector Williams leading the way, they walked through wide corridors, passing rooms filled with desks, computer screens and untidy stacks of paper-work.

She didn't want to be here and she certainly didn't want Owen to be here. Her son was involved with pirated goods! Even if he hadn't known too much about it, the people he worked with were breaking the law.

What if the market stall guys were here too? Gangster film plot-lines began speeding through her mind . . . what if they were going to try and stop Owen talking? She broke into an anxious sweat.

But there was Harry, striding towards them, cheery greetings not just for them but also for the inspector leading them through the station. Harry was as neatly suited and booted as if he'd just strolled out of his office, rather than been shaken from his bed.

'Hello, hello there, lovely to see you.' He swooped down on Annie for a cheek to cheek kiss, as if they were meeting at a garden party.

'Owen, *splendid* to meet you.' Harry held out his hand for a bemused Owen to shake. 'Now, Inspector Williams, before we get settled down for any sort of formal interview, I'll need to know all about your allegations, then I'll have to have a jolly quick chat with my man here –' he put his hand on Owen's shoulder. It was a firm, protective hand and it signalled to Annie that Harry would take good care of Owen.

Once Harry had spoken in private to the inspector, a tiny interview room was found and Annie, Harry and Owen were ushered inside.

Here, Harry made sure Annie had a cup of tea at her side before he began calmly questioning Owen.

'So what was the stall selling, Owen?'

'CDs and DVDs.'

'And you actually took part in selling these?'

'Yeah.'

'You offered them for sale and you took the cash?'

'Yeah.'

'Did you know that the CDs and DVDs were illegal copies?'

'Well . . . some were proper second-hand, we bought them used from customers. But some looked a bit dodgy,' Owen admitted.

'Owen!' Annie hissed, but she bit her lip at a glance from Harry.

'Did you have anything to do with copying CDs or DVDs?'

'No.'

'Absolutely certain about that?' Harry asked.

'Yeah.'

'Did you see anyone making copies?'

'No.'

'Totally positive about that too?'

'Yeah.'

'But you sold some CDs and DVDs that "looked dodgy" to you.'

'Yeah.'

'Did you sell porn DVDs, Owen?'

'Not many,' Owen said, giving his mum a guilty glance.

'Right . . .' Harry paused to make some notes. 'So how did all that equipment end up in your bedroom?' he asked.

'The guys who run the stall asked me to look after it because they were moving flats.'

'Did they drop it off?'

'Yeah . . . they did it when I was the only person at home.' Owen at least looked slightly shamefaced about this.

'I see. What are the names of the people who run your stall?'

'Does he have to tell the police?' Annie squeaked, vividly imagining gang bosses turning up at their house in the dark of night intent on silencing her son . . . *aaaaargh*!

'There's Dimitri, Sandy and Rob,' Owen replied.

'Do you know their last names?'

Owen screwed his eyes with concentration: 'I think Dimitri's is Theodopolus. Don't think I know anyone else's.'

'Do you know their addresses?'

'No. We just meet at the stall every week.'

'How did you get to know these guys, Owen?'

'We just got talking at the market one day.'

'I see,' Harry said lightly, but Annie felt her face burn with shame.

She'd let her 14-year-old son work on a market stall with people she'd not even met. Somehow she'd assumed maybe Ed had met them . . . or that Owen knew them through school friends. It had never occurred to her that these were dodgy blokes who'd got talking to her son one day and drawn him in to a *life of crime*! She should probably be grateful that Owen was only involved in DVD piracy. He could have been *abducted* and sold into *sexual slavery* by now. Quickly, she began to look in her handbag for tissues, convinced she was going to cry.

'Do you have their mobile phone numbers?' Harry continued.

'Yes. On my phone.' Owen reached into his anorak pocket, brought out a mobile and held it out to Harry.

Harry took it from him and slipped it into his

own jacket pocket. 'OK, I think just for now, we'll say you haven't brought your phone . . . if it comes up.

'Right, so you knew them by their first names, you didn't do any copying, but you did sell their stuff for them. Did you apply for the market stall licence?'

'No, don't know anything about that,' Owen shrugged.

'They've put the stall in your name, I believe.'

'How?' Annie wondered.

'Maybe they just sauntered along to the town hall with some forged documents in Owen's name.'

'But why not just use another made-up name?'

'Indeed.'

With his fountain pen, Harry wrote further notes. As Annie watched his loopy, illegible hand-writing form across the page, she once again felt soothed.

'OK Owen, here's the plan,' Harry said when he'd finished writing. 'Be very, very nice and polite to our officers. Tell them everything you've told me – except the tiny bit about your phone – and if we're extremely lucky, we might get off with a caution.'

As Harry led Owen in for his police interview, Annie had to wait on a hard plastic chair outside and brood. Her son was in a police station being interviewed about things he had done while she was gallivanting on the other side of the world. The guilt was going to kill her. She should have been right here, looking after him. She should have meddled right into his business. The money he was making! No way should she have turned such a blind eye to it. Money didn't appear out of nowhere! People had to work hard for it. How much more of an alarm bell had she needed than for her 14-year-old son to be sending his dad to New York for a weekend?!

'Annie, they're just going to caution Owen now,' Harry said, suddenly at her shoulder. She'd been so lost in guilt, she hadn't even heard him come out. 'You can come in for this . . . if you'd like to.'

Feeling dazed and mentally bruised, Annie walked out of the police station with a jaunty Owen and the ever-charming Harry, who clicked open the locks on his Bentley, held out the door for Annie and insisted that he give them a lift home.

There were so many things Annie needed to say to Owen. She had to make sure he was OK. She needed to ensure that he'd understood exactly what had happened here today. But these things would have to wait until they were back home, because right now, there was an urgent question for Harry burning in her mind.

'Harry . . . thank you so much for what you did here for us today.'

'Don't even mention it,'

'There's something else I really need to talk to you about.'

'Go on,' Harry said.

'Those people were copying porn in our house – on Owen's computer. Is there any way that what they were copying could have somehow got on to the computer system at Owen's school?'

'Oh God!' Owen slapped his forehead dramatically, 'that's it! That's how it happened!'

Annie looked round at Owen in the back seat.

'What?' she asked.

'Well, I know all about Dad's suspension. I mean, I know you and Dad haven't told me the full details but it's all anyone can talk about at school. But that's it! That's how the viral stuff has ended up all over the school system and been traced back to Dad's computer. Dimitri and the guys said they needed more back-up, so I gave them the password . . .'

When Owen saw the horrified look on his mother's face, he exclaimed: 'I didn't know they were copying porn. Honestly, I had no idea.'

'Owen!' she hissed, 'you are grounded . . . for the rest of the year! For the rest of your bloomin' life!'

'So, what's all this about Ed?' Harry wanted to know.

The more Annie told him about the situation, the more astonished Harry looked.

'I don't believe it,' he spluttered. 'I mean, yes, I can totally believe that Owen's dodgy Daves have managed to infect the entire St Vincent's system, but I can't believe you let Ed stew about under a simply horrendous cloud like this without phoning me immediately! The school has suspended him, without a single shred of evidence. That is outrageous! Good Lord, Annie, by the time I've finished with them, they will rue the day. They will jolly well rue the day!'

CHAPTER 32

Mr Ketteringham-Smith:

White shirt (M&S)
Grey suit (Austin Reed)
Blue tie (same)
Black shoes (Jones)
Watch (Timex, gift from mother)
Total est. cost: £450

'I will be writing to your parents . . .'

St Vincent's was an old-fashioned, traditional, private school. It was all about Victorian Gothic cloisters, lashings of wood panelling and children with regulation neat hair wearing woollen blazers.

So it was a little strange to see a bright yellow banner hanging over the school gates which read: 'Bring on Mr Leon.'

'That's nice,' Harry said from behind the wheel of the Bentley as he drove them smoothly into the courtyard. Whenever Svetlana went out in the

337

family's car, she hired a driver for the day. But Harry wasn't flashy, he liked to drive the Bentley himself.

Ed, sitting in the front seat beside Harry, was blushing about the sign. Annie could tell even though she couldn't see his face, because his ears always went red when he blushed.

'Look, Dad,' Owen spotted the banner for the first time: 'someone's put that up there for you! There was talk of everyone wearing badges as well. I wonder if anyone made the badges!'

'You have got to be joking,' was Ed's astonished response.

'I should bloody well think so! After all they've put you through,' Annie said.

The Bentley glided to a standstill in the court-yard and immediately one of the sixth form prefects appeared to open doors and guide the party into the school's reception area.

'Time for me to split,' Owen announced and ducked out of the way to join the rest of his class for the morning's assembly. 'Cheers for the lift, Harry!'

Not long after, the headmaster, Mr Ketteringham-Smith, appeared and shook everyone by the hand, including Ed, who looked increasingly awkward.

'Ms Valentine – or do we call you Mrs Leon?' Ketteringham-Smith asked as he took Annie's hand and pumped it vigorously.

'I'm Mrs Leon today,' Annie told him, trying to

make her smile genuine, but Kettingham-Smith and Annie had never quite seen eye to eye. There had been too many little awkward run-ins in the past. And as for the sight of the school bursar over there, Annie just about shuddered, remembering all the times in the past when she'd had to scrimp and save and pay the fees with a wing and a prayer and a totally over-extended credit card. How he'd looked down his nose at her then. She could never forgive him for that.

'I'm absolutely delighted we can put all this behind us,' Ketteringham-Smith was telling Ed. 'So glad you could all join us for our special assembly. Mr Roscoff, you included.'

Harry shook the head's hand brusquely.

'Well, just want to make sure it's all absolutely up to scratch, sir,' Harry said, smiling with charm, then adding lightly, 'otherwise I'll be advising my client to sue.'

'Oh, there will be no need for that,' K-S laughed nervously.

'I do hope not,' Harry said and smiled just as sweetly as if he'd ordered a Pimm's.

A bell rang, the sound of hundreds of footsteps thundering through the corridors followed and finally Harry, Ed and Annie were led in by the headmaster to take their seats up on the podium beside the other members of staff for this special assembly.

It was only after a hymn, a prayer and various notices for the day ahead that Mr K-S began his speech.

'I would like to welcome back Mr Ed—'

He was interrupted by a cheerful round of applause punctuated with several whistles and whoops.

Annie had always known that Ed was a popular teacher, but such a vivid demonstration brought a lump to her throat.

'I'm sure everyone here has heard all sorts of gossip and rumours about why Mr Leon has been away from school for a brief period. There was a computer virus which spread through the school's system. I'm afraid this virus was, mistakenly, linked to Mr Leon's computer.'

Mr K-S paused, looked up at the school then continued to deliver the difficult speech which Harry had thoroughly vetted.

'I took the decision to suspend Mr Leon. I realize now that this was entirely the wrong decision. Mr Leon is a valuable member of staff who has given us many years of devoted service. There has never, ever been the slightest question as to his conduct or character. So when he told me he was entirely innocent, I should have believed him.

'I am truly sorry that he has had to endure any gossip, rumour or hint that he behaved inappropriately. We should all hold Mr Leon in the highest regard and I will be writing to your parents to explain this situation fully. Thank you.'

As Mr K-S drew to a close, loud applause broke out, accompanied once again by whistles and cheers. Ed, shy and overwhelmed, blushed deeply pink and gave his audience a smile and wave of acknowledgement. Annie reached over to hold his hand in hers and to whisper in his ear: 'Fantastic! You're going to be the school star for a week or two.'

'Looks like it,' Ed whispered back. 'Thanks for being here.'

The pianist struck up a jaunty tune and as the staff got up to file out of the room, the pupils clapped along in unison.

'Well, that's the liveliest assembly we've had in a while,' one of the teachers told Ed and Annie once they were out of the hall. Then Ed was surrounded by staff wanting to shake his hand and welcome him back.

Annie landed a quick kiss on his cheek, told Harry she'd meet him back at the car as soon as she could, and went off in the direction of the headmaster's office.

Right outside, she could see Owen already sitting waiting on one of the chairs set out for this purpose. 'Hey there,' she greeted him and sat down in the chair beside his, 'not feeling too bad about this, are you?'

'The only thing I feel bad about is that it caused Dad so much trouble,' Owen replied, then he ruffled a hand through his hair slightly nervously.

'He knows. He knows how bad you feel,' Annie assured him, 'so you don't have to worry about that. He knows you wouldn't have done any of this on purpose. You just made some very silly mistakes.'

'So what do we tell the headmaster?' Owen wondered.

'We tell him everything, just as simply as we can. We explain it all. He's heard it from Harry and from Inspector Williams, now he wants to hear your version . . .'

'And give me a great big telling off,' Owen added glumly.

'Well, I think you better expect that. He suspended a member of staff over this.'

'Hmm.'

The door opened and Mr Ketteringham-Smith was standing in front of them, pushing his glasses up to the top of his nose. 'Mrs Leon, Owen, time for the high jump, I'm afraid.'

CHAPTER 33

Micky and Minnie on the motorway:

Matching denim dungarees (Baby Gap)
Matching tops (one pink, one blue) (Petit Bateau)
Matching white socks (Baby Gap)
Total est. cost: £55

'Waaaaaaaah!'

On Saturday afternoon, the car wound through busy roads out on to the clogged up motorway towards Annie's mother's house in Essex.

Minnie and Micky were tired and reluctant back-seat passengers, gurning and whingeing despite the relentlessly cheerful *Sesame Street* songs blaring from the iPod. Annie turned from the passenger's seat and stroked their feet, suggesting things to look at out of the window. Finally Minnie fell asleep, and then Micky.

The Muppets sang on, until Ed reached over and pressed the stop button.

'So Owen is playing at a school football match,' Annie whispered to Ed, 'then he's going over to Pete's house and Pete's mum knows there is to be no cinema trip, no outings and we'll collect him at 9p.m.'

'Correct,' Ed confirmed quietly.

'Silly old Owen – how's he going to spend his weekends now that there's no market stall?'

'Oh, you've not heard his new plan then?' Ed glanced over at Annie. 'He's suggested the pupils run a weekly bring and buy sale at school – second-hand stuff, games kit, uniform, toys, DVDs and so on, a percentage of profits to charity. He's going to run it. The headman's OK-ed it. It's quite a good idea, really.'

Annie couldn't help smiling. 'He's going to go far. A born salesman.'

'A chip off the old block, you mean.'

Annie took her phone out of her handbag. 'I want to see how the other one is doing. You know I think some of the Annie sales genes have been passed on in Lana's direction too.'

'No doubt.'

Annie dialled Lana's mobile number and heard the faraway, transatlantic dial tone.

'Mum?' Lana answered.

'Baby! How's it going?' Annie said, so excited to hear her girl she forgot to speak quietly, causing Minnie to stir.

'Great!' came Lana's verdict. 'Dresses flying out! *Flying* out! We've had to take new fabric up to Brad and he's working all weekend to get us more in stock.'

'Fantastic! That is such good news.'

'Elena's on NBC breakfast news tomorrow – it's just unbelievable. They love her Svetlana love-child background. They love it.'

'Did you get good fabric? Good colours?'

'Oh yeah, sea-green silk, just like the colour of your bag. Some buttermilk . . . lots more cotton jersey too because it's so popular. People seem to love the idea of tossing on the dress and feeling comfortable.'

'Brilliant – and you, are you OK?'

'I'm great.'

'Forgotten all about . . . what's-his-face.'

'Totally.'

'Is there a new what's-his-face?'

'Mum! I'm far too busy. We just work and work and then dash out to Whole Foods for a box of dinner.'

With those words, Annie pictured the walk from the apartment, over Fifth Avenue, down 15th Street to buzzing Union Square, and she felt weirdly jealous.

'Any TV news?' Lana asked.

'Well . . . it took a bit of persuading, but Tamsin has suddenly got enthusiastic about doing a celebrity fitness programme. I think she's going to try and speak to Gawain, suss him out a bit more . . . but it's all very early stages. She doesn't have an interested buyer yet.' Annie was trying not to sound too downhearted as she said this: 'We'll see.'

'Poor old Mum,' Lana sympathized, before adding, 'Look, I'm going to have to go. I have a lunch date with Sye and Elena.'

'Ooooh is love in the air?'

'Like, definitely!'

'D'you think if Elena married him, she could wear a Perfect Dress wedding dress?'

'Ooh, great idea. I'll tell them over lunch!'

Annie hung up and turned to Ed. The twins were asleep, her phone was quiet, this was their first chance at a conversation so far today.

'How's Lana?' he asked.

'Fantastic,' Annie told him, 'I don't think she'll be too keen to come home, especially as we've not lined up anything else for her to do yet.'

'We'll work on that.'

'Yeah . . . and how are you?'

'Not too bad. Not too bad at all,' Ed said, shooting her a smile, 'everyone's being very nice to me at school.'

'Bloody right!' Annie said.

'I've had letters and cards from some of the parents.'

'That's very nice, but I should bloody well think so. You didn't deserve to go through one moment of all that.'

His face serious now, Ed added, 'It's been

absolute hell. But knowing that you believed in me totally, that was the one thing which kept me going. I hope you know that.' He reached over and squeezed her hand.

'Well . . . internet porn, it just doesn't seem like your kind of thing. It takes you half an hour to send an email, babes.'

'Back issues of *Vogue* are more my kind of thing.'

'Oh really . . .?'

'But how are you?' he wondered. 'You come all the way back from New York to find out your son's a porn dealer, your husband's suspended and your agent still hasn't signed you up to a new series . . . that's quite a lot to deal with.'

'I know. It's rubbish! I wish I was Lana,' Annie said, more loudly than she'd intended, which had the unfortunate effect of waking Micky, who promptly burst into tears.

'That's done it,' said Ed. Then Minnie began to cry too.

Still, Annie knew there were a few things she wanted to air, so she might as well get them said, even if it was over the cacophony of two screaming babies.

'Ed, I miss New York! I really, really miss New York. I feel the way you do after a bad break-up. I dream about it, I can't help thinking about it all day long. I just want to go back.'

Ed looked over at her, clearly surprised at this outburst, but Annie was in full flow.

'It was so glamorous there. So fashion, so

career-focused, so go-ahead. I felt as if anything could happen. Any plan could come off if I just tried hard enough. It just felt very me, that's the only way I can describe it. Ed, a big part of me hates the fact that I'm back here, dealing with school problems and the TV standstill and the domestic grind.'

Finally Ed managed a quiet, 'Oh.'

Then he pointed ahead. 'Look, there's a car park. We'll stop for a minute and sort out M&M. But Annie, you'll be back to work soon and then you'll feel much better.'

'I don't know if I want to go back,' she confessed. 'Nothing Tamsin sorts out is going to be as good as *How Not To Shop*. I had my own show on Channel Four, Ed! I don't want to step down from that. I can't run the same programme on a much smaller channel. It just wouldn't be as good.'

'Maybe there will be a different programme altogether?'

'Maybe. But I don't have a good feeling about it. Tamsin's all excited about another new project she has lined up. I'm feeling *over*. Just like Connor warned.'

Ed parked the car, causing the cries of the twins to nudge up another level.

'Step out of the vehicle,' he said to her with a little bit of a smile.

He got out too, shutting his door and telling her to do the same. She immediately reached over to open the back door and scoop up the babies.

'Just a minute,' Ed urged and walked round to her side of the car. 'Please, just a tiny minute of silence.' Annie looked in on the babies: they were red-faced with crying, but she couldn't hear them through the window glass. It was tempting to enjoy just one moment of peace. 'We have the whole day to dote over them,' he told her. 'Can we just look after us for a second?'

He put his arms around her and held her close. 'This has all been very hard for you. Me and the school, Owen and the police! Your show getting cancelled. It's been a tough few days.'

'You should have phoned Harry straight away like I told you to.'

'Yes, I should have. I totally should have. But Annie, what about you?' Ed ran his hand over her hair soothingly. 'What do you want to do? What do you really want to do?'

'I want to move,' she heard herself blurting out. 'I used to move all the time. Now it's been years and years and I want new places, new chances. I want to be part of the whole thrilling *thing* again.'

'You want to move . . .' Ed began hesitantly, 'to New York?'

She didn't answer, or dare to move. Did she really want to move to New York? Did she really want to leave London for Manhattan? Had Ed guessed at her heart's desire before she had really decided for herself?

Ed's voice had a new, slightly nervous tone to it as he asked, uncertainly, 'With all of us?'

CHAPTER 34

Fern in the garden:

Pale green cardi (John Lewis)
White and green blouse (Hobbs)
White trousers (Lands' End)
Comfy green sandals (same)
Total est. cost: £180

'. . . going out in a blaze of glory.'

As the car pulled up in front of the home Annie's mother had lived in for many years, Annie's mind was racing with plans. Could they move? Could they really move? Would they rent out the house? Sell the house? What could Ed do in New York? Could he teach music there? Would it be easy to move if Annie was working with Svetlana's company? Would they all be able to get visas?

What about Owen? Would he want to leave school for a move like this? And Lana? All her friends would be left behind in London.

It would be easy enough for the babies to move – but then what about Dinah? When Annie asked herself this question, she felt a big pang. Dinah couldn't move with them. Dinah had a husband, Bryan, and a daughter of her own, Billie, and they were all very happily settled in London.

With no beloved sister to look after the twins, she would have to find one of those New York nannies. The kind she'd seen in Central Park, wheeling the tiny 'Hudson Juniors' about in the most up-to-the-nanosecond strollers.

Maybe Owen could go to business school . . . he'd probably get in early. Maybe Lana would want to work for Perfect Dress—

'Annie!'

Her mum was already at the front door, smiling delightedly, waving them all in.

'Hello Mum!'

With Minnie in her arms, Annie walked up the path, marvelling at how luscious and beautiful the garden still looked for October. She hugged her mother hello.

'Hello, hello, my girls,' Fern smiled at them, 'and how are my boys?' she asked, turning her attention to Ed and Micky.

Annie studied her mum closely. She looked just a little smaller and frailer today. Sometimes when Annie saw her, she thought her mum looked better and stronger. Sometimes, like today, she thought she looked just a little more vulnerable.

Just over a year ago now, Fern had been diagnosed with early-onset dementia and every time Annie saw her, she was frightened that the condition would be worse.

Fern didn't need care yet, but a student nurse rented a room in Fern's house as a temporary solution, so there was someone on hand who could let Fern's daughters know in between their visits if their mother wasn't looking after herself properly.

'How are you?' Annie said, giving her mum another hug and slipping a hand around her waist. Fern felt comfortingly solid. 'You're eating well then,' Annie said, relieved.

'Yes, too well. Stefano is a very good cook. Did you know that? Whenever he has an evening in, he makes us both a wonderful supper. He's not nearly as good as Ed, though,' she added quickly, reaching up to kiss both Ed and Micky.

'The garden looks beautiful,' Annie told her.

'I know, doesn't it just? I've been working away all summer long and now it's going out in a blaze of glory.'

Fern proudly gave a mini-tour of the bushes and plants she was most pleased with this season.

Annie tried to listen with interest but really, gardening was not her thing. Maybe in some dim and distant time in the future, when all her children had grown up, she might enjoy pottering round the flower beds planting things and taking as much delight in the new season's flowers and shrubs as she did in the new season's clothes and accessories. But right now, her garden was a simple patch of irregularly mown lawn, strewn with toddler toys and the odd unhappy plant in a tub which she struggled to keep alive.

'So tell me all about New York,' Fern said, as they went inside to the sitting room and sat down, 'I want to hear everything. The Empire State Building, the museums, the shops. That must be a wonderful city, I'll bet.'

Annie did tell, thinking of all the places she'd been, all the sights, the hustle and bustle, the noise, the roaring sense of ambition to the place.

'People are so focused,' she said, 'they're all looking fantastic, they're all jostling, they've got things to do, places to be, ladders to climb . . .'

'You *loved* it, didn't you?' Fern asked, smiling, pouring tea and understanding her daughter perfectly.

'I did. I absolutely loved it. Now that I'm back . . . I think I feel homesick.'

Ed laughed quietly, while Fern shook her head. 'But you're not planning a move or anything dramatic, are you?' she asked, her eyes catching Annie's.

'Well . . . you never know. It might be really interesting to go for . . . well . . . a year or so.'

She saw the stricken look in Fern's eyes straight away. 'But I can't move over with you, you know,' her mum said, stirring her tea, 'there's the garden.'

Oh for goodness' sake! This is what gardeners got

like – they couldn't leave the country for a fortnight, terrified they'd miss the philo-dilo-whatsit presenting its one and only blossom of the year.

'Then there's . . .' Fern carried on stirring, 'there's the problem with the . . . you know . . . oh, what is it again?' The infuriated look which accompanied every one of Fern's regular senior moments crossed her face.

'Planes? You don't like to fly?' Ed wondered, trying to be helpful.

'Love flying . . . No the – what's it called? That nice man who's in charge. He's trying to sort it out. Oh! What's his name? I can't remember anything . . .' she looked upset now.

'Relax, Mum,' Annie soothed, 'yoga breaths, it will come.'

'The money you have to pay, for doctors . . .'

'Health insurance,' Ed said, understanding now.

'Thank you Ed. Health insurance. How can I possibly move over there in my state? It would probably cost £100 a day just to let me come in. I'm not sure if I could even visit you very often. And who is the nice man in charge?'

'Barack Obama?' Ed said.

Annie moved along the sofa so that she was right beside her mother. She put an arm around her and leaned her head so that it was on her mum's shoulder. She breathed in Chanel No. 19, plus the liquid soap which had been used to gently handwash the beige cashmere cardigan draped over her mum's shoulders.

Annie closed her eyes for a moment and went through the pros and cons in her mind. What if something happened to her mum when she was on the other side of the Atlantic? She tried to imagine having to make some terrible, lonely and tormented journey home.

Then she thought of Dinah and Billie: the one growing older and the other growing up. She would miss so much of that time, wouldn't really know either of them as incredibly well as she did now.

She thought of Owen trying to fit in at a new school. He'd never had to move school before.

And Ed might have to look after the babies all day long because he didn't have a work permit.

But then Fifth Avenue crept temptingly into her thoughts: hot and heady, sparkling with lights, shop windows, the steady stream of yellow cabs, honking horns, packed with life, energy and excitement.

She thought of Elena and the thrill of the dress sales. They'd made a dress together which Emily Wilmington had chosen to wear on her date with Josh Hartnett! It still amazed her. Emily Wilmington, who could pick any dress from the *Vanity Fair* rails which took her fancy, had worn their dress for her film-star date.

'Mumma.' Minnie, clutching at the table leg for support, threw her head into Annie's lap. 'Mummmmmma,' she repeated, burying her face

355

against Annie's leg. Annie touched the silky hair on Minnie's head.

Just as she'd told Ed in New York, she *loved* having attachments, and she wouldn't have it any other way.

CHAPTER 35

Lana homeward bound:

Black and white maxi dress (Banana Republic sale)
White flip-flops (pavement stall)
Big Apple pendant necklace (gift from Elena)
Huge black and white tote (Macy's)
Total est. cost: $70

'I'll miss you too . . .'

The sharp blast of the buzzer startled Elena. She looked up from her computer screen at Lana, who was sitting on the sofa bed, surrounded by luggage and dresses in long plastic wrappers.

'Your cab?' Elena asked in surprise.

'I think so.'

Lana went to the door and lifted the speaker phone from its cradle.

'Hi . . . yes, OK . . .' She turned to inform Elena, 'it's the cab.'

'Already?' Elena sounded sad.

'Yeah . . . I guess I have to go.' Lana sounded sad too.

'It is terrible,' Elena said. She got up from the table and flung her long arms around Lana.

'When will I see you again, my wonderful worker? When are you coming back to Perfect Dress?'

'We've talked about that,' Lana reminded her.

'No one looks as good in the navy jersey as you,' Elena said, pulling away from Lana reluctantly.

'Thanks, but you rock the magenta.' With that Lana picked up her handbag and two large holdalls.

'No, I help. I come down with you,' Elena insisted.

They rode the elevator down chatting about the busy week Perfect Dress was about to have. The dresses were out on sale now and Elena and Svetlana were launching an all-out PR offensive. Elena was still trying to persuade Emily Wilmington in person to come on board as an official face of Perfect Dress.

'When do the next lot of new fabrics come in?' Lana asked.

'Tomorrow. Is so, so sad you miss them. Navy silks and deep pink chiffon for winter. Turquoise for spring.'

'And how about pewter silk?' Lana asked, 'to carry on the elegant, understated theme.'

'Good idea!'

Out on the pavement, they hugged tightly once

again and as Lana got into the cab, they promised to stay in touch.

'I'll let you know, just as soon as I can,' were Lana's parting words as she hung from the open cab window, waving.

'I'll miss you!'

'I'll miss you too. I'll miss Manhattan more!' Lana called.

Then the cab was off down the street. Elena followed it for a moment or two, then realized someone was walking along the pavement towards her – waving.

She watched, not just with her eyes, but somehow also with her heart. And her heart beat faster and opened wide. Wide as the grin now stretching across her face. And his.

'Sye!' she called.

He ran the last 20 metres or so towards her. Once he'd snatched her up, whirled her round and kissed her on the mouth, he asked, 'Have you missed me just as much as I've missed you?'

'Well . . .' She laced her fingers behind his neck, let her eyes melt into his, 'maybe . . . maybe just a little bit.'

'How long has it been?'

She looked at her watch, 'Seven and half hours.'

'Too long, way too long.'

'You are early.'

Sye shook his head: 'No, I'm taking you on a little trip before our very important *appointment*.'

'A trip, I can't go on a trip. I have very busy

schedule,' Elena protested but she kept her arms around his waist and her face turned to his, playfully willing to be persuaded.

'Let's call it your lunch break. C'mon, we'll go up to the apartment, get your bag and then we'll go.'

But the privacy of the elevator and then the even greater privacy of Elena's apartment – all her own for the first time in four weeks – was too much of a temptation for a couple so expressively in love.

Elena was attempting to undo Sye's belt buckle by floor nine and he'd already succeeded in unleashing her bra. They ran from the elevator to the apartment door and kissed and caressed while Elena fumbled with the keys. As soon as the lock was opened, they hurried inside and began to make love right up against the other side of the door.

She felt his pulse leap under the touch of her lips on his neck. He was pushing against her, sliding his hand up her leg, moving her dress out of the way, then the wispy slip of underwear.

Up on her tiptoes, leaning against the apartment door, she took him inside, her fingers clinging to his buttocks.

'Sye. Yes . . . yes . . .' she heard herself gasping as she ran her hands over her breasts, desperate to bring the tingling, shuddering tension to breaking point.

★ ★ ★

'Is there still time . . . to go on your trip?'

'The trip!' Sye sat up from the doze he'd fallen into on Elena's bed and glanced at his watch. 'Quick! Clothes back on. I think there's still time, if we hurry up.'

Outside again, Sye took Elena's hand in his and hurried her towards the subway station where they got onto a train bound for the Lower East Side.

'Are you going to tell me what this is about?' Elena asked, sitting as close to Sye as she could, fitting her shoulder snugly under his arm.

'No. Surprise.'

They got off at the last stop before the train tunnelled under the water and out towards Brooklyn, then Sye led her by the hand out of the station and through several streets much shabbier than the glittering midtown she was used to. Discount food stores, drugstores and all the smaller, cheaper shops of a neighbourhood like this, lined the streets.

'And here we are,' Sye announced, pulling Elena to a stop in front of a nondescript luggage shop. Cheap bags and suitcases filled the windows and a pavement display of plastic shoulder bags and multi-coloured shoppers had been set up outside.

'What is this?'

'This is 135 Orchard Street.'

'So?'

'This is a very important address for my family. What you need to know is that the ultra-glamorous Mrs Westhoven of the Upper East Side, married to

Sam Westhoven, and chief buyer for Bloomingdale's, grew up in a tiny apartment on the top floor of number 135.'

Elena's eyes widened in surprise. 'No!'

'Not only that, but Sylvia Westhoven once worked in her parents' grocery store which used to be right there where the luggage place is now.'

'Really?' Elena could hardly believe it.

'Yeah. And her parents were . . .' Sye paused, knowing Elena would find this almost unbelievable, 'immigrants who came to New York with . . . nothing.'

'No,' she breathed. 'From where?'

'Poland.'

'Poland? Are you kidding me?'

Sye shook his head.

'She is an Eastern European girl, just like me. Why you wait so long to tell me this?' There was an accusing flash in Elena's eyes.

'I don't know . . . I didn't know my grandparents, I never think of my mother as "foreign", it was only when this meeting came up that I really thought about it.'

'Sye, why is she so against me?'

'I don't know. Maybe you remind her too much of everything she used to be but isn't any more. She's not a person who wants to look back. She considers herself High New York Society now.'

'She used to work in a grocery store on the Lower East Side? And her parents came to New

York from Poland?' Elena wanted to make sure she'd heard all this properly.

'Yes . . . I think I've got that right.'

'And now she lives in Upper East Side with very rich lawyer husband and has big important department store job?'

'Yeah . . .' Sye pushed his hair from his face and looked almost embarrassed by the grandeur of his family.

'American dream, huh?' Elena gave him a little smile.

'I guess.'

'Did they want you to be lawyer?' Elena slipped her arm through Sye's and gazed up at the building.

'Oh boy yes. A smart lawyer son to take over the family firm one day. But instead, they got an Arts Major who wanted to take fashion pictures. Their only son! They were *terrified* I was gay, so that's a relief for them, at least,' he said, letting his hand slide down onto Elena's pert behind.

'But now,' Elena was working it out, 'they want a rich wife and clever grandchildren who will be lawyers in the family firm.' She might have grown up in the Ukrainian countryside but after two years in Svetlana's company, Elena was catching on fast to the ways of the wealthy.

'Oh yeah,' Sye said gently.

'I could be a rich wife,' Elena said, also in a quiet voice, 'my mother a multimillionaire and I run very successful dress business.'

'True . . .' Sye said.

'But we don't need to think about all this now.' She slipped her hand into the back pocket of his baggy combats and squeezed.

'No,' he shook his head, turned and kissed her on the lips, 'but if you have any visa problems, don't worry, we'll just get married.'

'Your starter wife?' she teased, feeling a thrilled leap in her stomach.

'Yeah,' he agreed, feeling the same tingling thrill.

They turned and began to kiss properly, clinging together, oblivious to the street hustle going on around them; deaf to the catcalls from the man at the ramshackle stall close by selling water-melons and mobile phone holsters.

When the kiss was finally over, they stood looking deep into each other's eyes, electrified by the emotion fizzing between them.

'I . . .' Sye began.

'I . . .' Elena wondered.

Their lips were just inches apart.

Elena put her finger up against Sye's mouth. 'Shhhh . . .' she urged and began to kiss him once again.

Then Sye dug into one of his trouser pockets and brought out a pale blue envelope, a little battered by its journey. 'This is for you.'

Elena's eyebrows shot up, but she began to tear the envelope open. Inside she found a sheet of folded pale blue paper. She opened it up to see the words 'Sylvia Westhoven' embossed in the corner and then a letter, handwritten in navy blue ink.

'"Dear Elena,"' she read aloud to Sye, '"I owe you an apology. I understand now that you are a hard-working, ambitious girl of *considerable means*" . . . what is this?' Elena asked, needing a translation.

'You have your own money – very important to Mrs Westhoven,' Sye said.

'Oh . . . "and if my son thinks you are a wonderful person, then you must be very special. I would like to get to know you much better. I look forward to meeting you at Yakowski's Deli today. The latkes are amazing, just like my mother used to make. My very best wishes, Sylvia."'

Elena looked up at Sye in astonishment.

'If I was not holding this letter in my hands, I would not believe it,' she said.

Sye nodded his agreement and added: 'Maybe that's why she wrote it.'

CHAPTER 36

The client:

Violet evening gown (Zac Posen)
Gold sandals (Russell & Bromley)
Satin bow clutch bag (MaxMara)
Total est. cost: £1,600

'Did you recognize me . . . or the dress?'

At almost exactly the same time as Elena and Sye were stepping into Yakowski's Deli, Ed was letting Annie go first into the lift which would take them up to the restaurant on the very top of London's OXO Tower.

'You look great,' Ed told his wife for about the tenth time this evening, 'whatever you and your iPod are doing on the bedroom floor every morning, it seems to be working.'

'Thank you. It's all down to Gawain. He talks to me through the iPod. I train with Gawain every morning. And hey, you're looking pretty smokin' yourself.'

'You are a sucker for a shirt, jacket and tie.'

'Every girl's mad for a well dressed man.'

'Are you misquoting the works of Mr ZZ Top?' he asked, making her snort, in a way entirely unbefitting a woman in a spectacular new D&G floral-print cocktail dress.

'This is sooooo fancy,' Annie whispered as the lift doors opened and they were ushered into the glittering restaurant right up on the top floor. The panorama of London at night was set out before them.

'Nothing but the best for my girl,' Ed assured her as they were led to a table right beside the window.

A bottle of wine was ordered and the happy pair clinked glasses. 'Here's to date night,' Annie said, smiling, 'may it come round slightly more often than once a year.'

'We've been very busy,' Ed admitted, 'far too busy to go out for dinner and enjoy ourselves . . .'

'And get dressed up.'

'Whenever I see you all dressed up, I assume that you're about to leave the house and go to work.'

'Poor old you,' she sympathized, 'you brought me all the way up here for a reason, didn't you?'

'Yes,' Ed smiled, liking the way that she could almost always guess what was going through his mind.

'You thought: take her up a very tall building, treat her to a swanky night out and she'll be convinced that London can be just as glamorous and exciting as New York.'

'We've been through this quite a lot lately,' he reminded her.

'I know and I've made my decision, I really have. I'm going to be just fine with it. Honestly, the Big Apple will just have to wait for me. But I'll get there, one day.'

'We'll make a plan,' Ed told her.

'Maybe M&M will be New Yorkers.' Annie reached out across the table for Ed's hands, 'I'll be fine about it, honest. Just as soon as I've got something else to keep me occupied.'

'No word yet?'

'Meeting Tamsin for lunch tomorrow,' she said, 'there's something on the cards. But we need to talk it through.'

'It's going to work out.'

'Yes. Especially now that I don't have to worry about you any more.'

'Me?'

The waiter appeared to take their order but they hadn't even glanced at the menu, so had to send him away again.

Over the top of her menu, Annie said: 'Yes you, getting suspended, worrying me half to death with all that.'

'You know how much I owe you for getting Harry involved.'

'Yeah, about £5,000 with travel costs an added extra.'

'Has he sent us a bill?' Ed asked, looking aghast.

'No. We're his friends, he's done it as a favour . . . but if we'd had to pay . . . different story, especially Owen. Imagine how much Harry normally charges for getting up at dawn and coming to police stations – probably £100 a minute.'

'Do you think Owen's going to be OK?'

'We'll talk about Owen, just as soon as we've ordered,' Annie said, spotting the waiter hovering into view again, 'but I think he's going to be just fine. I think he'll go to business school and do really well.'

'As long as he doesn't go to jail, I'll be proud of him.'

'He won't go to jail, he doesn't have a single crooked bone in his body. He was just a bit naive. He'll wise up. Look at the menu, Ed, quick! The waiter is coming.'

'But you look so lovely,' he said and winked.

As she was just finishing her main course, Annie took a moment to look around the packed dining room just to make a surreptitious check on the other diners. What were they eating? What were they wearing? Where was the fun in eating out if you couldn't do a little people spotting?

There was a woman over on the far side of the room who caught her eye. She just looked so good in that wonderful, possibly Halston, dress. It framed her face, set her apart . . . it had almost definitely been chosen for her . . . by Annie!

'I've just spotted a client,' Annie told Ed, 'I think I'll go over and say a quick hello.'

'Go for it,' Ed said, 'but if you spot any St V parents, I'm hiding. I don't want any conversations about the up and coming violin exams.'

As she approached the table, the woman in the beautiful dress looked up, and recognized her immediately.

'It's Annie Valentine, isn't it? Guy, look, this is the lady I was telling you about, the one who helped me buy the dress. Did you recognize me, by the way, or did you recognize the dress? I'm Joanne Kettner, in case you've forgotten.'

'Joanne, of course I remember you. You sent me to New York,' Annie said and reached over to take Guy's hand which was being offered to her. 'Hello, Guy.'

Annie did remember the dress and the day when she was in The Store mourning her lost TV series, and how Joanne had told her that if she had to go to New York to be true to herself, then she had to go.

'How was New York?'

'New York was fabulous. Unbelievable. I'm kinda homesick,' she said with her best accent.

'How did the dress business grab you?'

'I loved it. I loved it just as much as television. It's very hard to choose.'

'Who are you here with, tonight?'

'My husband, Ed, we're at the should-we-or-shouldn't-we have a dessert moment.'

370

'Us too! Why don't you join us?' Joanne suggested, 'we'd love that.'

Guy smiled and waved his hand welcomingly over the table. 'Please come over, my wife was just talking about you and I'd love to meet you properly.'

'Guy's in business, finance,' Joanne began, 'but he's currently obsessed with the idea of making a personal finance TV series . . . something with a popular touch.' Joanne's eyebrows raised and Annie understood her meaningful look immediately.

'Right, I'm going to go and get Ed, then I definitely think we should have dessert. I'm hearing the siren call of the crème brûlée. And yes, I'm prepared to risk the seams on my Spanx just for that.'

Guy looked baffled, but Joanne gave a hoot of laughter. 'I know, damn dresses. Really we should all just wear elasticated waists out to dinner.'

'There is no good way to wear an elasticated waistband.' Annie said. 'Believe me, I have tried.'

Ed and Annie strolled arm in arm along the riverfront, wrapped up against the stiff October breeze.

'I love this walk along the Thames,' Annie told him, 'all the lights reflecting in the water. Plus, this is the watery, beating heart of London: Houses of Parliament up that way, Tower Bridge and the Tower of London down there, swanky riverside apartments, everywhere you look. It's old, it's brand new, it's brilliant.'

'But it's not New York.'

'No-oo.' She pulled his arm in tightly: 'It's OK. New York is always there. It'll still be there when I'm ready to go.'

'What about Perfect Dress? Will it still be there?'

'Yes! It'll be a multinational superbrand that I'll be honoured to have such a good connection with. Hopefully, Svet and Elena will be able to give me a great job.'

'Are you sure?' Ed stopped, so that they could face each other properly, 'I don't want to be the person who pressed the pause button on your dreams.'

'Very poetic,' she said and kissed him on the mouth. He tasted of coffee and Ed and just . . . home.

'It's not just you,' Annie told him, 'it's me, who I am. I want to live a wonderful life and do all kinds of wonderful things. I already have . . . but I'm also a mum and a wife and that's really important, babes. It's hard to make a good job of all those things. Sometimes the dreams have to take a little step back. They're not going away. I'm not giving up on a single one of them, but I think I have to put some important people first.

'And anyway, you don't want to leave St Vincent's.' She looked hard into his eyes, wondering if there was the slightest sign that maybe he would.

'Not right now, but maybe in the future.'

'Exactly. Owen doesn't want to leave it now either. But in the future, he might want to do something new and exciting. With a little luck . . .' she swallowed and crossed her fingers, 'life is long. And I've always believed that all kinds of exciting adventures lie ahead.'

'If you're around, Annie, that will always be true!' Ed said, moving his arms tightly around her.

'I love you,' she told him with a smile full of all sorts of shared understandings.

'I love you too, Annie Valentine.'

'It was supposed to be Annie Leon, remember, I said I would change.'

'I know, but you suit Annie Valentine. It's fine, Valentine is a crucial part of who you are.'

She leaned her head on his shoulder and gazed out at the inky waters flowing smoothly by. 'Yeah . . .' she agreed softly.

He was so good for her. She pushed her hands into his coat pockets. Who else could possibly understand how important it was for her to keep her late husband's name? The name Valentine connected her, Owen and Lana to Roddy. His name was the visible thread which kept them all still bound up with him.

She turned her head and kissed Ed's neck tenderly, just below the jaw. 'I have a feeling it's all going to get interesting again.'

'Not more interesting! What next?'

'How serious do you think Guy was about a personal finance programme? He seemed to know an awful lot of interested people. And he's going to get in touch with Tamsin.'

'The idea of you doing a personal finance programme is actually quite funny,' Ed said.

'Why?!'

'Because your personal finances are always a little bit . . .'

'Optimistic?'

'Yes, optimistic. That's about right.'

'So I'd be perfect, I'd be learning as I went along, just like my viewers. That's the best kind of programme.'

She kissed him again. Properly. Pulling him tight, shutting her eyes and feeling all the rush of emotions which this man stirred up in her. He kissed back, interested and very alive.

It felt like a kiss from back in the pre-twin days.

Parenting small children – it really was the kiss of death to any sex life. Maybe with good reason, otherwise there would be crazed parents all over the place with whole troupes of pre-schoolers.

'This is very promising,' Ed said, breaking away but running his hands over her silky D&G derrière.

'I know, very . . . but we'll get to the tube station, ride the train home, pay the babysitter, go upstairs, light the candles, put the music on, brush our teeth, start kissing, hear crying, put a baby back to bed, then fall asleep.'

'I promise to have sex with you when we get home, no matter what,' Ed said, pulling her in tight, so she could feel the stirring happening there.

'You know,' she whispered against his ear, 'I think I'd rather go for a seriously saucy cuddle on that bench over there than take the risk of staying interested all the way back to the bedroom.'

Ed ran his fingers lightly over the exposed tops of her breasts, causing her skin to tingle with pleasure.

'Just how saucy were you planning to get?' he asked in a whisper.

'Follow me, big boy . . .'

CHAPTER 37

Connor's gym kit:

Black running tights (Adidas)
Green vest top (Nike)
Black and green trainers (Saucony)
White socks (Nike)
Total est. cost: £180

'Move your sad and saggy ass.'

'THis is very, very exciting, baby. I am loving it. Ohhhhh, yeees. Yes! Give me more . . . Harder. Punish me. Make. Me. CRY!'

'Do you always shout at the cross trainer like this?' Annie asked Connor, who wasn't just shouting, he was panting, sweating, *suffering* on the machine beside hers.

'Work, Annie, work!' he urged her, 'what would Gawain say? He would tell you to smell victory, baby, to close your eyes and reach for the gold.'

'Gawain, ha, this is all Gawain's fault!' Annie

puffed. 'If I'd never met Gawain, I would not be here right now.'

'Gawain is going to be here in London in just four days' time,' Connor reminded her, 'so you better move your sad and saggy ass or you are going to be in supersized trouble.'

Annie nudged her treadmill up from 1 (i.e. barely moving) to 2. 'You're right. I'm going to be a totally, totally different woman when he is here.'

Over the last few days there had been some very interesting developments. Connor had begun his time on *Strictly Come Dancing* and been all over breakfast TV like a rash, flirting, showing off his buns and abs of steel and boasting about his 'unbelievable' New York personal trainer.

Connor had also happened to mention that said personal trainer was in talks with a well-known British TV producer about a celebrity fitness show.

Well . . . *then* the phones had started to burn red hot.

Connor's agent was talking to Gawain's agent who was talking to Tamsin who was talking to Annie's agent.

Would Connor consider appearing on the celebrity fitness show? Would Annie consider hosting the celebrity fitness show? And how on earth would everyone get the money together to make it worth Gawain's while to appear on British TV?

'Baby, as soon as they said unfit celebrity guinea pig . . .' Connor began.

'You thought of me. Sweet,' came Annie's reply.

'And you have other news, don't you?' Connor asked, 'I can tell . . . you look smug.'

'Ah well, nothing definite yet . . .' Annie began.

No sooner did the four special episodes of the Celeb Fit Show look as if they were really going to happen than Tamsin had been on the phone with more news.

'Please tell me someone's going to buy the *How Not To Shop* format?' Annie had just about pleaded.

'No. But I'm not giving up on it,' Tamsin had assured her, 'it's a great show with a very loyal audience. But Annie, for now, I've been talking to a Guy Kettner, I believe you know him?'

'Oh . . . the night of the crème brûlée.'

'Well, he loves you. He may have mentioned to you that he's got plans for a personal finance programme. Well, he's very keen on you and I think he's getting keen on me too. We're meeting tomorrow.'

'That is interesting, babes, very interesting.'

'But meantime, you're signed up with Connor and his new fitness phenomenon. So that is brilliant. That keeps you on screen and right in our minds and hot, hot, hot. Plus, you'll get into shape too, which never hurt anyone. Not that I'm a body fascist.'

'I thought you liked the "real" me.'

'Real yes. You don't need to go size zero on me . . .'

'As if.'

'But supersized, no,' had been the brutal reply.

So that was why, right now, Annie was in the gym with Connor, who kept leaning over and nudging up the speed on her machine.

'Stop it!' she warned, 'or I'll be a *dead* celebrity guinea pig and no use to you at all.'

When the mobile in her back pocket began to ring, Connor protested, 'A mobile! In the gym? You can't have a mobile in the gym, it's against the rules. How can you feel the pain with Gawain if you stop and chat on the phone?'

Annie wasn't listening. She'd already jumped off the machine with relief. Anyone could be calling, she didn't care, as long as she had an excuse to get off the treadmill.

'Annah!'

There was no mistaking the voice at the other end of the line.

'Svetlana, how are you?'

'Vonderrrrful. Dresses sell out all over New York, everybody want one. Now we are worrrking very hard to get new range in place. New fabrics, new colours, playing a little with the styles. Is all so good and so fascinating, no? I go over again next week to make sure everything going well.'

Annie felt the pang of jealousy in the pit of her stomach. Back to Manhattan. Back to the fashion business . . .

'So I phone you to talk again about our plan.'

'Yes . . .'

'I think it is a very, very good plan. I think it

will be amazing. I already organize a bigger apartment.'

'In the same area?'

'Almost. Very nice, very safe. But Manhattan much safer than London. No?'

'So you really think this will be OK?'

'Yes, I already organize work permit with the consulate.'

'Really? And it wasn't a problem?'

'No problem. All organized. So you need to book ticket.'

'Really?' Annie gripped the phone tightly. She could feel her heart thud with the heady mix of excitement and fear. 'I can't quite believe it,' she said. 'Thank you so much. It's amazing. It's a really amazing opportunity.'

'I know. But good for us too. And the weather is still warmer than London, but winter is coming and maybe there will be lots of snow. When are you going to come?'

CHAPTER 38

Annie at Heathrow:

Trench coat (Aquascutum)
Skinny jeans (Gap)
Highest black heels (Jimmy Choo)
The sea-green bag (Mulberry)
Beige and green scarf (Otrera)
Minty gum (Wrigley's Extra)
Pocket hankies (Kleenex Balsam)
Total est. cost: £1,600

'It's not like I'm retired yet . . .'

The ticket and the passport were checked by the slightly exhausted but nevertheless smiling lady behind the counter, and the two large suitcases were tagged with labels bearing the big black letters: JFK.

'This flight begins boarding at 8.30a.m., gate number 54, so if you'd like to make your way through security. Have a pleasant journey.'

Annie held the boarding card in her hand and

walked at an unusually slow pace through the airport with Lana, trying to stave off the moment when they actually arrived at the entrance to security.

'Thank you so much for coming to see me off. You really shouldn't have. It's a long journey and so early in the morning.'

'Don't be mad, of course I was going to see you off.'

'I'm going to miss you.'

'Not half as much as I'll miss you, darlin'.'

'Mum, I'll be OK, won't I?' Lana looked at Annie with a half-nervous, half-smiling expression which Annie understood perfectly.

Lana was scared.

Annie was terrified.

But it was Annie's job to hug her daughter very, very tightly and tell her that of course she would be OK. Because that was her job here. She was the very good mum who was going to give her fledgling bird the nudge out of the nest, so she could learn to fly.

Putting both arms around her and nearly squeezing the life out of her girl, Annie insisted: 'Yes, my darlin', you're going to be more than OK. You're going to be brilliant. Fantastic. You'll take NYC by storm! You will love your new job and you'll be so fantastically good at it. Plus, you've got a great new place with Elena, with your own room! And Elena will look after you . . . she'll be the big sister you always wanted.'

'It's only for a year, though – and you'll all come out and visit. You will come out, won't you?' Lana's big blue eyes fixed on Annie's anxiously. 'You promise?'

'Babes, my November winter shopping spree is already booked. Then you're back with us for Christmas. We'll see more of you like this than when you were spending all day moping in your bedroom,' Annie said, sounding brightly cheerful but suddenly aware that tears were rolling down her cheeks.

'Don't cry!' Lana exclaimed, but now she was crying too.

'Oh, I love you,' Annie said, hugging her daughter again, 'I love you. This is so exciting, I am so jealous! I wish I was moving to New York to work for a wonderful new dress label; swanning about Fifth Avenue with a Ukrainian executive and her super-mum. It's so exciting!'

'I wish you were coming.'

'I know . . . but I have babies, and a day job, and Owen at school – and Ed.'

Lana nodded with understanding.

'But you . . .' Annie ran her finger over Lana's cheek and brushed away the tears, 'you're eighteen. You have a whole fabulous new grown-up life ahead of you.'

'Oh . . . Mum,' Lana said and hooked her chin over her mum's shoulder for the last time . . . in a long time.

'Obviously I have lots of fabulous new exciting

things ahead of me too,' Annie added, mainly to cheer herself up: 'it's not like I'm retired yet or it's game over . . . or anything.'

'Ooh, I've got a present,' Lana said, remembering.

'Oh no . . .' Annie dragged a paper hankie across her face, she didn't know if she was strong enough to make it through a present: 'me too!'

For a moment they both searched in their handbags and brought out small wrapped gifts. Then they each sniffed hard, tried not to cry and fumbled with wrapping paper.

Annie was the first to gasp out her thanks. In her hand was a framed photo of Lana, taken by Sye for the Perfect Dress campaign. Annie hadn't seen it before and now that she looked at her daughter's beautiful, serious, oh-so-grown-up face, she felt a fresh wave of pride, mingled with nostalgia and a growing sense of loss.

'Oh thank you, you're beautiful, babes. Look after yourself over there, won't you? Beware all the Taylors, find yourself a nice boy . . . or be too busy with work to find any boy at all,' she said gruffly into her daughter's hair as she hugged her again.

'Oh Mum! You shouldn't have!' Lana exclaimed, holding up the beautiful bright blue, hideously expensive patent wallet which was her present.

'Yes, you're a working girl now, you have to have a lovely purse,' Annie insisted, 'for your business receipts and travel tickets and . . . oh . . . all grown-up.'

For a moment, Annie wasn't sure if she could bear to let Lana go. Then she remembered: it was her job. This was what she had to do. The nest would always be here. She would always welcome Lana back. But now she had to give her the little push to go.

'Send Manhattan my love,' Annie said, setting a big smile on her face and somehow managing to let her arm pull back from Lana's slight shoulder.

'I will,' Lana said, brightening at the thought of the huge adventure she was about to set off on.

'See you very, very soon, my darlin'.'

'Yeah . . . OK . . .' Lana took a deep breath, 'I guess I better go then . . .'

'The duty-free perfume counter is waiting for you,' Annie tried to joke.

Lana tucked the brand new purse into her handbag. She hugged and kissed her mother one last time, turned to go, turned back once again to smile and wave. Then she was gone.

Annie stared at the space where Lana had been, needing this time to try and compose herself enough for the walk back through the airport.

As she turned to face the airport again, she saw a young mother hurrying towards the departure gate. Holding her hand tightly was a serious-faced girl of about five or six with long dark hair. In the girl's hair was a little clip with a blue gingham bow.

As soon as Annie registered the hair clip, she felt undone.

All that time! All that very happy, peaceful time she'd spent brushing out Lana's long dark hair, over so many years, ever since she was tiny. Brushing it, plaiting it, clipping it back from Lana's little pale face. That time had passed.

Annie felt as if her heart might break.

CHAPTER 39

Gawain ready to train:

Silky black boxing shorts (Lonsdale)
Grey sweatshirt (Nike)
Black boxer boots (Lonsdale)
Total est. cost: £90

'Are you ready to roll?'

'**M**um!! I'm phoning from the pavement outside Bloomingdale's. One whole window . . . a whole window, Mum, is Perfect Dress. I'll send you a photo right now!'

Annie heard the thrill in Lana's voice and told her: 'You should be very proud, very proud, darlin'. You and Elena.'

'And you!' Lana insisted, 'it was your idea to go skip hunting in Brooklyn and to have the fashion show *and* to send a dress to Emily Wilmington!'

'Aw, thank you, babes. I do feel proud. The window of bloomin' Bloomingdale's, no less! But you're the ones supplying the orders, manning the

business. Be very proud of all you've done. Darlin'
I have to go. I'm filming! Yes . . . right now. You
should see me, I look like a freeeeeeak! See
you very, very soon. It's less than a fortnight now.
Love you. Mwah! Byeeeee.'

Annie hung up and took care to switch off. She
now had first-hand experience of what Gawain
did to people who let their mobiles ring when he
was training them.

It involved many, many press-ups and it wasn't
at all nice.

'Annie, c'mon, we're all ready for you!' the
director called from the centre of the studio.

There, a treadmill, a cross trainer and several
other instruments of torture were set out for her.
Gawain, glistening oiled skin popping with
muscles, was standing beside the treadmill in silky
shorts and a cut-off sweatshirt, his dark locks
pulled back from his face with a sweatband.

'Hello, girl,' he said, looking friendly, but with
his hands on his hips, meaning business.

Annie felt a little nervous, but OK. This was
going to hurt. Again. But somehow when she was
being filmed, when she knew she was going to
share the pain, the agony, but also the ultimate
triumph with her viewers, it didn't hurt quite so
much.

She shuffled along to the treadmill, the plastic
clothes she was wearing scrunching as she walked.

It was an experiment. She was in a tight T-shirt
and tight cycle shorts (grotesque, every dip and

rise of cellulite on view), and over this she was wearing a top and trousers both made of clear, elasticated plastic. Apparently this was to keep her hot and sweating so she could work her muscles and lose weight more effectively.

'I look like a boil-in-the-bag,' she said directly to the camera, then gave a little twirl.

Bob, the man behind the camera – who had filmed most of the episodes in Annie's *How Not To Shop* series, not to mention the disastrous digital TV show they'd been involved with before – began to laugh.

'Don't forget your chicken,' the director said, pointing to an assistant who was holding a red plate studded with tiny cubes of white meat.

'Chicken boil-in-the-bag!' Annie joked, then straight to camera she explained: 'OK, as well as working out and swathing myself in plastic, I'm also going to be eating a piece of lean protein every fifteen minutes. Apparently this will stoke my metabolism to a raging furnace and burn, baby, burn.'

Annie tried to check the smirk that was threatening to break out over her face.

Gawain was shaking his head in an 'I didn't sign up for this' kind of way. 'Are you ready to roll?' he asked Annie.

She nodded, and he pointed to the cross trainer.

As she slid her feet into the stirrups, he began to encourage her in the inimitable Gawain way. Crouching low so he could talk right into her ear, he began to tell her all the good things she was going to achieve as he whacked the speed up higher and higher.

'No gain without pain, that's why we train, train and train with Gawain!'

Now the loud, cheesy, disco music Annie had chosen began to thump out of the speakers, and she pushed her feet forward and back, forward and back, faster, faster, until she began to pant with the effort.

'C'mon now, you can do this. I've seen you go much faster. You can run, girl, feel the wind in your hair,' Gawain urged.

'Whooooooo-hoooooo!' Annie cried, then began to sing along with the music. She reached over for the chicken cube the assistant was offering her. Her plastic clothing flapping in the wind, she carried on speeding along, chewing, sweating and singing.

Bob pushed his lens forward and zoomed in on her face.

'Annie!'

Annie looked up. There, at the edge of the studio space, was Tamsin's assistant, Amelia, committing the cardinal sin of interrupting a shoot.

Annie whacked the stop button on the machine and jumped off, feeling a rush of panic. 'Is everything OK?' she panted, gasping for breath.

'It's Tamsin . . .' Amelia began, holding out her mobile phone. 'She says she has to tell you something right now. She doesn't care what you're doing.'

It was Tamsin . . . Annie gulped down a lungful

or two of air and tried to calm herself. This was a work call. No family emergency had occurred.

'Hi—' she began, trying not to pant too hard down the line.

'ANNIE! I know your phone's off, I know you're filming . . . but I've just had incredible news. Guy Kettner – Guy Kettner and the BBC!' Tamsin was so excited she could hardly tell the story straight.

'Yes?' Annie's fingers clutched the mobile tightly.

'We've just put the deal together. You're going to have your very own show again. But this time on BBC TWO. The real deal! A twelve-episode first series. *How To Be Fabulous.* Covering money, health, work, lifestyle but loads of fashion included, don't worry – and just for you, one entire episode to be filmed in Manhattan!'

'No. NO! You have got to be joking, girl.'

For several moments, as Tamsin went into the detail, Annie tried to take it all in. She closed her eyes and found she was squeezing out tears. It was just so strange, sometimes, the way things worked out.

Suddenly it didn't seem so long ago that she'd been out on the town in her moment-of-shopping-madness red Valentino dress, celebrating her husband Roddy's unbelievable new television deal. The amazing lead part that he'd never been able to play; the one which would have put enough money in the bank to take care of them all for years and years to come.

Then all those terrible times had followed, when

she'd been alone and bereaved, so broke and so desperate to provide for her shattered children. She'd worked incredibly hard and just willed her way through it . . . but even then she had *always* allowed herself to dream. To dream of the next deal, the next pay-rise, the next genius new outfit she'd treat herself to *when* . . .

So a moment like this . . . a *triumph* like this . . . Annie knew now that precious few of these came around in a lifetime, and that when they did they had to be savoured to the full.

'Just a second,' she told Tamsin and carefully set the phone down on the floor. In a minute she would call Ed, Lana, Owen, Dinah, her mum and Connor to tell them this incredible news. In fact, no – even better – she'd throw a full-on party and everyone from The Store would be invited too.

But right now, still encased in the see-through plastic suit, Annie just had to throw her arms up into the air and begin a victory lap of the studio, shrieking: 'Yeeeesssssss!' at the top of her voice. First the director was treated to a sweaty hug and kiss, then the assistant, then the sound guy and the girl on lights, then it was a startled Gawain's turn, and finally Bob.

To his astonishment, Bob got a kiss on each cheek and a damp smacker right on the lips.

'I love you,' Annie told him, 'I love the camera . . . and my family . . . and isn't life just fabulous, babes?'